BY THE SAME AUTHOR

The Black Door
The Third Figure
The Lonely Hunter
The Disappearance
Dead Aim
Hiding Place
Long Way Down
Aftershock
The Faceless Man (as Carter Wick)
The Third Victim
Doctor, Lawyer . . .
The Watcher
Twospot (with Bill Pronzini)
Power Plays
Mankiller
Spellbinder
Dark House, Dark Road (as Carter Wick)
Stalking Horse
Victims
Night Games
The Pariah
Bernhardt's Edge
A Death Before Dying
Dead Center
Except for the Bones
Switchback

A LT. HASTINGS MYSTERY

HIRE A HANGMAN

Collin Wilcox

AN OWL BOOK
HENRY HOLT AND COMPANY
NEW YORK

Henry Holt and Company, Inc.
Publishers since 1866
115 West 18th Street
New York, New York 10011

Published in Canada by Fitzhenry & Whiteside Ltd.,
195 Allstate Parkway, Markham, Ontario L3R 4T8.

Library of Congress Cataloging-in-Publication Data
Wilcox, Collin,
Hire a hangman / Collin Wilcox.—1st ed.
p. cm.—(A Henry Holt mystery)
I. Title.
PS3573.I395H57 1991
813'.54dc20 90-40317
CIP

ISBN 0-8050-0980-9
ISBN 0-8050-3121-9 (An Owl Book: pbk.)

Henry Holt books are available for special promotions
and premiums. For details contact: Director, Special Markets.

First published in hardcover in 1991
by Henry Holt and Company, Inc.

First Owl Book Edition—1994

Designed by Lucy Albanese

Printed in the United States of America
All first editions are printed on acid-free paper.∞

1 2 3 4 5 6 7 8 9 10
1 2 3 4 5 6 7 8 9 10
pbk.

To Pete and Carolyn,
my old friends

HIRE A HANGMAN

Monday, September 10

9:45 PM

Hanchett turned to his right side, glanced at the bedside clock. By ten-thirty he should be home. But first he must kiss her, stroke her, partially arouse her. Promises made, promises to keep. Then he could leave her bed. Ten minutes to shower and dress. Bringing him to ten o'clock. Another ten minutes, fifteen, perhaps, to kiss her again, stroke her again, keep the flame burning low. Then the drive home: fifteen minutes, portal-to-portal, her place to his.

If Barbara didn't awaken, he could be asleep by eleven. Seven hours to restore the body, let the heart rest, let the organs relax. Then a new day would begin. Tomorrow, Tuesday, September eleventh. The struggle would begin anew: life, struggling against the inevitability of death, his stock-in-trade.

The struggle that made men rich.

As the hours of September eleventh passed, the sexual pulse, already waxing, would begin to throb: that beat, growing stronger—and stronger. Until he returned here, to her bed.

Lying beside her. Beginning. Once more, beginning. He and Carla. Burning bright.

He knew that now, just now, she would speak. It was predictable. After three months together, it was predictable.

It was also predictable that when she spoke it would be preemptive—the predictable, preempting the predictable:

"I know," she said. "You're running late."

"Ah . . ." He turned toward her, smiled. "You noticed."

"I like a man who takes his domestic responsibilities seriously."

"Is that a fact?" He touched her stomach, just above the navel. Her stomach was wonderfully taut. The tennis, the aerobics, the daily sessions on the stationary bike—all of it compounding to gratify his touch, determination defeating flab. Aware that he was quickening, he moved his hand lower. God, the wonder of her body. It was poetry. Pure, sweet poetry.

"I'd appreciate it," she said, "if you wouldn't do that. Not unless you intend to put your organ where your hand is."

He chuckled, withdrew his hand. It wasn't only her body. It was her élan—her don't-give-a-damn-flair. Carla was brash. And smart. And essentially ruthless. His kind of woman.

He chuckled again, kissed her, pushed away, slid out of bed. "I do have responsibilities, you know. While you're working on your forehand tomorrow, I'll be at the office."

"I'd rather work on my foreplay. And your foreplay, come to think about it. We mustn't forget your foreplay. Must we?"

10:07 PM

It was as if she were awakening from a dream to discover the dream incarnate: this same quiet street, these trees, the streetlamp high overhead. Yes, there was his car, a tan Jaguar. To make sure, there was the personalized license plate: BRICE H.

"Check the license plate," she'd rehearsed, "just to make sure. Absolutely sure."

And, meek as a little girl, herself so long ago, she'd nodded. Yes, she would check the license plate.

Soon, she knew, he would come to her. It was promised, that he would come to her. The door of the small apartment building across the street would open, and he would begin walking toward his car. He would most certainly pass within a few feet of where she now stood, close beside a large, tall tree. The branches of the tree arched high overhead: dark, mysterious shapes against the night-blue sky. Sometimes dark shapes in the night frightened her. Witches' wings, overspreading.

Once when she was small—much smaller, even, than she felt now—a bat had flown above her, so close she could hear the dry graveyard rustle of wings. She'd been alone that night. All alone.

But she wasn't afraid. Even though she was alone, she was not afraid.

When they'd come to the door that night—when she'd heard the sound of footsteps outside the door, that night—she'd known she would never again be afraid.

Because after death, there was nothing more to fear.

Even the cold steel touch of the pistol did not frighten her. Always, for as long as she could remember, guns had terrified her. Even the sight of a gun had made her curl up inside, tight as a sow bug, and just as tiny.

But no more.

Instead, now, just as she'd been instructed, she gripped the pistol with her right hand and drew it from the canvas carryall bag. She'd bought the bag especially for this purpose. She'd bought it at a sporting goods store downtown. It was an expensive store. The clerk, she knew, had looked down his long, aristocratic nose at her. But she hadn't cared. She and the sow bug, neither one of them cared.

10:16 PM

Hanchett glanced at his watch, touched the knot of his tie, touched his fly. His car was just ahead; miraculously, he'd found a parking spot hardly a hundred feet from her apartment. Would the Jag still be intact, stereo in place, hubcaps attached?

Aware that muggers preyed on drivers fumbling to unlock their doors, he took out his keys, ready. The night was warm, the sky was clear. The remembrance of the last two hours was still palpable, still incredibly immediate, flesh-to-flesh replete, sensation sated. When Carla lit the fuse, the rocket soared. Never—never—had they fizzled, he and Carla.

Was marriage on her mind? Children—conceivably children, the whole nine yards?

He could still remember the moment he'd first seen her. There'd been an art opening, a provocative show of semi-abstract landscapes, at the Mooney Gallery. Carla had been—

Ahead, only five paces ahead, a figure was stepping out from the shadow of a tree. It was the figure of a woman, unmistakably a woman, wearing a man's clothing: slacks and a jacket and a cap. Did he know her? Was she—?

Her arm was coming up. Pale streetlamp light glinted on a metallic shape in her hand, level with his chest.

A gun. A—

Orange flame blossomed; the quiet of the night was shattered, a cataclysm of sound. Erupting. Rolling. Deafening. Finally fading.

Lost. All of it. Lost.

10:17 PM

Still naked, with her hand on the knob of the bathroom door, Carla heard the shots: one shot, a pause, then two more shots.

Shots?

Or backfires?

Had she ever heard the sound of shots, identifiable shots? Short, staccato sounds, yes; sounds of the city, of people, of cars and trucks. But had she ever—

Voices. Someone shouting. A man's voice. What was the word? Police? Was that the word?

10:18 PM

Was this the way? In the darkness, the shapes were unfamiliar, constantly changing. Had she lost her way? Would they find her wandering, helpless? Would they—?

The gun.

She could still feel its weight, inside the canvas bag she'd bought where the sales clerk had been so rude. But it was wrong, she knew, that she still had the gun. It was a promise broken.

But where was the sewer grate? In the darkness, she'd lost that particular sewer, with that particular grate, large enough for the gun.

And where was the rapture?

Please, God, where was the rapture?

10:20 PM

"There." Bob Miller pointed ahead. "There it is. As advertised." As the squad car angled across the steep Russian Hill slope of Green Street to park in a driveway, Miller keyed the microphone he'd taken from its hook, called Dispatch, identified himself.

"Go ahead, Unit three-twenty-one." It was Diane Granger's voice. Starchy, by-the-book Diane Granger.

"We've got a victim down in the eleven-hundred block of Green Street, between Hyde and Leavenworth. Maybe ten onlookers. We'll need an ambulance and another unit. Maybe two units."

"Roger, three-twenty-one. Are you going to your hand-held?"

"That's affirmative."

"Channel three."

"Channel three," Miller acknowledged. He replaced the microphone, automatically verified that the shotgun was shackled and the keys were in his pocket, safe. As he pushed open the door, held it against the steep hill's gravity, and levered himself out of the cruiser, uphill, he sighed heavily. Whichever it was, either homicide or aggravated assault, the same chain-of-evidence rule applied: first on the scene, last to leave. Meaning there was no way, no way at all, that he'd be relieved when his shift ended at midnight.

10:35 PM

Alone in the Homicide squad room, eight desks, seven of them unoccupied, seated at his own desk, feet propped on the open lower file drawer, Canelli felt the numbness of sleep descending. Since eight o'clock he'd been alone in the squad room, the officer in charge. Until the fifteenth of September, his turn in the rotation, he was the after-hours duty officer. The after-hours duty tours were fifteen days. So, multiply fifteen days by eight—no, by seven—and he would know when his turn would come again, the graveyard shift. And even after midnight, the duty officer was hooked up to his pager, score another point for science, the electronic revolution. The last time he'd caught the duty, three, four months ago, he'd—

When his telephone rang, he realized that his eyes had closed. Really closed. Guiltily reflexive, he looked at the glass walls that separated him from the two lieutenants' offices as he picked up the phone.

"Homicide. Canelli." Automatically he drew a notepad closer, clicked his ballpoint pen, checked the time.

"It's a call from the field, Inspector." It was a woman's voice.

Bored. Plainly bored. The two of them, bored. "It's Patrolman Miller. North Station."

"Oh. Yeah. Right." He remembered Bob Miller: a big, good-natured man, a whiz at slow-pitch softball.

Or was that another Miller?

He waited for the patch-through: two clicks, a pause, then two more clicks. Finally: "This is Unit three-twenty-one."

"Yeah. This is Canelli. Homicide. That you, Bob?"

"Hey, Joe. Yeah. You sound sleepy."

"I know. What've you got?"

"I got a dead one for you, Joe. Russian Hill, eleven-hundred block. Upscale neighborhood, upscale guy, looks like. We got two units here, got the yellow tapes up, even got some witnesses for you."

"Eleven hundred Green Street, you say?" Trying to visualize the neighborhood, Canelli frowned.

"Between Hyde and Leavenworth, that steep hill. At the top of the hill, everything's gold-plated. Here, it's—" Unable to find the word, Miller broke off.

"Nice, though," Canelli offered.

"Yeah. Nice. One of the witnesses says the victim was a doctor. Big-shot doctor. She's a friend, this witness. And she's a beauty, too. A real beauty."

"A doctor, huh?"

"Right. A doctor. Or so this lady says. I'm not going to go for his ID, though. I'd have to move the body to get to the wallet. But he's got a key ring in his hand, with Jaguar keys on it. The car's right here, at the scene. Very fancy car."

"So what d'you think? A robbery that went wrong? Is that how it looks?"

"Like I say, I don't know about his wallet. Maybe he's got it, maybe he hasn't. So about robbery, I'm not going to guess. And I haven't really interrogated the witnesses. I wanted to call you guys first."

"Okay, I'll be right there. Twenty minutes, probably, by the time I call the coroner and the crew. Hang on to the witnesses, okay?"

"Yeah. Sure. Obviously." In Miller's voice, Canelli caught a note of faint irritation. The reason: Canelli should have assumed that Miller, the pro, would keep the witnesses at the scene. Was an apology called for? No. An apology would only make it worse—for him.

Canelli said good-bye, broke the connection, checked the time again, then sat motionless for a moment, eyeing the phone. According to departmental guidelines, he should call out the equipment, then go to the crime scene. He should secure the scene and make a preliminary examination. At that point he must decide when to call a lieutenant. If the hour was late and the homicide routine—a small-time drug dealer, or a hooker killed in the line of duty—the call could wait until morning.

But a doctor with a Jaguar, killed on posh Russian Hill, was a headline grabber, guaranteed. Meaning that, yes, a lieutenant must be called—Lieutenant Hastings, on this duty tour.

Meaning that, since the time was almost eleven o'clock, Hastings's bedtime, the call might better be made now, while Hastings was still awake.

10:55 PM

Hastings was brushing his teeth when the phone began to ring. As Ann quickly picked up the extension in the living room, Hastings rinsed the toothbrush, rinsed his mouth, put the toothbrush in the rack beside Ann's. They shared one rack; Ann's two sons shared another rack. As he turned off the water, Hastings heard Ann's voice, amiably chatting. Conclusion: Canelli was on the line. Of Homicide's rank-and-file inspectors, Canelli was Ann's favorite. It was probably her inherent sympathy for the underdog. A chronic, amiable bumbler who tipped the scales at two-forty, not all of it muscle, Canelli was the only detective in squad-room memory who constantly got his feelings hurt. Almost always, the wounds were self-inflicted.

"It's Canelli," Ann said.

"I know." He took the phone, kissed her on the cheek, patted her buttock. "Go to sleep. I'll lock up."

She patted him in return, smiled, waved good night.

11:20 PM

Hastings suppressed a smile as he watched Canelli park his unmarked car in a driveway directly across from the murder scene. Because Hastings lived within a mile of the scene, it had been predictable that he would arrive at the Green Street address before Canelli, who'd come across town. Just as predictably, Canelli's broad, swarthy face registered mild consternation when he saw Hastings. His soft brown eyes were earnest, his voice solicitous:

"Oh, hi, Lieutenant. I guess I should've—I mean, I figured that if it got to be twelve, one o'clock, whatever, before I got things sorted out and called you, then I figured—" Once more he broke off, plainly irked with himself.

"I'm glad you didn't wake me up." Hastings spoke slowly, deliberately. He was a tall, heavily built man. His face was solidly squared off, matching the pattern of his movements and the measured economy of his speech. He wore a light poplin jacket, corduroy slacks, and running shoes. As he spoke, he turned his attention to the crime scene. The body lay on the sidewalk, in the approximate middle of the block. A small, docile cluster of perhaps a dozen onlookers stood behind the yellow tapes, some of them talking, most of them simply staring. With their spotlights trained on the victim and their doors standing open, two black-and-white units were parked in adjoining driveways. Two uniformed officers stood at the yellow tapes, their eyes on the onlookers. A third officer stood leaning against one of the black-and-white units, monitoring the radio. As Hastings surveyed the scene, Canelli came to stand beside him, awaiting orders.

"Who called it in?" Hastings asked.

"Bob Miller. The one on the radio."

"Where do I know him from?"

"Softball. He's a hell of a slow-ball pitcher. A real ace. Nice guy, too. Real—you know—easygoing."

"I'll talk to him, see what he's got. The other two, I want them to take their units to either end, here"— Hastings gestured up and down the hill—"get this block sealed off. You monitor the radio."

"Yessir." Canelli turned away, gave the orders, then returned to his unmarked car, and the radio. As the two squad cars pulled out of their parking places and went to opposite ends of the block, Hastings clipped his badge on his jacket, ducked under the tape, and gestured for Miller to join him as he stood looking down at the body. With the two squad cars gone, the body lay in the dim light of a streetlamp.

"Here, Lieutenant." Miller took a four-cell flashlight from his equipment belt and handed it to Hastings.

"Thanks." The flashlight circle revealed the face and head of a middle-aged man: regular features, stylish rimless aviator glasses, medium-long, medium-mod brown hair graying at the temples. The face had settled into peace; the eyes were open, rolled upward. The victim lay flat on his back, right arm crossed over the body at the waist, left arm flung wide. Beside the open left hand, a ring of keys lay on the sidewalk. The right hand was tightly closed. The body was angled so that the right foot hung off the curb. The torso was almost completely blood-soaked. Because of the steepness of the hill, the blood had run in three long rivulets down the sidewalk. Two of the rivulets ended about five feet from the body. The third rivulet, the center one, continued for several feet more. The blood was still viscous, just beginning to congeal. Probing, the pale yellow cone of light illuminated a tweed sport jacket, gray flannel trousers, brown loafers, argyle socks, a white button-down shirt, and an old school tie. Added up—the hair styling, the tweeds, the flannels, and the argyles—the effect was Brooks Brothers casual.

Hastings straightened, handed back the flashlight, and gestured for Miller to come close enough to let them talk without being overheard by the onlookers.

"So how's it look? Anything?"

"There're two eyewitnesses," Miller said. "And their stories are pretty consistent." He pointed across the street. "One of them was delivering a pizza. That's him, in that Honda, there." Miller pointed to a white sedan illegally parked parallel to the curb on the far side of the street. As in most of Russian Hill, parking in the eleven-hundred block of Green Street was desperate. Because the hill was so steep, parking was perpendicular to the curb. Because the street was so narrow, parking was permitted only on the south side. Because they would have had to be blasted out of solid rock, there were no garages on the north side of the street. The upper half of Green Street's south side was a stepped series of towering retaining walls, leaving only four garages for the entire eleven-hundred block. All of the buildings were more than fifty years old, almost all of them small apartment buildings. Like much of San Francisco's premium real estate, they clung to the hills that offered the best views. And the views from Russian Hill were superb.

"The other witness lives right here." Miller pointed to a narrow, three-story building that had been built over a double garage. "His name is Bruce Taylor, and he lives on the second floor. There're three flats in the building. Taylor was putting out the garbage." Miller gestured to a trash container and two plastic garbage bags. "He saw it happen. He tried to help the victim, but it was too late. And by that time, according to the way I get the story, the perpetrator had disappeared. So then Taylor went inside his house and called nine-one-one."

"And you and your partner were the first ones on the scene?"

"Right. We were only three blocks away when we got the call. If Taylor's telling the truth, which I think he is, he called nine-one-one maybe two, three minutes after the shots were fired."

"So you were on the scene within five minutes."

"Give or take a minute. No more."

"Did you talk to both of them—Taylor and the pizza guy?"

"Yessir. His name is Jeff Sheppard."

"And?"

Miller pointed across the street to another three-story building, this one without a garage. "The victim came out of that building. The number is eleven-forty-eight. He crossed the street diagonally, uphill." As Hastings followed Miller's moving forefinger with his eyes, the finger traced a path across the street, coming toward them. "He got on the sidewalk here, at about Bruce Taylor's garage. Then"—the finger continued to move—"then he started walking uphill." Now the finger was pointing to a tree about ten feet uphill from the body. "At that point, as I understand it, the perpetrator stepped out from behind that tree, there. They were just a few feet apart. Five feet, maybe."

"Did he fall in his tracks?" Hastings asked.

"That's my impression, Lieutenant."

"Do both witnesses' stories agree?"

"Pretty much, yeah."

"How do you rate the witnesses?"

Miller shrugged. "Compared to what?" He hesitated. Then, explaining: "This is only the second homicide I've ever caught."

"Okay—so what'd the assailant do?"

"Apparently he went to the body and stood over it for a few seconds, looking down. Then he walked down to Hyde Street"—Miller gestured downhill—"and turned left on Hyde."

"Walked?"

Emphatically, Miller nodded. "Walked. Definitelv walked. He didn't run."

"Did either Taylor or Sheppard try to follow the guy?"

Miller shook his head. "Taylor went to the victim, to see if he could help, like I said. And Sheppard, who'd parked by that time, he stayed in his car. Which was smart, of course."

"It would've been nice," Hastings said ruefully, "if he'd followed the guy in his car."

"Yeah. Well . . ." Miller shrugged again. "What can you do? At least he's willing to talk to us. There's that."

"Yes," Hastings agreed, his voice resigned. "Yes, there's that."

11:27 PM

Because the shop windows and the cars parked at curbside and the garbage pails set on the sidewalk moved and changed and appeared and disappeared, she realized she was walking. But there was no sensation, no contact, no conscious movement. Even if the sky tilted and the earth shifted, there would be no sensation. Only the night had meaning, only darkness had substance. From darkness come to darkness returned. Was it a poem? Was it the truth?

Could she remember?

Yes, always she would remember.

The eyes, dead, rolled up in their sockets. The bloodstain. blossoming as she'd watched. Always, she would remember. Always.

So that now, finally, she could rest.

Finally it was finished. Finally the pain had been numbed. As darkness had returned to darkness, so death would return to death.

11:32 PM

The door swung open to reveal a tall, slim, balding man dressed in faded blue jeans, scuffed white running shoes, and a sweatshirt imprinted with a Porsche logo.

"Mr. Taylor?"

"Right." Taylor nodded—a small, semi-spastic inclination of his narrow head. Taylor was probably still in his thirties. His face was delicately drawn, hollow-eyed and hollow-cheeked, an invalid's face. His small mouth was permanently pursed, a worrier's mouth. His round hazel eyes, blinking, were vulnerable as they fixed on the gold badge pinned to the breast of Hastings's jacket.

His voice, too, was vulnerable: "Have you—is—" Shaking his head, he broke off. Then he stepped back, gesturing for Hastings to come inside.

Like the Russian Hill neighborhood, Bruce Taylor's flat was elegant: antiques that were obviously authentic, paintings that were obviously originals. Abruptly showing Hastings to a damask settee, Taylor sat facing him across a small wooden table. A heavy cut-glass tumbler, half-filled, stood on the table. For a moment Taylor sat rigidly, staring down at the tumbler. Then: "I'm—I'm having a drink. Would you—" With an obvious effort, he raised his eyes. "Would you like one—a drink?"

"No, thanks."

"Ah . . ." As if he'd received a rebuke, Taylor first nodded, then sharply shook his head, suggesting that he couldn't control his own impatience with himself. "I—I'm sorry. But the truth is . . ." Shakily he gestured to the window that overlooked Green Street. He frowned, licked his lips, then looked directly into Hastings's eyes as he said, "The truth is, this thing—it's gotten to me. I mean, I'm thirty-seven, and I've never seen a body. Not—not even in a funeral home. I . . ." Shaking his head again, this time helplessly, forlornly, Taylor reached for the tumbler, drank half of the dark amber fluid, and replaced the tumbler on the table. "I mean, Jesus, you see someone like that, dead, and—" As if confused, he broke off. His eyes were still cast down, fixed on the tumbler.

"It's not easy," Hastings said. "It's never easy. Believe me."

Taylor nodded, his head bobbing loosely. Then, making a visible effort to collect himself, he said, "I suppose you're here—I suppose you want to—to find out about it—about what happened."

"That's right, Mr. Taylor. I'm sorry to make you go over it again so soon. But there're only two eyewitnesses, at least so far. So we've got to know what you know. Now. Right now."

"Yes . . ." Uncertainly, Taylor nodded. "Yes, I—I understand."

"So start at the beginning." Hastings spoke quietly, dispassionately. Whatever distress Taylor was suffering, the problem didn't concern Hastings. Not here. Not now.

"Well, I—I was taking the garbage out. The garbage can is in the garage. And there were a couple of bags of clippings in the garden. So I opened the garage door, and I put the can outside, on the sidewalk. It's still there."

Hastings nodded. "Yes, I saw it."

Quickly, Taylor gulped at the drink. "As I was putting the can out, I saw him coming toward me, from across the street."

"The victim, you mean."

Spasmodically, Taylor nodded.

"He was coming from"—Hastings glanced at his notebook, open on his knee—"from eleven-forty-eight. Is that correct?"

Taylor waved a fretful hand. "I suppose that's the number. Anyhow, it's diagonally across the street, downhill."

"Did he live in that house, do you know?"

"I don't think he lives—lived—there. But I've seen him there several times. He has a—" Taylor broke off, stole a speculative glance at his interrogator. Hastings recognized that look, and knew its meaning. Taylor was deciding what to tell him—and what not to tell him.

"There's a woman who lives there. They—I've seen them together, several times."

Watching Taylor carefully, listening to his inflection as he pronounced *woman,* Hastings decided that Taylor was probably a homosexual.

"Do you know the woman's name, Mr. Taylor?"

"No. I—she's only lived there for a few months. But you shouldn't have any trouble locating her. That building's like this one. Three flats. Besides, after the—the shooting, she came outside. She talked to one of the policemen."

"Describe this woman."

"Well, she's in her thirties, probably. Good-looking, I guess you'd say—" It was a grudging admission. Yes, almost certainly Taylor was gay.

"Dark hair? Light hair?"

"Dark hair. Lots of dark hair. And she drives one of those new little sports cars." He frowned. "It's Japanese. Red. Two-passenger." The frown remained.

"A Miata?"

Promptly, Taylor nodded. "Right. A Miata."

"All right. Good." As he said it, Hastings heard the sound of an engine coming up the hill, and voices slightly raised. The coroners had arrived. Or the lab crew. Or both.

"So what happened then?" Hastings asked. "After you took the garbage out, and you saw the victim walking across the street toward you, what happened? Did you speak? Nod?"

"No. We didn't—that wouldn't—I mean, we weren't really acquainted, you understand. I'd just noticed him, that's all."

"What happened next?" Mindful of the personnel on the street below waiting for his orders, Hastings spoke briskly.

"Well, I—after I saw him, like I said, I went back inside the garage, for the clippings. I got them, one in each hand, and I was trying to get both bags out, between my car and the bikes that the goddam neighbors leave in the garage, when I heard the shots."

"How many shots?"

"There were three. One, and then a slight pause, and then two more."

"What'd you do when you heard the shots?"

"Well, I—" Taylor drained his glass, then waved a hand in a short, delicate arc. "Well, I—I just continued, just took the bags out. I—at the time, you see, I didn't think they were shots. I thought it was a car backfiring. So when I finally got the trash bags around the bikes, I took them outside and stacked them beside the garbage can. And then, God, I saw him. It was—I can't tell you—it was horrible. Just horrible. I'll have nightmares. I—" He shuddered. "I *know* I'll have nightmares."

"What about the assailant? Did you see him?"

"Well, I—I guess so. I mean, there was someone walking away, down the hill."

"Did you get a look at him, at his face?"

"No. His back was to me."

"Was he running?"

"No. Walking." As if he were baffled, Taylor shook his head. "Just walking, down to Hyde Street."

"How was he dressed?"

Taylor frowned. "Just—you know—just a jacket, it looked like. A windbreaker. And slacks." He eyed Hastings. "Pretty much like you're dressed, I'd say."

"Bareheaded?"

Another frown. "No. I think he had a hat. Or rather a cap. Maybe it had a visor, but I'm not sure. I mean, there's not much light, you know. These streetlights, they're not much, on this block. We're supposed to be getting sodium-vapor streetlights. But some people think they're too bright, too garish. Not me, though. I always wanted the new lights. And this proves I was right. I mean—" He drew a deep, ragged breath. "I mean, if there'd been more light, this might not've happened."

"What about a gun?" As he spoke, Hastings rose to his feet. Down on the street, men were waiting. City employees, some on time and a half. "Did you see a gun?"

Decisively, Taylor shook his head. "No. No gun. God, if I'd seen a gun . . ." Shuddering, he gently stroked the side of his face with an unsteady hand, as if to comfort himself.

"What about the victim? You went to him, I understand. Did he say anything to you?"

"God, no. He—he was past that. All he was doing was twitching. His hands, and his feet too, they were—" As if the memory of the moment had numbed him, Taylor suddenly broke off. Hastings rose, thanked him, and quietly left the apartment. Before he reached the bottom of the stairs, he heard Taylor bolting the door.

12:10 AM

As Hastings walked toward the body, he saw Canelli and the pizza deliveryman standing together beside the deliveryman's car. Hastings beckoned and waited for Canelli to join him.

"So how'd it go?" Hastings asked. "Is he cooperating?"

"Yeah." Canelli nodded. "He's an eager beaver. You know, a cop fan. He's only nineteen. Nice kid."

"Okay . . ." Hastings gestured to the body. "You get the techs started, your responsibility. Clear?"

Canelli lifted his chin, squared his shoulders. This, he knew, was a significant moment. "Yessir, that's clear. Thank you."

Hastings pointed to the building across the street. "I'm going over there, see what I can find out."

"Yeah." Canelli nodded. "Sheppard—the pizza guy—he said it looked like the victim came from there, one of those buildings across the street. But he couldn't see which building, not from his angle."

"I know which one it is." Hastings looked at the victim and at the waiting technicians. "You get things going here. Tell Bruce Taylor and the pizza guy to stay available. You know, the usual."

"Shall I do the whole thing?" Canelli asked. "Sign the body off? Everything?" He spoke hesitantly; his soft brown eyes were hopeful. It had been months since Hastings had let him do it all: supervise the technicians, consult with the medical examiner, decide when the body could be moved, conduct a search of the victim's person, finally sign off the body for release to the coroner for autopsy. If the job wasn't done properly—the whole job, down to the most minute detail—then the vital first link in the chain of evidence would be compromised. And, always, it was that link that the defense lawyers tested first.

"Yeah," Hastings said. "Go ahead." He gestured to the building across the street. "I'll be over there. At eleven-forty-eight."

12:20 AM

As she watched, she was aware that her perceptions had skewed. After two hours, frozen here at this window, helpless, the scene had become surreal, a manic animation of flashing lights, official vans and station wagons, police cars, the monotonous, monosyllabic sputter of the police radios, the eerily immobile figures simply standing there, waiting for the ritual to begin, inscrutably alert for their subliminal cues. All of it centering on the figure lying dead on the cold concrete sidewalk—the figure none of them looked at directly.

They were waiting. Watching. Expecting some secret signal, some significant presence, some nameless, faceless authority—the same presence that she awaited.

All of it focused on the inert shape illuminated by two floodlights that had just been set up, each one on its own tripod, shades of a Hollywood set.

Brice.

Dead.

Three hours ago, they'd made love: a complex, urgent, intense coupling, herself receiving him, her essence enveloping his essence. Lovers. Antagonists. Explorers of sensation's limits, rivals for the prize.

And now he was an amorphous shape lying on the sidewalk. In the two hours of her vigil, the shape had become flat on the bottom, as if Brice's clothing covered a gelatinous sack of thick, viscous liquid that resembled a . . .

One of the plainclothesmen—the tall, muscular one with a large golden badge pinned to his poplin jacket—was coming down the staircase of the building across the street. She saw him walk toward the other plainclothesman. The second detective was a large, lumpy man with a swarthy face, whose manner marked him a subordinate. Now the two detectives were talking together, the swarthy one nodding anxiously, the first detective gesticulating, obviously giving orders. The first detective was bareheaded. His hair was thick and dark, his manner calm, self-sufficient.

Now, suddenly, the tall detective turned, raised his head, looked directly toward her.

Then, yes, he began crossing the street. Standing now on the sidewalk directly beneath her window, he was looking up at her, his head tilted. The moment held; a confirmation passed between them. Then, a measured greeting; he nodded. Gravely she returned the greeting. Then she turned away from the window, walked out into the hallway, stood at the head of the stairs. Waited. When the buzzer sounded, she pressed the button in return. He came in, closed the door, carefully tested it. Then: "I'm Lieutenant Hastings. Homicide. I understand you can help us." Looking up at her, he gestured behind him, toward the street. Toward Brice—the viscous, gelatinous husk of Brice.

"Yes. I—I guess I can. Come up."

"Thanks."

She stepped back from the upstairs landing, waited for him to join her. Then: "I'm Carla Pfiefer."

"How do you do." The detective looked expectantly through the living room doorway. "Can we—?"

"Yes. Certainly." Conscious of an overwhelming weariness, a sudden heaviness of her legs, she led him into the living room. Choosing a chair that let her keep her back to the street, she gestured for him to sit facing her. As she waited for him to speak, she could hear the continuing mutter of the police radios.

With a small spiral-bound notebook opened expectantly on his knee, ballpoint pen poised, Hastings said, "I understand that you know the—the victim."

"Yes, I knew him." As she said it, she could see satisfaction registering on the detective's face. Seen up close, he was an attractive man: a squared-off face, a generous mouth, thick brown hair graying at the temples, calm brown eyes. His voice, too, was calm: "What's his name?"

"His name is—" Her voice caught. God, this was where it started. Here. Now. With her very next words: "His name was Hanchett. Brice Hanchett."

"He was a friend of yours." It was a statement, not a question. The neighbors, then, had been talking. Always, it was the neighbors.

"He was with you tonight." Another flat, calm statement. He knew his business, this quiet-spoken detective. Behind his words, she could sense the ponderous weight of the law. He ordered, the others obeyed. Now she knew why.

"Yes . . ." Aware that it was a reluctant admission, aware that he could hear the reluctance in her voice, she nodded. "Yes, he was with me tonight."

He nodded in return, let a beat pass. Then, pen poised, he said, "What I'd like you to do is give me a rundown on Mr. Hanchett. Everything."

For this question, she was ready. For this, during the past two hours, standing at the window, looking down, she had prepared herself.

"It's—actually, it's *Doctor* Hanchett. He works—worked—at the Barrington Medical Center. He's—was—very well known Famous, I guess you'd say. At least in medical circles."

As she'd expected, his face remained impassive, his voice noncommittal. "Famous in what way?"

"Well, he—he was a surgeon. A very good, very successful surgeon. He was head of surgery, in fact, at BMC."

"Ah . . ." Hastings was nodding. "Yes. Thank you." Then, still the flat-voiced inquisitor: "You were . . . friends?"

This time it was a question. Not a statement, but a question.

"Yes . . . friends." She drew a long, deep breath. "My, ah—my husband works at BMC, in fact. He's a surgeon, too. A neurosurgeon."

"Your husband . . ." As he said it, Hastings circled the room with a perceptive, inquisitive gaze. Then, inquiringly, he turned his dark eyes directly on her. The message: she didn't fit his image of a married woman. Neither did the flat, or its furnishings.

"Hmm . . ." Speculatively, he cocked his head. It was an appealing gesture. What would he be like in bed, this strong, silent policeman?

Holding his eye, she spoke quietly. "We're separated."

"So? . . ." He raised one hand, a gesture that matched the inquiry in the monosyllable. The unspoken question was clear: Had she and Brice Hanchett been lovers?

If she denied it, he would continue probing. She could see it in his eyes, hear it in the one-word question. The thought—the certainty of policemen probing the secret recesses of her life—it was an obscenity. Requiring that she meet his gaze squarely. Then requiring that she speak firmly, disdainful of his questions, contemptuous of his policeman's petty insinuations.

"If you're going to ask whether we were lovers, Brice and I, the answer is yes. I'm separated from my husband, as I said. And Brice—well, you'll have to speak to his wife, I guess."

Surprisingly, the detective smiled—a small, noncommittal smile but, nevertheless, a smile. "You come right out with it." Approvingly, he nodded. "Good."

She lifted her chin, sat straighter in her chair. The worst was over. Until the next wave of horror overtook her, probably when she was in bed—the bed they'd shared, a few hours ago—the worst was over. "I don't have anything to hide, Lieutenant."

"I didn't think you did, Mrs. Pfiefer."

They sat silently for a moment, eyeing each other. Her expression, she could feel, was holding: a silent challenge. His expression, too, was holding: implacable but respectful.

Was that the word? Respectful?

Now he pointed to the window. "You have a direct view of the street. Did you see it happen?"

"No. I was in the bedroom, in back. The bedroom, and the bathroom."

"Did you hear the shots?"

"Yes."

"How many shots did you hear?"

"There were three. First one, then two more." As she said it, she saw him nod. It had been the right answer, then. Why did she feel so pleased, seeing him nod?

"What'd you do when you heard the shots?"

"Well, I—as I said, I was—" A momentary pause, a single defiant beat. Then: "I was using the bathroom. So, afterwards, I put something on. Then I went to the front of the apartment, to the window. And then—" Suddenly her throat closed, a sharp, sudden spasm. "Then I—I saw him. He was—" She couldn't finish it. She could only shake her head mutely. Perhaps to give her time, Hastings was rising, crossing to the window, looking down. Then he returned to his chair, saying, "He's lying across the street, and the light isn't very good. How could you be sure it was him?"

"I knew. I just *knew.*" Was she talking loudly? Too loudly? Too insistently?

"You knew? How?"

"Well, he—he'd just left, for one thing. And his car was still there, across the street. I—I think that's how I knew, how I was sure. Because of the car."

"Did you take any action? Call the police? Call nine-one-one?"

"No, I—I didn't. I—I couldn't seem to think."

He nodded. "That's understandable. You were . . ." He paused, searching for the word. "You were close, the two of you."

"Yes—close." Somehow she suddenly felt ridiculous, repeating the single word *close.* Was that all there was to say? Lovers—passionate lovers—for three months. All reduced to *close.*

"After the first policeman arrived, though, you talked to him?"

"Yes."

"Did you go downstairs and talk to him? Or did he come up here?"

"I went down. I—I thought I should help. Tell them his name, tell them about the car."

"I wonder . . ." The detective paused, studying her. Then, apparently having come to a decision: "I wonder whether you could tell me what kind of a man Brice Hanchett was."

"I . . ." She frowned. "I'm not sure what you mean."

"I mean, give me a description of him. Was he even-tempered? Hotheaded? Did he make enemies? Was he cautious, or was he reckless? Things like that." Transparently trying to put her at ease, reassure her, he smiled. "I'm looking for impressions. No big deal. I won't repeat what you say."

Her answering smile twisted ruefully. "Hot-tempered, even tempered, that's easy. He had a terrible temper. At least on the job, he supposedly had a terrible temper."

"What about privately? Did he have a temper privately, would you say?"

Considering the question, how best to answer, to be fair, she let her eyes wander. Then, speaking deliberately, she said, "Brice was a very intelligent, very attractive, very vital man. He was one of those people who have it all. His personality—well, it was very powerful, very compelling. And he had the ego to match. He was a very egocentric man. When everything was going his way, he was charming. But cross him, and sparks flew. Big, bright sparks."

"Did he hold a grudge? Was he that kind of a man?"

She nodded. "I suppose he did. But no more than the next man, I'd say. If Brice got in a fight, he usually won. And winners don't hold grudges. At least Brice didn't. As long as he got his way, there weren't any problems."

"By 'fight,' I presume you mean verbally. Not physical fights."

She hesitated. Then she nodded again. "Yes. Right."

Hastings folded his notebook, clipped his ballpoint pen to an inside pocket. "This'll probably turn out to be a street hoodlum who panicked and pulled the trigger by accident. An attempted robbery, in other words. At least that's the way I'd bet." A pause. Then, quietly: "Is that how you'd bet, Mrs. Pfiefer?"

Behind the question she could sense some secret meaning. But what? Why? How much did Hastings *really* know?

"I—I'm not sure what you mean."

"What I mean is, if it turns out not to be robbery, or attempted robbery, do you have any idea why someone would want to kill Dr. Hanchett?" A moment passed as they eyed each other.

Then: "Your husband, for instance. Is he—was he—jealous of Dr. Hanchett?"

"Are you saying—suggesting—that Jason would—" Incredulously, she began shaking her head as she felt anger growing, warming her. A small glowing ember of anger. "Are you saying that Jason could have done it, killed Brice?"

"I'm just looking for information, for opinions. I gather it's your opinion that your husband couldn't have done it."

"Yes," she answered. "Yes, that's definitely my opinion. Definitely, yes."

1:20 AM

In silence, Hastings watched the doors of the coroner's van close. With their measurements checked and their evidence bagged and tagged and their pictures taken, the lab technicians were switching off their lights and taking down their yellow tapes. In an hour the night would reclaim the murder scene. In the morning, bright and early, the householders responsible for this section of sidewalk would be out with hose and broom, washing down the blood.

Standing beside Hastings, Canelli noted the time in the log as Hastings glanced across the street. Was Carla Pfiefer still watching from her darkened living room? How would she sleep tonight? Had she been in love with Brice Hanchett? Or had they been using each other? If Hanchett was an egotist, what did that make Carla Pfiefer?

And what had Carla Pfiefer made of her husband except a cuckold?

He waited for Canelli to make his log entries. "So what's it look like?"

"Well," Canelli answered, "it turns out that he had his wallet and his money—about a hundred dollars—and a ring and a fancy wristwatch. So it doesn't look like robbery. Except if the bad guy got spooked, the old story. But from what Taylor says, and what the pizza guy says, the whole thing was pretty—you know—deliberate. The victim—his name was Brice Hanchett, and he lived on Jackson Street, in Pacific Heights—he was just walking calmly, not expecting a thing. It seems like the assailant was waiting for him, standing behind that tree"—Canelli pointed—"in the shadows. So that was it. Three shots. Hanchett went right down, apparently. So then the assailant, very cool, stood over him for a few seconds, then walked off. The M.E. says Hanchett probably died right where he fell, by the look of the wounds. Two shots hit him, it looks like, large caliber, in the chest. So the third shot went wild, probably. We got two shell casings, by the way. Two out of three, not bad." As he said it, Canelli looked hopefully at Hastings, for approval.

Hastings nodded. "Great. That's great. By the way—" He pointed to the tan Jaguar, parked a short distance up the hill. "That's his car, that tan Jag. Did you hold on to the keys?"

"Yessir. I figured they wouldn't take prints."

"Okay—good. Well—" Hands in his pockets, Hastings surveyed the scene. "Well, let's wrap it up. Or rather—" Hastings smiled, yawned, took his hands out of his pockets, stretched his arms overhead. "Or rather, let's *you* wrap it up. After the towtruck comes, unblock the street. Then . . ." He hesitated. At one-thirty in the morning, was he presuming too much on Canelli's amiable good nature? No. Canelli was the officer in charge at the scene. It was a trial run for command, for promotion. In for a dime, in for a dollar. "Then you'll have to find his family, break the news."

"Right." Canelli nodded. Then, tentatively, he gestured toward Carla Pfiefer's flat. "What about the lady? Carla Pfiefer? What d'you think, Lieutenant? Should I mention her to the guy's family, or what? I mean, if his wife asks where he was—where he'd been, before he got killed . . ." Letting the question linger, Canelli furrowed his brow. His brown eyes were anxious. "I mean, if you were me . . ." Once more, his question trailed off.

"If I were you," Hastings said, "I'd discharge my duty to notify the next of kin. If they're in shape to answer questions, I'd find out what they know. But I wouldn't volunteer anything. And I wouldn't answer any questions—not any hard questions, anyhow. I'd just do it by the book—get through it. And then I'd get out. That's best."

"Yeah . . ." Gravely, Canelli nodded, then repeated dubiously, "Yeah . . ."

1:30 AM

She turned her gaze from the bedside clock to the ceiling of the bedroom. It had been just a little after ten o'clock, she knew, when she'd arrived at the Green Street address.

Three and a half hours . . .

The pistol had been a snake in her hand, deadly and alive, the dark metal tracking him like a cobra's head. The flame licking out to find him, touch him—

Kill him.

Wands were metal, too. Magician's wands, touchstones of her childhood. Wands come alive, reincarnated, the flame that could kill.

A touch of her finger on metal, flame finding flesh, death unto death.

Vengeance is mine, saith the Lord.

And hers, too. Finally hers.

Tuesday, September 11

9:10 AM

As Hastings mounted the broad stone steps of the Barrington Medical Center, the realization suddenly surfaced, paired with a name: Susan Parrish, someone he'd known in high school. Newly promoted, Susan was head nurse at Barrington. She'd married young, just out of high school. Quickly, she'd had two children. Her maiden name had been Jessup; she'd married Arnold Parrish, whose father was a dentist. After she'd had two children, a girl and a boy, and after the children were in their teens, Susan had decided to go to college and become a nurse. When he'd returned to San Francisco, soon after he'd gotten his shield, Hastings had discovered Susan working at San Francisco General, in the emergency room. They'd both been rookies, both in their thirties, both of them taking a second look at life. For Susan, the career move had been voluntary, a search for another dimension. For him, the move had been involuntary, a retreat from the failure of his marriage and the sudden end of his playing days with the Lions. Followed by the final defeat: he and the bottle, no contest.

At the reception desk, a young black woman with quick eyes and a melodious voice asked whether she could help him.

"Susan Parrish, please. Tell her it's Frank Hastings."

Moving efficiently, the woman nodded, wrote the name on a small notepad, punched out a number on her telephone console. "Susan Parrish. Frank Hastings is here." She listened, nodded, smiled at him. "She says for you to come right up. Do you know the way?"

"Afraid not."

She produced a printed floor plan of BMC and deftly began laying out his route with a felt marker.

9:36 AM

When Hastings had finished his account of the murder, Susan Parrish smiled broadly. "God, this is great. Obviously, everyone at BMC'll be talking about Hanchett. But I'll be the only one with an inside track. Wait'll I tell Arnie tonight."

Sternly, Hastings raised a forefinger. "You can tell Arnie. But that's it."

She nodded, a deep, good-natured inclination of her head. She was a stocky, robust woman, with the mannerisms to match. In high school, Hastings remembered, she'd almost always been on the honor roll. During the twenty-odd minutes they'd been talking, Susan had taken three calls, each obviously involving problems only she could solve. In each case, Susan had dealt with the problem smoothly and efficiently. It was a talent Hastings envied.

"So what can you tell me about Hanchett?" Hastings asked. "The inside stuff, I mean."

"The truth?"

"The truth."

"The *whole* truth?"

"The whole truth."

"Well, the truth is—let's see—" She broke off. Crow's feet showed around her eyes as she considered. Without realizing it, Hastings sat up straighter in his chair, sucked in his stomach.

"The truth is," she said, "Dr. Hanchett was a stuffed shirt and a petty tyrant and a bush-league megalomaniac—and a hell of a surgeon. And, oh yes, a philanderer. You already know that part. Scandals—triangles—didn't faze him. If he saw a woman he liked, he went after her." She shrugged. "Maybe he couldn't help himself. Dr. Pfiefer and his wife were only the latest triangle. There were others. Always."

"Did he make enemies, would you say?"

Promptly, she nodded. "All the time. Excluding lovers, I can't think of any friends he had, at least not at BMC. But he definitely had enemies."

"Did anyone hate him enough to kill him?"

"That," she answered evenly, "is a judgment you'd have to make, Frank. What causes someone to murder someone else?" She spread her hands. "That's outside my area of expertise." She paused, looked at him speculatively. "Was it premeditated? Is that what you're saying?"

How much should he tell her? How much should he hold back?

"The way it came down," he said, "the way it seems to've happened, it could've been premeditated. That is, there wasn't anything taken, no robbery. However, that can happen if a potential robbery victim resists, and gets shot. The bad guy usually forgets about the wallet or the purse, and runs."

Her smile was mischievous. "So what're you saying? What is this, the either-or game? Premeditated, not premeditated, take your pick?"

"What this is," he answered, "is a guessing game. I don't have the faintest idea who killed him, or why. But if it's premeditated, then the murderer was known to the victim, that's the first rule. Someone who knew the victim, and someone who hated him, that's the profile. And so far, the guy I know about that best fits into that profile is Jason Pfiefer, the jealous husband."

Susan Parrish's smile turned inward as she reflectively shook her head. "Doctors—those two doctors, especially—they've got three-hundred-pound egos. At least."

"Was Jason Pfiefer jealous of Brice Hanchett, would you say?"

"I have no idea, Frank. None."

"Carla Pfiefer said Hanchett was chief of surgery."

"Yes."

"And Jason Pfiefer is a neurosurgeon."

She nodded.

"So they worked together."

"Right. But except for the transplant team, they really didn't have much to do with each other."

"There wasn't any friction between them, then."

Wryly, she shrugged. "If Hanchett was involved, there was friction. Guaranteed. But the only time Hanchett and Pfiefer worked together was on transplants, like I said. Still, there wasn't any unusual friction between them during the operations, that I know of."

"Transplants . . . you mean hearts, livers, like that?"

"No hearts," she answered. "Livers and kidneys, at Barrington. We specialize, you see. That's the secret of Hanchett's success in transplants. Specialization. Which is why we have a worldwide reputation, especially for livers. And it's all thanks to Dr. Hanchett and his ego."

"How do you mean, 'specialization'?"

"I mean we don't take chances. We do one kind of operation—livers and kidneys—and we do it very well indeed. We don't experiment. That's when you fail, you see. Which is why . . ." Her voice began to fade, her eyes began to lose focus. A random thought had surfaced, something significant.

He prompted her. "Which is why?"

Thoughtfully, she responded, "Which is why, occasionally, Hanchett had problems. Not with the doctors. With recipients. Or, rather, with their families."

"Someone needs a liver and doesn't get one. Is that what you mean?"

"For every organ that's available, there're always a dozen candidates. Someone has to rank them, give them a priority number, one to twelve, whatever. Actually, it's a committee of three that assigns the priorities—the Recipient Selection Committee. And Hanchett, of course, was the chairman of the committee, which means—meant—that it was a one-man show, really." Now, mischievously again, she smiled. "Some cynics say playing God came naturally to Hanchett. But whether it came naturally or not, the fact remains that someone had to decide who got a chance to live. Which meant, of course, that someone else would probably die. And Hanchett had to make the decision."

"How'd he decide? What were the guidelines?"

"Mostly it's a medical decision. It's very complicated, really. But basically it comes down to how successfully the recipient will get through the operation—and how long he'll survive, assuming the operation succeeds."

"So a ten-year-old kid has a lot better chance of being chosen than someone who's eighty."

She smiled. "Try fifty."

"What about money? Does a forty-year-old millionaire have a better chance than a ten-year-old whose family's on welfare?"

She let a beat pass before she decided to say, "I hope not." Another moment of silence. Then, as if to divert his next question, she said, "The primary consideration is need—how sick the patient is, how long he can live without a new liver or kidney. Sometimes that translates into"—she paused, searching for the phrase—"into geography."

"Geography?"

" 'Harvesting organs,' as it's called, is a minute-to-minute operation. It's distance, and it's time. The ideal source is a nineteen-year-old kid riding a motorcycle without a helmet. He hits his head, goes into a coma. His parents agree to donate his organs, if and when. Barrington is notified that a liver and kidney might be available. A couple of transplant surgeons pack their instruments and a change of underwear. If the organs are in Sacramento or San Jose, they drive to the hospital—and wait. Otherwise, they get into a corporate jet—and hope the weather is flyable. Because once the donor dies, those surgeons have got to get the organs and pack them in ice, and get in their Learjet and get back here. They always come in an ambulance, sometimes with a police escort, from the airport.

"And while all that's going on, the recipient has got to get to the hospital—time and distance again. He's got to be on the operating table. Because once that organ comes through the doors, the surgeons start cutting. So, obviously, the recipient who can get here the soonest has an edge. Which is why, just last month, a young couple with a twelve-year-old girl who was dying of kidney failure got in their motor home and drove down from Redding. They drove to San Francisco, and they started living in our parking lot. They parked there for almost two weeks before—" She broke off, looked away. Meaning, without doubt, that the girl had died.

"So are you saying Hanchett made enemies, playing God?"

"I'm saying that he had to deal with some pretty distraught people. Especially parents with young children—mothers. Believe me, Frank, you always hear about the ferocity of the mother fighting for the life of her young. And I'll tell you, it's all true. You see it constantly in this business. But never more dramatically than when there's a mother whose child is going to die unless he gets a particular organ from a particular donor by a particular time. The mother will do anything—*anything*—to get that organ. And a mother who sees an organ go to another woman's child, then sees her own child die . . ." Susan shook her head. "I only dealt with it once, when the woman went off the deep end. But it was awesome. Really awesome. Most times, I like being a nurse. But dealing with that woman . . ." She turned up her hands. "That night I about decided to go into real estate. Even after one of Arnie's double martinis and a backrub, I still thought about real estate."

"How long ago was this?"

"Six, seven months, I'm not really sure." She smiled ruefully. "I'm trying to block it out, obviously."

Thoughtfully, Hastings nodded. A distraught mother whose child had died because Hanchett had decided to give an organ to another child . . . it was a possibility worth exploring. Both witnesses had said the murderer was a man. But all they'd seen was a figure wearing slacks and a jacket and a cap. The closest streetlight had been a hundred feet away; the block was badly lit. The closest witness, the pizza deliveryman, had been at least fifty feet from the victim.

He opened his notebook. "What's this woman's name?"

"Her name is Bell. Teresa Bell."

"Do you know her husband's name?"

She frowned—"It's Fred. I'm almost sure it's Fred."

"Do they live in San Francisco?"

"Out in the avenues." She smiled. "Not too far from where we grew up, Frank. The old neighborhood."

He returned the smile, closed the notebook, moved forward in his chair. "Thanks, Susan." He rose. "I've taken enough of your—"

Her phone warbled—a different, louder note. Was it an

alarm? Yes, he could see it in her face as she listened briefly. He could hear it in her voice: "Okay. Two minutes." Quickly she rose. "Sorry, Frank. Duty calls. You know how it is."

"I know how it is. Thanks, Susan. Can I use your phone?"

"Dial nine." She hugged him, kissed him on the cheek, went to the door. "Let me know. Promise?"

"Promise." He watched her leave the office, closing the door as she went. Sitting in her swivel chair, he touch-toned Homicide, asked for Canelli.

"Sorry, Lieutenant, but Canelli isn't—oh, wait. Here he comes now. Just a second." And, moments later, Canelli came on the line.

"Hi, Lieutenant. How's it going?"

"I was just going to ask you the same question."

"Well, his wife took it pretty cool, Lieutenant. Very cool, in fact."

"What time did you talk to her?"

"It was twenty minutes after two when I finally got there." As Canelli spoke, Hastings could hear him suppressing a yawn.

"And?"

"Well, she was alone in the house. It's a real fancy house on Jackson, near Scott. I mean *real* fancy. Big bucks. *Real* big bucks."

"Had she been asleep, did you think, when you got there?"

"Hard to tell. Like I said, she was real cool, made me show my ID, the whole nine yards. All this with the night chain on the door. So, jeez, with her coming on so strong, not letting me in, and demanding that, you know, I tell her what it was all about, me standing on the goddamn stoop, well, jeez, I didn't have any choice. I mean, I had to tell her through the crack in the door that her husband was dead. So then—finally—she let me in."

"She wasn't upset, eh?"

"Not that I could see, Lieutenant. Mostly—well—if I had to

pick a word, I guess it'd be 'hostile.' I mean, we just stood in the hallway, you know? She didn't even ask me in, or anything. It was like—you know—I'd delivered a real smelly load of fish or something, and she couldn't wait for me to leave. And—oh, yeah—the first thing she asked me—after I told her that her husband was dead, and that he was shot by an unknown assailant on the street—the first thing she asked me was where had he gotten killed. What street, what address? Well, even though I knew we weren't giving out that stuff to the press, or anything, not now, at least, I figured that, jeez, I couldn't very well refuse to tell her. So I told her it happened on Green Street. I mean, I figured she'd find out anyhow, sooner or later. So I—" Partly to catch his breath, partly because of uncertainty, Canelli broke off. Hoping for the best, he waited for Hastings to speak.

The pause was Hastings's cue. "That's right, Canelli. What else could you do?"

"Ah." It was a grateful sigh. "Right. What else could I do?"

"So how'd she react, when you gave her the location?"

"She didn't really react, not that I could see. She just wanted me to leave—get lost, it seemed like. So then, the next thing I know, I'm standing on the goddamn porch again, looking at the door."

"I think I'll talk to her. Then I'll come in. Tell Lieutenant Friedman I'll be there by about noon. Okay?"

"Yeah. Sure, Lieutenant. Okay."

10:50 AM

"If you'll please take a seat"—the uniformed maid gestured to a large leather armchair—"Mrs. Hanchett will be right with you."

"Thank you." As Hastings sank into the luxury of the chair, he glanced around the room. It was a small study. Two walls, floor to ceiling, were bookshelves. A third wall was dominated by a huge, multicolored, leaded-glass window that was certainly an authentic antique. There was a library table and a leather-topped desk, also antique. Another leather lounge chair matched Hastings's chair. The desk chair, on casters, was also leather. The wall behind the desk was covered with framed pictures, certificates, and mementos.

"Would you like some coffee?" the maid asked. "Rolls?" She was Filipino; her *café au lait* face was as smooth as polished stone, and just as bland. Her voice was expressionless.

"No, thanks."

"Mrs. Hanchett is with . . ." The maid hesitated, searching for the right word. As the silence lengthened, she began to frown. "She's with the undertakers."

"Ah." Hastings nodded. "Yes."

The maid nodded politely in return and turned toward the door, which she left open as she walked out into the spacious entry hall with its curving staircase that led up to the second floor. The door was carved oak, thick enough to have come from a castle. The massive handle was brass.

A maid; a Pacific Heights town house; bookcases filled with leatherbound books; a Jaguar; a young, beautiful lover: Hanchett had had it all.

But the Jag was in the police lab. And Hanchett was in a drawer at the morgue, awaiting the autopsy surgeon's knife.

From the hallway came the sound of voices, hushed male voices, a restrained woman's voice. Contracts in their pockets, the morticians were departing. Through the open door, Hastings saw two men in dark suits gravely shaking hands with a dark-haired woman wearing beige slacks, and a loose-fitting brown sweater. Slim but full-bodied, carrying herself with the arrogance of a desirable woman aware of her own desirability, Mrs. Brice Hanchett bore a remarkable resemblance to Carla Pfiefer. Had Hanchett's choice of lovers followed a pattern?

She was coming toward him now. With her dark, elegant, arrogant good looks, with her chin raised, shoulders and hips working together, moving as provocatively and as economically as a model might, she came into the study, swung the door closed, and took one of the two deep leather chairs facing him. All of it—the entrance, closing the door, sitting down, crossing one slim leg over the chair—was accomplished as if it were one movement, smoothly choreographed, flawlessly executed.

Carla Pfiefer, the girlfriend, was a sensual, exciting woman.

But the wife had the class.

After Hastings introduced himself, Mrs. Hanchett said, "I've already talked to a homicide detective this morning. Do you know that?"

Hastings nodded. "Inspector Canelli. Yes. This is a—a follow-up. I've just finished talking with Inspector Canelli, as a matter of fact."

Watching him with her dark, calm eyes, she made no response. Her face revealed nothing. It was a lean, aristocratic face. The mouth was small and firmly set, the nose aquiline, slightly pinched.

Like I'd delivered a load of smelly fish, Canelli had said.

Score another one for Canelli.

As, still, she waited calmly, her eyes effortlessly meeting his.

"I'm sorry it had to be so late when Inspector Canelli rang your doorbell," Hastings began. "But it's departmental policy to notify the next of kin in person, not by phone."

She nodded. "Of course."

"Is there anything I can do, Mrs. Hanchett? Anything I can help you with?"

She smiled, a slight, humorless movement of her impeccably drawn lips. "You can catch whoever did it."

"That's why I'm here, Mrs. Hanchett."

She frowned. It was the first spontaneous expression she'd revealed since she'd made her entrance. "I don't understand."

"It's beginning to look like your husband might've been killed last night for personal reasons."

The frown deepened, the nostrils thinned, the mouth hardened. "What d'you mean, 'personal reasons'?"

"I mean enemies."

"Enemies?"

"Whenever someone's killed, we look for two things—motive and opportunity. So, we're trying to find someone with a motive for killing Dr. Hanchett. Usually, in a killing like this—a street killing—it's either a fight or else it's robbery. Sure, there're the nuts, the random killers who kill for kicks, or because their voices tell them to do it. And it's possible that your husband's killer was one of those. But my hunch is whoever killed your husband did it for a reason."

"What kind of a reason?"

"Usually it's either gain or revenge. Or jealousy, one of those three." He decided to smile, to make a gesture of invitation. "Take your pick. Please. We need all the help we can get."

"Lieutenant . . ." She let a hard, deliberate moment pass. "I really don't have time for guessing games. And I don't have the patience, either. Not this morning."

"Sure. I understand." Briskly he withdrew a notebook from an inside pocket. "This won't take long, Mrs. Hanchett. I've already been to BMC, and I've gotten a pretty good idea of Dr. Hanchett's, uh, professional situation. So now, if I can get a rundown on his personal life—his relatives, his family situation—then I'll be on my way." Expectantly he clicked his ballpoint pen, at the same time experimenting with another smile.

"What is it you want, exactly?" Her voice was cold, impersonal. But something stirred in the depths of her eyes. Was it caution? Concern?

Concern for what? Why?

"I'd like vital statistics. From his driver's license I know he was fifty-two years old, and I know he lived at this address. But that's all I know. And I need more. Lots more."

"He was married before," she said, reciting now. "And so was I. His first wife's name is Fiona. She lives on Washington Street, not too far from here, in fact. They have a son. John. He lives with his mother."

"Is that Fiona Hanchett?"

She nodded. "Yes. She never remarried."

"What's your name—your given name?"

"It's Barbara." She hesitated, then decided to say, "Barbara Gregg Hanchett."

"How long have—were—you married to Dr. Hanchett?"

"Almost four years. It'll be—" She broke off, bit her lip. "It would've been four years in two months—November."

"You were married before. Could I have your first husband's name?"

Instantly she bristled. Hastings recognized that mannerism: the upper-class matron harassed by a mere civil servant.

"Why do you want my first husband's name?"

Tactically, his response was textbook-clear: never answer a hostile question.

"Have you ever seen a transcript of a murder trial, Mrs. Hanchett?"

"What's that got to do with it?"

"A transcript can run to thousands of pages, the most minute detail. That's what this business is all about, Mrs. Hanchett. Details."

Jaw set grimly, eyes bright with rigidly suppressed anger, voice edged with bitterness and scorn, she said, "His name is Edward Gregg. He's remarried, and lives on Cherry Street. He's a lawyer. A very rich, very successful lawyer. He's forty-five years old, and—" Contemptuously, she shrugged. "And I'm forty-three, if that's the kind of detail you're looking for. We—Edward and I—have a daughter named Paula who's a model and lives in North Beach." About to say more, she frowned, then fell into a brooding, patrician silence.

Calling for a calm, cool response: "Thank you, Mrs. Hanchett." He flipped a notebook page, made a final entry, flipped the notebook closed, returned it to his pocket, the businesslike policeman doing his job. "That's very helpful."

"Good." Sitting in her chair, chin lifted, back arched, legs elegantly crossed, a finishing-school posture, she nodded, a slight, stiff-necked inclination of her impeccably coiffed head.

All of it making an irresistible target.

Holding her gaze, Hastings let a beat pass. Then, quietly, he said, "Did Inspector Canelli tell you the, uh, circumstances surrounding your husband's death?"

"Circumstances?"

"It happened a little after ten P.M., in the eleven-hundred block of Green Street. That's on Russian Hill, between Hyde and Leavenworth."

She made no response. But, deep behind her violet eyes, something shifted. He'd touched another nerve. Or was it the same nerve?

"Would you like to hear the details?" Hastings asked. "Or would you rather not? Your choice." Aware that whichever way she answered he could only win, he was also aware of the smugness he felt. Friedman's favorite targets were the rich and the famous. Sometimes Hastings could understand why.

"Do you mean that—" Watching him attentively, she broke off. When she spoke again, her voice was lower, tighter. "Do you mean that you know how it happened? Why it happened?"

"We've got two witnesses. There're probably others, there usually are. It can take time for witnesses to come forward. But we have a good idea of Dr. Hanchett's movements right up to the time the shots were fired."

"And?" As she spoke, she held her finishing-school pose. If it was a performance, it was flawless: the lady of the castle, composed, ready to receive tidings that would daunt a lesser person.

The only possible response was the truth. "Well, he—Dr.

Hanchett—spent approximately two hours in the company of a woman named Carla Pfiefer, who lives at eleven-forty-eight Green Street." Covertly watchful, he let a second pass. Her face remained rigid. Another second. Then it began: raw, elemental hatred, clouding the eyes, twitching at each corner of the beautifully drawn mouth, constricting the muscles of the throat. Her voice dropped to a low, clotted whisper:

"So you know about it—about them?"

Silently, he nodded.

"She's not the first, you know. She's just the latest."

"I know."

"You've talked to her, then."

"Yes. Last night. Today or tomorrow, I'll probably talk to her again."

"What'd she say? What'd she tell you?"

"I—ah—I don't think I should get into that, Mrs. Hanchett. It's—"

"Did she talk about me? That's all I want to know—whether you talked about me."

"No," he answered quietly. "No, we didn't talk about you."

She was breathing more deeply now, round, taut breasts thrusting against the cashmere softness of her sweater. Her chin was still raised, her posture still disdainfully stiff. But she'd lost control of her mouth, and her eyes were balefully fixed. Finally: "Was it a man? Was the killer a man?"

"We don't know that." He looked at her attentively. "Why?"

"Because her husband," she said, biting off each word, "is insanely jealous of her, that's why."

Until he could keep his voice level, his expression neutral, Hastings made no response. Then: "Her husband works at BMC. He's a doctor. Is that correct?"

"Yes. A surgeon."

"Has he ever made any threats against Dr. Hanchett?"

For a long moment she sat rigid, each hand clamped on the

arms of her chair. Finally, after carefully clearing her throat and once more elevating her flawless chin, she said, "That's up to you to find out. You find the murderer, Lieutenant. I'll bury my husband."

10:55 AM

"Please, Jonathan, don't scratch. It only makes it worse, when you scratch."

"But it *itches.*"

"I know it itches. But if you scratch, it'll get infected. Remember what the doctor said."

"Have you ever had poison oak?"

"No, I never have." Wearily, Jane Ryder smiled down at her son. Should she send him to school tomorrow? School had only been in session for seven days, since Labor Day. If she let him—

"Has Dad ever had poison oak?"

"Yes. He told you that last night."

"I think I'll watch TV. Can I have a cookie?"

"How about a bran muffin?"

Resigned, Jonathan sighed. "Okay."

"First, though, I want you to go outside and pick up those papers in the hedge. Take a wastebasket. Then come back for the muffin."

"Aw . . ." He began scratching at his chest, where the poison oak was the worst.

"Jonathan—*don't scratch. Please.*"

"Aw . . ."

"Here." She took the plastic wastebasket from under the sink. "Pick up those papers and put them in the basket, and then empty the basket into the garbage can. Then come back and have your muffin and milk."

Carrying the wastebasket hugged close to his stomach, he waited for her to open the kitchen door. He stepped out into the bright, warm September sunshine and walked along the side of the house to the small front garden. He unlatched the gate, placed the wastebasket on the sidewalk. Did his mother mean for him to pick up just the advertising circulars? Or did she mean for him to pick up the candy wrappers and bits of paper, too? There were germs on paper like that, lying in the dirt. He sighed—and scratched his chest. Didn't his mother care whether he caught something from germs? One day she told him always to keep his hands clean, because of germs. But now, today, she—

Dark metal gleamed in the space between the thick-growing hedge. Something was lying on the ground. Using both hands, he parted two branches—

—and saw the pistol.

It was an automatic, and it looked real. Never before had he seen a make-believe gun that looked so real. He squatted, picked up the gun. It was heavy, the heaviest gun he'd ever felt. Not plastic, but metal. Just like a gun: a real gun, that could shoot.

Holding the gun in both hands, cops and robbers, he turned toward the gate, facing the house. He crouched, cops and robbers, and touched the trigger—

—and heard the whole world explode.

12:30 PM

Hastings took the microphone from beneath the dash, punched in the Command channel.

"Inspectors Eleven."

From Communications, an unfamiliar female voice answered, "Inspectors Eleven, go ahead."

"This is Lieutenant Hastings. Give me Lieutenant Friedman, please."

"Yessir."

A thirty-second pause. Then: "Friedman."

"It's Frank, Pete. What's happening? Anything on the Hanchett homicide? Any reports?"

"I'm expecting prelims from the lab and the coroner by four o'clock. How about if you and Canelli plan on a meeting here at four-thirty?" Uncharacteristically, Friedman spoke brusquely, his voice tight. Downtown, things were happening.

"Four-thirty. Fine."

"Okay. Gotta go. It looks like a couple of drug pushers are playing 'Gunfight at the O.K. Corral' out at Hunter's Point."

"Four-thirty. Where's Canelli?"

"Here. You want him, for the Hanchett thing?"

Irritated, Hastings spoke sharply: "I've *got* him, for God's sake. He's the officer of record on this."

"Okay. Calm down. I'll switch you." A long moment of dead air passed before Canelli came on the line.

"Leonard?"

"Wrong, Canelli. Guess again."

"Oh, Jesus, Lieutenant. Sorry. These goddamn phones. I thought you were Leonard."

"I want you to run three names for me. One of them—Fiona Hanchett—I want right now. She's Hanchett's first wife. She lives on Washington Street."

"Okay—just a second." On the other end of the line, the phone clattered as Canelli laid it on the desk. In the background Hastings heard the sounds of the squad room: typewriters clicking, a computer chirping, phones ringing, some voices mumbling, some voices raised. Finally: "Right. Got her."

"Good. Go ahead." Pen poised, Hastings waited.

"It's forty-one-seventy-four Washington. Sounds like money."

"I've got two more names. I don't need them right now. One is a woman named Teresa Bell, who lives in the avenues, I think. The other is Paula Gregg. She lives in North Beach." He spelled both names. "There's a woman named Susan Parrish. A head nurse at BMC. You can—"

"Excuse me, Lieutenant. BMC?"

"Barrington Medical Center. Where Hanchett worked."

"Oh, sure. Right."

"Teresa Bell's child died when BMC refused a liver transplant. Susan Parrish is an old friend of mine. Check with her to make sure we've got the right Teresa Bell. Susan and I have talked, so she'll know what you're talking about."

"Oh. Good."

Hastings could picture Canelli's expression, his dark eyes anxious, his broad, swarthy face probably sweat-sheened. Taking orders from superiors, anxious to get the instructions precisely right, Canelli often perspired.

"Do you want me to take an interrogation, Lieutenant?"

"Not right now. You catch for me. After I've finished with Fiona Hanchett, I'll get Teresa Bell's address from you. I hope I'll get some more names from her. There's a meeting with Lieutenant Friedman at four-thirty."

"Oh—okay." Then, solicitously: "Good luck, Lieutenant."

"Thanks."

12:30 PM

Already, she knew, the afternoon papers would have been delivered to Jamison's, only a block and a half away. By noon, most days, the *Clarion* was dropped off the truck—big, square bundles wired together, thudding on the sidewalk in front of the grocery store.

But they'd always taken the *Sentinel,* always had it delivered, early in the morning.

That morning, the *Sentinel* had been delivered at twenty minutes after seven. She'd been waiting for it, been ready for it, had her plans already made. Quietly—very quietly—she'd opened the front door and gotten the paper. She'd taken it into the kitchen. She'd put the paper, still secured by a thick rubber band, on the table. Then, as she always did, she'd put the kettle on for her tea. Next she'd put the toast on. And then she'd set out the breakfast things: the butter, the marmalade, the teabag, the sugar. All followed by the silverware.

By that time the water was boiling, and the toast had popped up. Allowing her to sit down at the table, as she always did. Which, in turn, allowed her to slip the rubber band from the *Sentinel,* and unfold the paper.

It was then that the newspaper began to shake—at first only a quiver, not bad enough to prevent her from searching the paper's first section. But then, when she learned that the *Sentinel* had not reported the monster's death, the paper began shaking so violently that the type blurred.

Meaning that it would be best not to risk what could happen if she walked around the corner to Jamison's and laid a quarter on the counter and took a copy of the *Clarion* in her hands. Because her hands, shaking, holding the *Clarion,* could betray her. She'd already had the warning.

But she had to know, had to see proof that the monster was dead.

Meaning that she must risk it, risk whatever awaited beyond the walls that had always sheltered her.

If rocks overturned exposed the wicked, then sunlight revealed the virtuous.

Brice Hanchett, dead.

At the thought, the trembling began again.

Virtue revealed—her own precious secret.

1:15 PM

"Mrs. Hanchett? Fiona Hanchett?"

Her face was bloated, her eyes pale and watery. Her hair, tinted a dusty blond, was in disarray. Her mouth moved uncertainly, as if the question confused her. Finally she nodded.

"Yes . . ."

"I'm Lieutenant Frank Hastings, Mrs. Hanchett." He held up his shield, watched her labor to focus on it. As she studied the shield, her whole body swayed. Was it booze? Drugs? Grief?

All three?

"You've come about Brice." Her voice was coarse, clogged by phlegm and roughened by too much liquor for too many years.

"That's right, Mrs. Hanchett." He looked past her, into the hallway of the two-story town house. The house was vintage Pacific Heights, market value more than a million dollars. Everything Hanchett touched, apparently, was gilded. Hanchett's current wife, his current girlfriend, his ex-wife—all of them lived the life of privilege. Hanchett's Jaguar cost more than most men earned in a year.

"Can we . . . ?" He gestured. "Can we go inside? There're a few things I have to ask you."

"Is it John?" Her eyes were anxious. Repeating querulously: *"John?"*

"Is John—?" He frowned. "Is he your son?"

As if she feared to answer, she first shook her head, then nodded hesitantly. Finally she said, "I'm sorry, Lieutenant—" Confused, she broke off. "I'm sorry, but I've forgotten—" Once more, she shook her head.

"It's Hastings. Frank Hastings." He gestured again. "Can we go inside?"

"Oh—yes—please." Hastily she drew back. "I—I'm sorry. It's just that all this—Brice, dead, it's made me—" Bemused, she waited for Hastings to step inside, then swung the heavy door closed. After an awkward moment, each deferring to the other, she preceded him into a large, sunny living room that had certainly been professionally decorated. She gestured him to a chair, and sat in a companion chair, facing him across a small antique cobbler's bench. She wore a full kimono-style garment that covered her whole body, falling to her ankles.

"Is there anything I can do for you, Mrs. Hanchett? Do you need anything?"

As if the question puzzled her, she blinked, then refocused her gaze on him. "Need anything?"

"Information. Help."

She began to smile, an ironic twisting of a mouth that age had begun to pucker. Or was it lipstick imperfectly applied?

Circling her eyes, also imperfectly made up, a network of lines had begun to deepen, a complicated tracery of chronic defeat. Her eyes were round and vague, Little Orphan Annie eyes in a tired, withering face.

"Help . . ." Still smiling, she slowly shook her head. "No, Lieutenant, I don't see how you can help me. I imagine you've come because you're trying to find whoever killed him. But the truth is, I don't care whether you find the murderer or not. Does that shock you?" Now the smile twisted, as if she'd experienced sudden pain. The watery eyes leered, a grotesque imitation of the flirtatious coquette.

"I'm looking for the truth, Mrs. Hanchett. That's what police work is all about."

"Well, then . . ." As if to encourage him, she nodded, an exhausted inclination of her head accompanied by a vague movement of her hand. The hand, Hastings saw, was a true extension of the body, flaccid and bloated, expensively bejeweled. "Well, then, we won't have any trouble, you and I. Because the truth is, I hated Brice Hanchett. I rejoice that he's dead. I rejoice because, wherever he is—wherever the fires of hell burn the hottest—he's now incapable of causing the rest of us any more pain."

Watching her carefully, listening to her, Hastings realized there was more to Fiona Hanchett than a bleary-eyed, self-pitying woman who lived alone and ate too much and probably drank too much. The longer she talked, the more sense she made. Her words were crisp now, and she spoke in sentences. Her eyes were sharp-focused, her gestures decisive.

Therefore, Hastings decided to challenge her with a smile as he said, "You're talking like a pretty fair suspect, Mrs. Hanchett. I don't suppose you'll mind if I ask where you were last night between the hours of ten and midnight."

Encompassing the room and the house, she raised both arms, hands poised in a self-mocking imitation of a ballerina's turn. "I was here, Lieutenant. I was right here. I was drinking expensive white wine and watching cheap TV. Is that when he was killed? Between ten o'clock and midnight?"

Hastings nodded.

"It was a street killing, I understand. Is that right?"

Still smiling, Hastings raised a hand. "Wait, Mrs. Hanchett. I'm supposed to ask the questions. You're supposed to answer."

"I've already answered. I was here last night. Alone. I was watching a TV movie. Two TV movies, in fact." She smiled ruefully. "A double feature."

"Okay, I've got another question for you. Or, rather, a request."

"A request?"

"I'd like you to tell me about Brice Hanchett. Tell me everything—his history, his enemies, his friends, his career, anything you can think of." He let a moment pass, watching her. Frowning now, she was watching him in return. Had he gained her confidence?

"To me," he said, "you seem like a pretty good talker. So talk. Start at the beginning, and talk to me."

Her answering smile was bitter. Her eyes were sharper, as if the memory of ancient hatreds had concentrated her attention. "A good talker, you say." She nodded wearily. "That's nice. I take that as a compliment."

"And so it was meant, Mrs. Hanchett."

"You seem like a thoughtful man. Do you like your work?"

Once more, he raised a hand. "Remember—I'm not here to answer. I'm here to ask."

"Yes. Well . . ." She sighed, shifted her bloated body. Her voice dropped to a lower, more introspective note. Her eyes softened reflectively as she said, "Well, there was a time, Lieutenant, before I met Brice, when I was considered a very good conversationalist. I was a good musician, too. I'm still a good musician, I think. But, unhappily, my opinion isn't the one that counts."

"A musician, eh? What's your instrument?"

"The cello."

"With what orchestra?"

"I played in the Boston Symphony." Her voice was soft. "I was only twenty-two when I got the chair. And then, two seasons later, I got an offer from San Francisco. San Francisco excited me, so I took the offer." She let her voice die, let her memory-clouded eyes wander away. "I've often wondered what would have happened if I hadn't taken the offer. I can't tell you how many times I've wondered."

"So you met Hanchett," Hastings prompted.

With what seemed infinite regret, she nodded. "Yes, I met Brice. I'd just come to town. I hadn't been here a month when I met him. We were married six months later. And a year later I had John." She pronounced her son's name tentatively, her voice shaded.

John . . .

Is it John? she'd asked anxiously.

Could John have killed his father, to avenge his mother? What was the ancient Greek play? *Oedipus?* No.

"John lives here," he said. "With you. Is that correct?"

She nodded. "He lives in back. There's an in-law apartment in the rear of the house." As she said it, the complex shading came back into her voice. "John's a casualty, too."

"A Brice Hanchett casualty, you mean."

Her lips twisted. Her voice dropped, as if hatred had smothered the words at their source. "Yes—another casualty."

"Tell me about Brice, Mrs. Hanchett. Tell me everything. It'll help. It'll help both of us. Start at the beginning. Take your time."

For a long moment she made no reply, but simply sat motionless, staring down at her hands, loosely clasped in her lap. Then she began to speak. "Brice had an ego that drove him like a demon. His father and grandfather were both doctors. His grandfather made a fortune in real estate, too. A multi-, multi-million-dollar fortune. And his father doubled the fortune. Maybe that's what drove Brice to excel as a doctor. I mean, there was already so much money, the only way he could distinguish himself, set himself apart from his father and grandfather, was medicine. So Brice went for it all: high-risk, high-profile surgery. And he succeeded, too. He was a first-class surgeon, there's no question. But he was—he was insatiable. That's the only word for it. Prestige, power, women, money—whatever it was, he could never get enough. Never."

"But you married him."

"Yes," she answered, "I married him. I was dazzled, that's the only word. I grew up in Grand Rapids. My father owned a lumberyard. A small lumberyard. I'd never met anyone like Brice. I was"—she paused, searching again—"I was mesmerized. That's all I can say. My whole life was music. It was all I knew. I was a virgin, for God's sake, when I met Brice. A twenty-four-year-old virgin."

"Obviously, though, he was dazzled, too."

"I was beautiful." As she spoke, she looked him full in the face, as if she were confessing to something shameful. "It's hard to imagine now, I know. But I was beautiful. And I was good at what I did. I was very good. I had a very good, very unique tone. My technique was sound, too. Looking back, I realize that I had class. And Brice could always recognize class, I'll give him that."

"How long were you married?"

"Almost twenty years. And all that time he was playing around. Always."

"Did you call him on it?"

"No," she answered. "I never did. Not for a long, long time." She grimaced. "A lifetime, as it turned out."

"Why'd you wait so long?"

"It was *this.*" Once more, she did the ballerina turn with her hands. "It was living here, in Pacific Heights. It was never having to think about money. Do you realize what that means, Lieutenant? Not to worry about money, that's one thing. But not even to have to *think* about money, that's something else."

"So you kept quiet about his playing around."

"I kept quiet about it—and I drank. So, of course, I lost my chair in the symphony. You can't drink and play cello."

"You have one child?"

As if she were confessing to another shameful secret, she nodded. "Some say—Brice, for one—some say I've spoiled John, made him a mama's boy. And maybe they're right. That's one of those things, it's not for me to say. The more I try to defend myself, the worse it seems."

"But you did ask for a divorce. Finally."

She smiled bitterly. "He and Barbara Gregg were practically living together. He'd rented a goddamn love nest for them. They started going places together—out to dinner, out to the theater. Finally they went to an opera opening together. There was a picture of them together, on the society page. That's what did it. I saw that picture and I called a lawyer."

"And now Brice is playing around—*was* playing around—on Barbara. Did you know that?"

"And Barbara was playing around on *him.*" This time, smugness softened the bitterness of her smile. "Did *you* know *that?*"

"No," Hastings answered. "Do you know his name?"

"His name is Clayton Vance." The smile widened subtly. "He's a car salesman. Jaguars, of course, very upscale. Still, I doubt that Brice was pleased, knowing Barbara was involved with a car salesman. He'd consider it a negative reflection on his status."

"Do you think he knew his wife was seeing someone?"

"I'm sure he did. That's the way Brice liked to play the game. Everything on the table, let the blood spatter where it may."

"He drove a Jaguar. Brice, I mean."

"He drove three cars. At least."

Hastings wrote *Clayton Vance* in the notebook. When he reinterrogated Barbara Hanchett, he'd drop the name on her, watch for the reaction. Could he dent her composure, shake her up?

For a long moment Hastings sat silently, his eyes thoughtfully unfocused. In an investigation that was barely twelve hours old, the list of potential murder suspects was impressive. Jason Pfiefer, Carla's estranged husband, still consumed by love, was a classic suspect. Barbara Hanchett could have been driven by a combination of jealousy and the prospect of gain, also classic motives. Teresa Bell, the woman who'd lost her child when Hanchett's decision went against her, was still to be interrogated. Could Fiona Hanchett, embittered by her own ruined life, have pulled the trigger? What about their son? How much would John Hanchett inherit at his father's death?

Those suspects, and perhaps many more . . .

It was time to play the guessing game: pick a suspect. Any suspect.

"I've got to be going, Mrs. Hanchett. But before I go, I'd like you to do something for me." To reassure her, he smiled. "Call it a game. Call it 'Who murdered Brice Hanchett?' "

She frowned. "A game?" It was a cautious question.

He nodded. "If you had to guess—if you had to pick a suspect from among the people you know—whom would you pick?"

"Is this a joke? Some kind of a joke?" As she asked the question, the words were slightly slurred. Her eyes were losing their acuity. She was regressing, once more the bleary, blowsy woman who'd opened the door. Was it an act? If it *was* an act, what was its purpose? To protect John? Someone else?

He let the smile fade. "It's no joke, Mrs. Hanchett. Murder is never a joke."

"But if I tell you—name a name—then I could be—" As if she were puzzled, she shook her head. "I could be sued."

"No. I'll never name you as an informant. I promise you that. And even if I did name you, there're no witnesses. It'd be just my word against yours."

It was a lie. But he'd told the same lie so often that it felt like the truth.

Now she was studying him with her bleary eyes. But deep in those eyes, he could see resolution sharpening.

Or was it calculation?

Finally: "Have you talked to Paula?" she asked. "Do you know where Paula was last night?"

He frowned. "Paula?"

She nodded. "Paula Gregg. She's Barbara's daughter by her first husband. It's common knowledge that Brice abused her. And now she's wild. She's wild, and she's dangerous."

2:05 PM

As the static-sizzling silence lengthened, Hastings drummed the steering wheel with impatient fingers. Finally, Friedman's voice materialized: "Frank? Where are you?"

"I'm on Washington Street. I've just finished talking with Fiona Hanchett, and I'm going to give Teresa Bell a try. But first I—"

"Teresa Bell?"

"She's the one with the kid who died when he couldn't get a transplanted liver."

"Oh. Right. So?" Plainly, Friedman was still short on time, as harassed as he ever permitted himself to become.

"So I've got another possible. Barbara Hanchett's daughter by a previous marriage. If someone can get an address for her, do a workup, maybe I can talk to her after I finish with Teresa Bell. Or, better yet, have Canelli talk to her. Tell Canelli that Paula Gregg is Fiona Hanchett's pick for the murderer. Apparently she hated Hanchett. *Really* hated him, because he abused her sexually when she was younger."

"Got it. Gotta go. See you at four-thirty down here. Right?"

"Right." Hastings released the mike's Transmit button and replaced the mike on its hook beneath the cruiser's dashboard. Parked across the street from Fiona Hanchett's town house, he was about to switch on the car's ignition when he saw a tall, loose-walking young man approaching the vintage wrought-iron gate that led to the Hanchett house. He wore blue jeans, running shoes, and a regimental khaki shirt, shirttail out. His dark hair was lank, half-long and half-combed. Against the pallor of his face, his lips were unnaturally vivid, his eyes unnaturally dark. As he walked, his gaze was fix-focused, the lusterless eyes staring straight ahead. The movements of his thin arms and legs were oddly uncoordinated.

With a practiced gesture the man tripped the gate latch, swung open the gate, and strode down a passageway beside the Hanchett house, disappearing behind a redwood lattice side gate.

This, certainly, was John Hanchett, going to his in-law apartment at the rear of his mother's house.

Is it John? Fiona Hanchett had asked distractedly. *John?*

Hastings picked up the microphone, cleared his unit, switched off the radio, got out of the car, and went through the iron gate. The lattice gate swung open to his touch, revealing a beautifully terraced garden of low-growing ferns, several small trees, and a series of low fieldstone retaining walls and flagstone walkways. The rear apartment's rooms featured floor-to-ceiling plate-glass windows that offered a full view of the garden.

Only a moment after Hastings had pressed the button beside the apartment's single outside door, the door swung open.

"Mr. Hanchett? John Hanchett?" As he spoke, Hastings offered his gold inspector's shield.

Staring down at the shield with his fix-focused eyes, Hanchett nodded. It was a rigid, stiff-necked nod, complementing the strange fixity of the eyes.

"I'm Lieutenant Frank Hastings, Mr. Hanchett. I'm co-commander of Homicide. And I'm investigating the death of your father. I know it's a bad time for you. But if you've got a few minutes . . ."

Immediately, Hanchett turned away and walked through the small kitchen to the adjoining living room, with its intimate view of the magnificent garden beyond. Both the kitchen and the living room were littered with the leavings of everyday life: dirty dishes stacked in the sink, food wrappers on the kitchen counters, newspapers and magazines and empty bottles and dirty glasses strewn about the living room, some of the mess on tables and shelving, some on couches and chairs, some on the expensive Oriental rug. The smell went with the litter: musty and pungent, the odor of indifference and defeat.

Hastings pocketed his shield, closed the outside door, and walked into the living room, where Hanchett sat slumped in a saddle-leather sling chair, his back to the view. Without being invited, Hastings cleared magazines and newspapers from one end of the couch and sat down.

"It's pretty tough," he offered, adding mechanically, "I'm sorry for your loss."

Sitting with his straightened legs spread wide, his long arms dangling, his head bowed moodily, Hanchett gave no sign of having heard.

"I—uh—I've only got a few questions," Hastings said, "and then I'll be—"

"He was never a father to me," Hanchett muttered. "If you know anything about him—about us—then you know that. Even when he was living here, he was never a father, never a husband." Like his dark, dead eyes, Hanchett's voice was fixed—a low, leaden monotone.

"I've already talked to your mother," Hastings offered.

"Then you know about him. If you talked to my mother, then you know."

As Hastings nodded in response, an instant's flash of memory erupted: his own mother, standing beside the kitchen table, reading the note his father had left propped against the salt cellar. He'd gone away with his girl Friday, his father had written. He was sorry.

Experimenting, Hastings decided to say, "Your father—uh—seems to've made a lot of enemies."

Beyond a sharp, contemptuous grunt, John Hanchett made no reply. His posture remained unchanged: legs spread wide, arms slack, chin resting on his chest. Signifying that, cautiously, Hastings could take the next step: "It's less than twenty-four hours, but already I've talked to several people, and heard about several more, who carried grudges against Dr. Hanchett. Deep grudges. Serious grudges."

No response.

"What I—uh—the reason I rang your doorbell," Hastings ventured, "is that I—uh—wondered where you were last night. It's routine, you see, for us to—"

A harsh laugh suddenly convulsed the long, sprawled body; the legs and arms contracted, the head jerked up. The voice was falsetto-shrill:

"You think I killed him."

Hastings drew a deep breath. "If I thought you'd killed him," he said, measuring the words, "I'd've given you your Miranda rights. It's the law."

" 'You have the right to remain silent—' " It was a manic

imitation of the TV-familiar ritual. " 'You have the right to—' *God.*" He interrupted himself. "Give me a break, Lieutenant. I might've *thought* about killing him—*fantasized* about killing him—hundreds of times. But—Christ—" Contemptuously, mock-sadly, John Hanchett shook his head. "You must be hallucinating, if you think I killed him."

"Do you have any idea who might've done it?"

John Hanchett's mouth twisted in a small, bitter smile. But the eyes remained coal-dead, sunken deep in the ravaged, sallow face. "If I had to guess," he said, "then I'd choose his wife, Barbara. Otherwise known as the Dragon Lady."

"Anyone else?"

"No."

"What about Paula Gregg?"

"Why would Paula do it?"

"Because," Hastings answered, "Hanchett is supposed to have abused her when she was a child."

"Who told you that?"

"No comment."

"It was Mother. Wasn't it?"

"Still no comment."

"Mother gets fixated on ideas sometimes. That story about my father and Paula is one of her fixations. You have to make allowances. Especially when Mother's drinking, which is most of the time."

"Then you wouldn't say Paula is a suspect."

"That's right."

"You'll stick with Barbara Hanchett."

"Also right."

3:00 PM

As Hastings turned in to the 600 block of Moraga, the predictable happened: a bittersweet pang of recall. It was here, in

San Francisco's Sunset District, that he'd grown up. At the turn of the century the Sunset had been nothing more than sand dunes rolling gently down from the highlands of Twin Peaks to the ocean, with only an occasional house dotting the dunes. In the 1920s the dunes had been subdivided, and in the thirties the real-estate developers began covering the sand with small stucco row houses, affordable housing for the workingman.

Hastings parked the cruiser and consulted the slip of paper attached to the dashboard by a small magnet: Fred and Teresa Bell, 643 Moraga. The house was exactly what he'd known he would find: a small stucco house, attached on both sides. Like most houses in the 600 block of Moraga, the Bell house was adorned with a few terra-cotta roof tiles and hand-hewn timbers meant to suggest a Spanish influence. The house looked freshly painted; the small front garden was well tended.

Hastings cleared his unit with Communications, switched off the radio, locked the car, and began walking toward the Bell house. As he drew closer, a sense of reluctance compounded his previous nostalgia. Interrogating the victim's widow and his ex-wife was part of the homicide detective's standard job description. Coping with parents who'd watched their child slowly die of liver failure was something else.

In response to a loud buzzer, the front door opened promptly. A bald, slightly built man stood in the doorway. His face was pale and narrow, his mouth permanently drawn, as if he'd always been in pain. When he looked down at the badge Hastings held in his hand, the man's eyes widened. It was a common response. A response of the timid—

Or the guilty.

"Mr. Bell?"

A nervous tongue-tip touched pale lips. "Yes. Fred Bell." He continued to stare down at the badge.

"I'm Lieutenant Frank Hastings, Mr. Bell. I'm in charge of the investigation into the death of Dr. Brice Hanchett." He spoke flatly, matter-of-factly, as if he assumed that Bell already knew Hanchett had been murdered.

Bell's instantaneous reaction was shock—sharp, stunned, spontaneous shock. The reaction was unmistakable, more revealing than the results of any polygraph. Until that moment, Fred Bell hadn't known of the murder.

But, just as certainly, just as irrevocably, Bell possessed guilty knowledge.

Susan Parrish hadn't spoken of Fred Bell, the husband, but only of the dead child's mother.

Instinctively taking a single step backward as he covertly unbuttoned his jacket and inched his right hand closer to the .38 holstered at his belt, Hastings drew a long, measured breath. It was important, he'd learned, never to reveal the excitement of the hunter at the first sight of his prey. Therefore, he must control both his facial expression and his speech. Thus the deep breath. Thus the carefully neutral voice as he asked, "Can we step inside, Mr. Bell?"

"Oh. *Oh.* Yes. Sure. Please." Anxiously, Bell stepped back, waited for Hastings to enter the hallway. Then Bell closed the door—and locked it.

For Hastings, the house's interior and its furnishings evoked another pang of recollection and recall. The narrow entry hallway, the crocheted antimacassars pinned to the overstuffed furniture, the ruffled curtains at the windows and the ruffled shades on the lamps, all of it was there. All carefully cared for, each item of furniture precisely placed, each dust-free surface gleaming.

As they sat down facing each other, Hastings said, "You didn't know about Dr. Hanchett's death."

Quickly, anxiously, Bell shook his head. "No. I—" He faltered. "I work nights, you see, and I sleep during the day. So I never hear the news. Not until later in the day."

"Ah." As if he were satisfied, Hastings nodded. "Yes, I see. But you knew him, of course."

"Oh, yes. I—"

From the hallway behind his chair, Hastings sensed movement, confirmed by the shift of Fred Bell's eyes, tracking the movement. Turning, Hastings saw a woman standing silently in the archway. The instant's evocation was of stark black-and-white photographs documenting the Great Depression. One of those photographs, Hastings vividly remembered, showed an emaciated, hollow-eyed woman standing in the doorway of a sharecropper's shack. The woman's face was wasted, a haunted mask of utter despair.

But Teresa Bell's eyes, abnormally large in her thin, ravaged face, burned with an emotion more desperate than despair. Plainly, Teresa Bell was deranged.

Instantly, Fred Bell was on his feet and at her side, his hand touching her arm as if to turn her aside, to deflect her. As though seeking some terrible truth, Bell's eyes searched her face as he moved protectively between his wife and Hastings, who was also on his feet.

"Teresa, this—this doesn't concern you. It's—please—" Bell increased the pressure on her arm, half turning her away.

"Wait." Hastings stepped forward. "It's all right, Mr. Bell. I'd like to talk to both of you."

"But—"

Preempting a response, Hastings gestured to the woman, inviting her into the living room. But, shaking off her husband's hand, she stood motionless, her dark, manic eyes fixed on Hastings.

"Teresa. Please. You—"

Sharply raising his hand to cut off the husband, Hastings

spoke directly to the woman: "Dr. Hanchett was killed last night, Mrs. Bell." It was a statement, not a question. It was an accusation.

Still staring, she made no response. Resigned, Fred Bell took his hand from her arm, stepped back. Hastings could hear Bell's breathing, shallow and rigid, as if an anxiety attack were imminent.

"You knew Hanchett was dead." It was another statement.

Slowly, gravely, she nodded. "Oh, yes. I knew." A pause. Then: "He killed Timothy, you know. Timmy died because of Dr. Hanchett." Her voice was hardly more than a whisper. She wore a shapeless housedress and run-over fuzzy house slippers adorned with felt rabbits. The dress revealed nothing of the woman's body beneath. Her short dark hair was hardly combed.

"I know about Timmy." Holding her feverish gaze, Hastings spoke softly. "It was terrible, about Timmy."

"But now Dr. Hanchett is dead."

"Yes," he answered. "Dr. Hanchett is dead." He spoke slowly, leadenly, in cadence with her.

"Teresa, I don't want you to—"

Hastings gripped Bell's arm hard enough to silence the smaller man. For a long moment there was no sound. As Teresa Bell's eyes slowly wandered far away, both Hastings and Bell stared at her with gathering intensity. Then the woman focused her gaze on Hastings as she said, "He's here, you know." She gestured vaguely. "Would you—"

"Teresa, for God's sake." Bell twisted away, broke Hastings's grip, went to his wife, and took rough hold of her arms as he forced her to look at him. "Teresa, I want you to go to the bedroom." He shook her. "Close the door. I want you to close the door and lock it. I'll handle this. You can't—"

Suddenly she threw her arms wide and flung him away. Shrieking incoherently, she crossed the living room in three strides to stand beside the fireplace. Hastings saw a large picture of a boy hung above the fireplace. It was a hand-colored photograph, elaborately framed.

Beneath the picture, on the fireplace's wooden mantelpiece, a bower of pine boughs was arranged. The arrangement was centered on a small amber-colored onyx urn.

As suddenly as it had come, Teresa Bell's agony passed, leaving her leaning with her head pressed against the fireplace's brick chimney, exhausted, her eyes fixed on the urn.

Timmy.

Timmy's ashes, in the amber onyx urn.

As the three stood motionless, the silence lengthened. Then, with his eyes still on the woman standing across the room, Hastings spoke softly to Bell.

"You said you were working last night." As he asked the question, Hastings half turned toward the man standing beside him. Visibly, Bell was surrendering to despair, shrinking from within. Still fixed on Teresa Bell, who was standing motionless, staring at the urn, Fred Bell's eyes had gone as hollow as his wife's.

"Mr. Bell." Hastings let a moment pass. "Answer me, please."

"Yes," Bell whispered. "Yes. I worked last night. The eight-to-four shift."

"And your wife was alone last night."

"She was here. Right here."

But the doubt was plainly readable in Bell's tortured eyes. "Right here," he repeated as he went to his wife, put his arms around her, let her head fall on his shoulder as she began to sob: deep, racking sobs that shook her whole body.

Finally her sobs faded to silence, but the grief-frozen tableau held: the woman's head buried against the man's shoulder, his arms holding her while her arms hung slack. Then, indistinctly, Hastings heard the woman speak. "I wanted him to die, Fred. I wanted him to die like Timmy died. I wanted it to be slow. Not fast. Slow." Suddenly she twisted in her husband's arms. Eyes blazing, she searched his face. "He's dead, Fred. You didn't pray for him to die. But I did. I prayed."

3:20 PM

He watched Hastings leave the Bell house, go down the steps to the street, walk to the Ford sedan parked across the street. The detective moved easily, confidently, as if he knew he carried with him the full force of the law, society's broad-shouldered guardian, the man with the badge and the gun.

The man who was stalking his prey. Closer—closer.

Hastings and all the others, searching, tightening the noose. A cliché. A dark, dangerous cliché, a morass. The mind of a murderer, meaningless tangles of insanity and lucidity: his only instrument of survival.

4:40 PM

Dubiously, Friedman shook his head. "I don't know, Frank. In my experience, loonies don't make very predictable suspects. Sure, she prayed for Hanchett to die. I'd be surprised if she hadn't."

"If you'd seen her, though . . ."

"I'm surprised you didn't hang in there, keep her talking."

"Her husband wouldn't let me do it. So before he got hot, decided to call a lawyer, whatever, I decided to back off. I'll wait till the husband's at work, talk to her again. Why don't you come along, see what you think?"

"Fine," Friedman said. "Incidentally, did you hear about the kid and the gun?"

"What kid? What gun?" Hastings asked the questions sourly. Friedman was building the suspense, working his audience.

"A little kid found a gun in some bushes a few hours ago. It was only two blocks from the murder scene. The lab's doing the ballistics right this minute, and then they'll do the fingerprints." Friedman smiled. "The kid fired the goddamn gun. At last report, the mother was still in shock. Not to mention the father, who's got a hole in the driver's door of his brand-new Celica." Friedman's smile broadened. "Can you imagine the insurance adjuster's expression?"

"Was the father inside the car?" Canelli asked.

"No."

As though relieved, Canelli settled back in Hastings's visitor's chair. Then, dolefully, Canelli began to shake his head. "Jeez, just think of it. That poor woman. Teresa Bell, I mean, with her kid dead. And now she'll be locked up, maybe. Sometimes—" Canelli sighed. "Sometimes there's no justice. None."

As Canelli said it, Friedman's smile faded. For a moment his face remained expressionless. Then, speaking quietly, looking down at his thick hands judiciously folded in his lap, Friedman said, "In this business, Canelli, justice is just a word. Haven't you figured that one out by now?"

As always uncertain how he should respond to yet another of Friedman's homilies, Canelli first shrugged, then shook his head. Finally he ventured an uncertain nod, followed by another shrug. Watching the two of them play their ritual parts in this long-running departmental skit, Hastings was once again struck by the similarities between the two men. Both weighed at least two hundred forty. Both men were swarthy. Their faces were smooth, their lips full, their eyes dark, their hair thick. Canelli's hair was dark; Friedman's hair was graying.

But their personalities differed dramatically. Lieutenant Peter Friedman, senior co-commander of Homicide, seldom revealed his feelings, never allowed himself to be put on the defensive. Hastings had never seen Friedman surprised or disconcerted or visibly frightened. First and last, Friedman kept them guessing.

"I thought," Canelli said, "that the witnesses both said it was a man."

"They said the assailant wore a cap, or a hat," Hastings said. "And slacks. Given a combination like that, if the light's bad, most witnesses will say they saw a man commit a crime, not a woman. They seem to be conditioned to think that—"

Millie Greenberg, Homicide's long-suffering receptionist, secretary, stenographer, and amiable object of lust, appeared framed in the aluminum-and-glass rectangle of Hastings's office door. When Hastings beckoned, Millie entered, deposited a sheaf of papers on the desk, and spoke to Friedman.

"Lab reports and the coroner's prelims on the Hanchett homicide." She smiled at the two lieutenants. "Can I leave? My kid's nursery school phoned. Donnie's got the shits, if you'll pardon the expression."

Saying something sympathetic, both lieutenants nodded in unison.

"Thanks," she said. "See you tomorrow." She flipped her right hand, used her left hand to pat Canelli on top of the head, and left the office. After duly studying the admirable action of Millie's buttocks and thighs, Friedman picked up the papers, slipped on a pair of black-rimmed reading glasses, and began reading the reports while Canelli asked Hastings whether Millie's divorce was final.

"I'm not sure," Hastings answered. "Why? What about you and Gracie? What's it been now—eleven years—that you're engaged?"

"More like twelve," Canelli admitted sheepishly.

Knowing that Friedman could listen to their conversation while he read the reports, Hastings said, "So what about Hanchett's stepdaughter, Paula Gregg? Did you talk to her?" As he asked the question, Hastings experienced a momentary pang of guilt. *She's wild,* Fiona Hanchett had said. *She's wild, and she's dangerous.* Meaning that he should have told Friedman, should have cautioned Friedman not to send Canelli alone to interrogate Paula Gregg. But Friedman had been harassed, working the telephones.

"Boy—" Canelli nodded enthusiastically. "Did I ever talk to her." Wonderingly, he shook his head. "I'll tell you, Lieutenant, too bad you weren't there. I mean, talk about a looker." Once more, Canelli shook his head. "I'll tell you, she's something else. She's one of those—you know—natural beauties."

"So what's her story?"

"Well . . ." Canelli took out his notebook, thumbed the pages back and forth, frowned, riffled the pages again. Finally finding his place, he began again: "Well, she lives in one of those old loading sheds down at the piers that's been converted into apartments. Nice place. Far out, but nice. You know—trendy. Funky, I'd call it. But anyhow, I got there a little after two, I guess. And, Jesus, it looked like she and some big black guy were just getting out of the sack."

Friedman laid the reports aside, took off his glasses, and studied Canelli as he continued. "The black guy took off, though. I mean, he took one look at the badge and he split. But the lady—Paula Gregg—it didn't faze her. She's like, you know, one of those real wild-looking types you see in the TV ads for perfume or something. Real long and lanky, with this real thick hair that's all over the place. You know, 'Jungle Passion,' like that. And, in fact, it turns out that's what she does. Models, I mean. She's got big blowups of herself on her walls, from magazine ads."

Marveling, Friedman shook his head. "You've got a gift, Canelli. A real flair."

Canelli's reaction was speculative. For as long as he'd been in Homicide, he'd never quite been able to divine Friedman's true motives.

"So what'd she say about Hanchett?" Hastings asked. "You *did* mention the murder, didn't you?"

"Yeah. And, boy, she didn't make any bones about it. She hated him. She's only twenty years old, but she's already been on her own for three years. As soon as she could get out of the house, she split. And before that—she doesn't make any bones about this, either—she was a ward of the juvenile court, and spent some time at that place in Idaho. That custody farm for rich kids, I forget the name."

"It's Orchard Lake." Friedman spoke quietly, thoughtfully. A suspect with a record—any record—was always taken seriously.

"What about last night?" Hastings asked. "An alibi?"

Canelli shrugged. "She was with that black guy, she says. I've got his name, but I haven't checked him out yet."

"Well"—Friedman gestured to the lab reports—"there's a little nugget here for us."

Canelli's reaction was an expression of hope; Hastings simply waited through the pause that always preceded something of substance from Friedman.

"It turns out," Friedman said, gesturing to the printouts he'd just scanned, "that the gun the kid found was the gun that did the job, no question. I had C. J. check the gun through Sacramento, and it was registered to a guy in Los Angeles. Then C. J. ran the guy." Friedman consulted one of the printouts. "His name is Foster Crowe, and he lives in Beverly Hills. A high roller, apparently, very big in Dun & Bradstreet. So I decided, what the hell, I'd give Foster Crowe a call. And it turns out that the gun was part of his gun collection. Which figures. I forgot to mention that the gun is a Llama, which is a Spanish automatic. Actually, I happen to know that, as a gun, the Llama is the shits. But this one is engraved, has carved grips, the whole thing. It turns out that part of the collection was ripped off a year ago. So I called old John Farrell, down at LAPD. John, it happens, owes me at least three favors, from that Custance homicide a few months ago. So he's going to see what he can do about tracking down the gun after it was stolen."

"What about the rest of it?" Hastings pointed to the other reports.

Friedman shrugged. "Not much we don't already know. There were two shots that did the damage. Your reports say three shots were fired, so one went wild. One bullet severed the aorta, which was fatal. That one went right through. The second shot punctured the lower abdomen and lodged in the buttocks. It's a seven-millimeter bullet, incidentally."

"So." Hastings spread his hands, glanced at his wristwatch. "So what we've got so far is zero."

"The game's just started."

"I don't know." Hastings shook his head. "Something about this case doesn't add up."

"Don't let me talk you out of Teresa Bell," Friedman said, "just because she's a loony."

"Her husband works nights, eight to four," Hastings said. "Tomorrow night, let's talk to her."

"Not tonight?"

Hastings shook his head. "I'm going to talk to Jason Pfiefer tonight. He's the estranged husband of Carla Pfeifer, Hanchett's girlfriend. "He's also a surgeon at BMC, and he was apparently very, very jealous."

"Ah." Friedman nodded puckish approval. "The jealous husband. Right." He smiled. It was the habitual Friedman smile: elliptical, inscrutable, knowing. "The case is assuming dimension. Who else've we got that hasn't been interviewed?"

"We've got a guy named Clayton Vance, who's Barbara Hanchett's boyfriend, at least according to Fiona Hanchett. Then there's Edward Gregg, Paula Gregg's father." He turned to Canelli. "Why don't you talk to him, since you've already talked to Paula? He lives in Pacific Heights. Meanwhile, after I talk to Pfiefer, I'll talk to Vance, hear what he has to say about Barbara Hanchett and her husband."

Canelli brightened visibly. "Maybe Vance and Barbara murdered Hanchett so she could get the inheritance and marry Vance."

"I think I saw that movie the other night on 'Golden Oldies,' " Friedman said. "Wasn't that John Garfield and Lana Turner?"

As Canelli was considering his response, Hastings spoke to Friedman. "So what about you?"

"I," Friedman answered, "will stick with the Llama. In fact"—he consulted his own watch—"in fact, I think I'll put in a call to the LAPD, see what they've found out. Also, I'm going to talk to a couple of police reporters." He glanced at notes he'd scrawled on the back of a printout. "All we really know for sure is that the assailant—man or woman—killed Hanchett at about ten-fifteen P.M. last night, at the eleven-hundred block of Green Street. Carrying the gun, he walked down the hill to Hyde Street, where he—or she—probably turned left. Then he probably turned right, on Vallejo. He walked a block and a half—probably—and then he dumped the gun in a hedge. Now Hyde Street between Green and Vallejo, I happen to know, is well traveled, even at that hour. There's the cable car, for one thing, and at least one restaurant on the block. So my plan is to give out that route to the newspapers and TV, see what we get."

"What we'll get," Hastings said, "is a lot of nuts calling up. You know that, Pete. It'll be more trouble than it's worth. It's *always* more trouble than it's worth."

Dark, heavily lidded, almond-shaped eyes hooded, swarthy face expressionless, Friedman studied his co-lieutenant. "Well, how about giving out the block where the crime was committed, and the block where the murder weapon was found?"

"And let them figure out the route for themselves," Hastings objected. "It comes to the same thing. There's only one route from the murder scene to the place where the gun was found."

"Trust me."

"Hmmm . . ."

7:10 PM

"*Frank.*" It was a woman's voice.

Hastings turned to see Susan Parrish—and her husband Arnie, reminding him again of the distant past, memories fugitive from the old neighborhood, half-forgotten high school days.

Arnie, in his forties now. Paunchy. Balding. Wearing a three-piece suit and an executive tie.

Arnie, who'd always been so skinny, so shrill. So pushy.

Still so shrill: "Hey, Frank. My God, all these years in the same city, Frank."

Followed by a hard, competitive handshake. Still pushy.

"Hello, Arnie. How've you been?"

"Never better. I'm in real estate, you know. Just like your dad. Only—" The smile, too, was competitive. The new Arnie now, condescending: "Only a little more successful, I guess you'd have to say. But, still—" A good-old-boy blow on the shoulder. "Still, I don't get on the six-o'clock news, like you do."

Smiling minimally, Hastings turned to Susan Parrish. "I've got an appointment with Jason Pfiefer. I'm late. He said he'd meet me in the lobby here, at seven."

She scanned the spacious lobby, and pointed. "He's over there. That lean, darkly handsome devil sitting beside the ficus tree. He's a little strange, maybe. But undeniably handsome."

As he turned to track her gesture, Hastings said, "That could be a description of Brice Hanchett."

"They're a lot alike," Susan said. "Same looks, basically. Same egos, too. Basically."

Hastings thanked her, smiled, managed to keep the smile intact as he shook hands with Arnie and walked across the lobby to stand before Jason Pfiefer. Plainly considering the meeting a waste of his time, Pfiefer rose, shook hands perfunctorily, and gestured Hastings to a chair. Pfiefer was tall and lean. His eyes were intense, revealing nothing, demanding everything. His close-trimmed beard lent a satanic cast to his pale, deeply etched face. He wore a green surgical gown and white running shoes. A stethoscope was thrust into the pocket of the gown. His hands, Hastings noticed, were in constant, restless motion. His body language was uncompromising.

"I don't have much time, Lieutenant. I told you that on the phone. And you're late."

It would be a mistake, Hastings knew, to apologize. Instead, trying to match the other man's intensity, Hastings leaned forward. "I'll come right to the point, then, Doctor. I'm investigating the murder of Brice Hanchett, as I told you on the phone. He was killed last night about ten-fifteen, as he was leaving your—as he was leaving Carla Pfiefer's apartment." Hastings watched for a reaction. Except for a slight compression of the thin lips, Pfiefer's expression remained unchanged.

"So?" It was a soft, sibilant monosyllable.

"So—how do you feel about—about—" A final hesitant beat. But there was no retreat. He'd boxed himself in, and was forced to come out with it: "How do you feel about Hanchett and your wife seeing each other?"

"*Estranged* wife. She's filed for divorce." Pfiefer's voice was icy. "I presume you knew that."

"You haven't answered the question."

"You're over the line, Lieutenant. I've no intention of telling you how I feel about Carla and Brice."

Studying the other man thoughtfully, Hastings finally nodded. "I can understand how you feel. But there's a man dead. There's a man dead, and there's a romantic triangle. Now, my business is like a lot of other businesses. It's percentages. And according to the percentages, in a situation like this—a romantic triangle—the natural suspects are the man's jealous wife and the woman's jealous husband."

Pfiefer's entire body tightened visibly as he rose to his feet. "Are you telling me—are you insinuating—that I killed Brice Hanchett?" Suppressed fury drew his voice taut. "Is that what you're saying?"

Moving deliberately in a choreographed pantomime of the moment's deadly delicacy, Hastings also rose. "We can make it real simple, Doctor." A final eye-to-eye confrontation. "Just tell me where you were last night between ten and eleven. Tell me that, and I'll be on my way."

Pfiefer's mouth twisted into a malicious smile. His voice matched the smile. "I was here, Lieutenant. I was here all night. There was a liver, you see, that we were waiting for. It was delayed because of bad flying weather. Then the airplane had a mechanical problem. The whole transplant team was here. All night. All sixteen of us."

7:30 PM

Now it began. The stillness that pulsated with a life separate from her own—the silence that beckoned from the darkness beyond the grave.

But somewhere in that silence, somewhere in that darkness, the voices would begin. First the small voices, whispering. Then the heavier voices, smothering the one voice—

Smothering her.

All of it shattered by the first explosion. All of it consumed by the orange fire blossom.

A trigger-touch of flesh on metal. Liberation. Silence. Peace. Promise.

But then, today, the stranger had come. The large, watchful man with the still, knowing eyes. Was he the devil, this man with the golden badge?

Was the watchful policeman her new tormentor, the one whose devil-voice would ignite the other voices, kindle the other eyes that always watched from the shadows?

This she must know.

Tonight, therefore, she must make the call—before it could begin again.

9:15 PM

"Mr. Vance? Clayton Vance?"

With the door open on the night chain, a pair of eyes looked down at the gold badge in Hastings's outstretched palm.

"That's right."

"I'm Lieutenant Frank Hastings, Mr. Vance. I'm investigating the murder of Dr. Brice Hanchett last night. Can we talk for a few minutes?"

"You're—" The four-inch door crack revealed a petulant frown and a peevish mouth pursed by either puzzlement or annoyance—or both. "You're—what—a policeman? Is that it?"

"I'm co-commander of Homicide. And I'd appreciate it if you'd let me in."

"Yes—wait." The door closed, the chain rattled, the door came fully open to reveal a man in his early forties. He wore tight, fashion-faded blue jeans and a tight T-shirt imprinted LE MANS. The red T-shirt was perspiration-stained. Anticipating, Vance explained: "I was working out."

"Ah." Taking the cue, Hastings looked him over: an improbably trim, muscular body, an improbably handsome male-model face. The mustache and the thick brown hair were complementary, both trimmed to suggest that they hadn't been trimmed. The mouth was full, the eyes narcissistic, self-indulgent, self-satisfied. Perspiration had dampened the hair at the neck.

Vance beckoned Hastings inside, closed the hallway door, led the way into a large single room that served as both living room and dining room. Vance's apartment building was a modern high-rise built on the flatlands of North Beach, east of Russian Hill. The building was shallow and wide, a concrete-and-glass slab constructed so that each apartment had a view to the east. Each apartment had a small deck; almost every deck featured a barbecue.

"Sit down, Lieutenant. I'll be with you in a second." Vance gestured to a chair, then abruptly ducked into a small hallway and disappeared. Reflexively, Hastings took his policeman's quick survey: an upscale one-bedroom apartment in an upscale building. Probable rent, fifteen hundred. All the furniture, all the wall decor, all the rugs and drapes and pots and pans hanging in the pullman kitchen were coordinated, each one a trendy fashion statement.

Wearing expensive-looking sweats, a towel draped around his muscular neck, Vance appeared in the doorway. Tanned hands gripping either end of the white towel, speculatively eyeing Hastings, Vance stood motionless for a moment, as if he were debating—or posing.

Finally, Vance inclined his head toward the kitchen. "Get you anything?" As he spoke, he smiled. It was a tactical smile.

"No, thanks."

Vance nodded, seemingly debated with himself for another moment, then strode into the living room to sit on a leather ottoman. Even sitting, Vance chose positions best calculated to display his body.

"It's getting late," Hastings said, "so I'll come right to the point."

Releasing the towel, Vance spread his hands. "Fine." But, reacting to the new note of purpose in Hastings's voice, the line of Vance's body tightened almost imperceptibly. The eyes narrowed slightly; a fine line appeared between the gracefully arched eyebrows. Plainly, Vance was on his guard.

Watching covertly for the other man's reaction, Hastings said, "I've just been talking to Jason Pfiefer."

The line between the eyebrows deepened; puzzlement clouded Vance's eyes. Was it genuine?

"Jason Pfiefer is Carla Pfiefer's husband. He's a doctor at BMC. Carla Pfiefer was Hanchett's girlfriend. His lover. He was leaving her place last night when he was killed."

Vance frowned, changing his pose to face Hastings fully. "I don't understand why you're telling me this."

"I already told you—I'm investigating Hanchett's death."

"So?"

"So—" Hastings decided on a flat statement of fact. "So Pfiefer is Carla's husband—and you're Barbara Hanchett's lover. It's two triangles, you might say."

"But—" In mute protest, Vance began shaking his head. "But you sound like you're saying that I—that Barbara—"

Still speaking quietly, matter-of-factly, Hastings explained, "It's a question of motive, Mr. Vance. We've pretty much ruled out a street killing—a robbery that went wrong, for instance. We think the murder was planned—that someone wanted Hanchett dead. So that means there's a motive. Premeditation, in other words. And generally, when we're looking for a motive, we think of things like jealousy. The unwritten law, in other words."

"If it's the unwritten law, then you should be talking to Jason Pfiefer."

"I told you, I've already talked to him."

"Ah." Vance nodded mockingly. "So now it's my turn."

Hastings decided to smile.

"So what's my motive, exactly?" Now Vance seemed to be enjoying their little game.

"You and the victim's wife could have the same motive. It's another classic one, after all—right behind the unwritten law." Hastings watched him for a moment. "The wife and her lover get rid of her husband so they can live happily ever after—especially if there's a lot of insurance money. And in this case, there'd be an added plus for Barbara. She'd make her husband pay for his philandering."

Suddenly Vance laughed—a harsh, hostile laugh. "Jesus. You're not serious, are you?"

Hastings's answering smile was polite. "Oh, I'm very serious, Mr. Vance. How about you? Are you serious? About Barbara Hanchett, I mean. About your relationship."

"That," Vance said, "is none of your business, Lieutenant. None."

"Well, then . . ." As if the interrogation were almost ended, Hastings shifted forward in his chair. "Why don't we get down to cases? Why don't I ask you where you were last night between nine o'clock and eleven?"

Vance's smile turned to smugness. "Last night was Monday, Lieutenant. That was my racquetball night. There was a problem with the water pipes last night—a broken pipe, I guess. We didn't get on the court until ten o'clock. By the time I'd showered and had a drink, it was midnight."

11:15 PM

"Let's go to bed," Ann said. "You look tired."

Hastings smiled, pressed the TV wand's Off button. "I was thinking you looked tired."

Her answering smile was wan. Now she sighed. It was a heavily burdened sigh. Something was bothering her.

Facing a dark TV screen, they were sitting at opposite ends of the sofa. He moved closer, touched her knee, let his hand linger on her thigh. She was wearing faded blue jeans and a much-worn, much-loved fisherman's sweater. Why, Hastings wondered, did the flesh beneath faded jeans arouse him more than the same firm flesh of the thigh encased in nylon?

"So what's wrong?" he asked.

The wan smile twisted bitterly. Hastings knew that smile. Victor Haywood, Ann's ex-husband, had called. Haywood was a society psychiatrist with a passion for Porsches and a penchant for picking at the wounds their divorce had inflicted on Ann.

"It's Victor," he said. "Isn't it?"

"Isn't it always?" Dispiritedly, she shook her head. "God, does it show that much?"

"To me," he said, "it shows." He moved closer, took her hand. "So tell me."

"It's the same old crap," she said. "Basically, that's what's so . . . so disturbing. The lines never change. It always starts with money. This time it was a bill he got from the orthodontist, for Billy. Then, of course, he gives me a free psychoanalysis, during which he explains why, basically, I'm not qualified to raise Billy and Dan. And then he takes a shot at you and me, about how we're living off him, off my alimony, that's what it comes to, the son of a bitch. Sometimes I feel like tearing up his goddamn checks. I really do."

"If you feel like tearing them up," he said, "then for God's sake, tear them up. Mail the pieces back to him. It'd probably do you good."

She turned toward him, searched his face. Her eyes were cornflower blue; over the years, those eyes had warmed him, comforted him, sometimes challenged him. These were not the eyes of an alimony junkie, the middle-class American divorcée addicted to those monthly checks. These were Ann's eyes. Ann, who had made him whole—finally, made him whole.

"You mean that, don't you?" she said. "It'd make *you* feel better, wouldn't it?"

"Definitely, it'd make me feel better."

She rose and gravely held out her hands to him. "Let's go to bed."

11:20 PM

"So he talked to you," he said. "Hastings. The police lieutenant. He talked to you. Is that what you're saying?"

"Yes, he talked to me. And he knew. I felt it. I felt that he knew."

"I'll have to think about it. Will you be there all night?"

"Yes."

"Alone?"

"Yes."

"Good." He replaced the telephone in its cradle.

11:21 PM

With great care, she replaced the telephone in its cradle attached to the kitchen cabinet.

She'd known the call would come. Today. This very hour. Tonight. This very moment. It had been destined. From the first, it had been destined.

So she must remember.

It was essential that she remember. Now. Beginning now. Beginning when it first began, not so very long ago.

Tragedy, she'd learned, could begin with the ordinary, the inconsequential, the trivial. The devil spoke like everyone else. There was no difference.

She'd been out of wine vinegar for the salad. The time had been about four o'clock in the afternoon; she'd never been sure of the exact hour. She'd gotten the vinegar and lettuce and tomatoes. Then she'd begun walking home.

Somehow she'd felt his presence behind her as she walked. And when she'd heard his voice, she'd known it was him: the one who'd come to liberate her, show her the way, cauterize the open wound.

Him.

Wednesday, September 12

9:20 AM

"It turns out," Friedman said, "that we might be getting warm on the gun." Drawing deeply on the first draught of the day's first cigar and executing three large smoke rings, each one flapped away irritably by Hastings, Friedman gestured to the sheaf of printouts he'd put on Hastings's desk. "In a nutshell, what we've got here is that, as I said yesterday, the Llama was originally owned by a Beverly Hills gun collector. He had fourteen guns stolen out of a collection of about fifty. The stolen guns were all pistols. That was a year ago, approximately." Squinting against cigar smoke, Friedman leaned forward to consult a sheet of yellow legal paper that accompanied the printouts. "Three of the guns were recovered immediately by the pawnshop detail in L.A., and four more were impounded as evidence in crimes, also in the L.A. area. That was during the first six months. Also during the first six months—" Frowning, Friedman put on a pair of black-rimmed reading glasses. "Also during that time, three more guns were recovered in New York and New Jersey. For a long while, that was it. My guess is that maybe the remaining guns"—he studied his notes—"four of them—were purchased illegally by ordinary citizens, for protection, whatever. That's to say, I assume they were purchased individually and not as a group, by one person.

"But then, surprise—" For effect, Friedman paused as, once again, he sent three rings sailing across the desk. Hastings got up, went to the window, opened it. Standing at the window, scowling, he waited. Unruffled, Friedman said, "Surprise, two more turned up at our old friend Floyd Palmer's pawnshop, just before he got busted. Floyd bought them on the same day. Which means, obviously, that he bought them from the same guy. Which means there's a chance the last four guns might've been owned by the same guy, not by individuals. Which means, in turn, that there's a chance, however remote, that the guy who sold the two guns to Palmer might've held on to the last two guns—the Llama and another one."

Hastings registered quick, avid interest. San Francisco's biggest, smartest, slipperiest pawnshop operator, Palmer had finally been busted only two months ago.

"I see," Friedman observed, "that I've succeeded in arousing your interest."

"What's Palmer's status?"

"He's out on bail, awaiting trial. He's been enjoined from pawnshopping, though."

"And? Have you talked to him?"

"I have indeed." Friedman smiled, a small, subtle, cat-and-mouse smile. Friedman was building the suspense. Again. Still.

"Come on, Pete." Impatiently, Hastings returned to his desk. "We're on the same side. Remember?"

Cheerfully acknowledging the point, all part of his favorite game, Friedman nodded affably. Now the words came more quickly, more crisply. "With Palmer, you know, it's all smoke and mirrors. He's a cockney, but he's got the soul of a Turkish rug merchant. Let him find out he's got something you need, and he'll add a zero or two to the price. Always. And, to be honest, I think I might've played my cards wrong, let him see I wanted something I'd pay for."

"He had to give you a name, though—whoever pawned the guns."

"Oh, sure. But, naturally, it was a fake name. So the question is, does Palmer know the true identity of the guy who brought the two guns in? I think he does know. And he knows I think he knows. And he intimates that he'll turn the guy for a price. Like immunity from prosecution for fencing. Except that, naturally, if he turns the guy, he cops to receiving stolen property. Fencing, in other words. Which makes it a very delicate transaction."

"So get the DA to make the deal. What's the problem?"

"The problem is that the DA's office are acting like real assholes on this one. Why, I'm not sure. I think I must've ruffled someone's feathers over there. Again."

"So twelve of the fourteen guns are accounted for," Hastings mused. "Leaving only the Llama and the other one."

Friedman nodded. "Right. If you wanted to be dramatic, you could say that the Llama is the thirteenth gun."

"What's the fourteenth gun?"

"It's a Colt forty-five automatic—a presentation model, so-called. That means it's a special issue. The action is hand-lapped, as they say. It's embossed, with mother-of-pearl grips. Nickel-plated, too. Very upscale. Like the Llama—and, in fact, like all fourteen guns. They're all collector's items."

"Big bucks," Hastings said thoughtfully.

"Big bucks indeed, at least originally. Whether your neighborhood dope dealer'll pay more for mother-of-pearl grips is something else, I guess."

"So what happens now? What's the plan?"

"I'm approaching the matter obliquely." Once more, cat-and-mouse, Friedman broke off. This time, though, he blew a plume of cigar smoke away from Hastings. They were getting down to cases.

Hastings sighed, looked at his watch. "Are you going to tell me?"

"There's a lady named Florence Ettinger, who works—worked—for Palmer. My plan is to bring her downtown, make a big deal of it, keep her overnight, make sure Palmer knows I'm interrogating her. I've already talked to the DA, and he's willing to give up Ettinger if she'll help with Palmer. That much, at least, he's willing to do."

"Does Ettinger know who brought the guns in?"

"I'm not sure. But if she does know, and if Palmer thinks she's telling us, then I figure we've got a chance with Palmer." Reflectively, Friedman paused. "What we've got going for us is homicide. If I can convince either one of them—or preferably both of them—that they're willfully concealing evidence in a homicide, and could take a heavy fall, then we've got a shot. Receiving stolen goods, that's one thing. Murder, that's something else."

"So when're you going to talk to Florence Ettinger?"

"Pretty quick. Parker and Sawyer are bringing her in right now. I hope."

"So what else have we got on Hanchett?" Hastings asked.

Friedman shrugged. "By me, nothing. The updated lab reports aren't much different from the prelims."

"What about the Llama? Fingerprints?"

"A few that're usable, on the gun itself. However, the prints on the gun, such as they are, don't match either the prints on the two ejected shell casings or the prints on the unused cartridges still in the gun, which are the same. Which might indicate that the gun was loaded by one person and fired by another person. Or the murderer used gloves when he killed Hanchett, but not when he loaded the gun. Except that the gun doesn't show smudges usually associated with gloves. So I'm tentatively figuring that maybe one person loaded the gun and someone else shot it. Which happens, of course, all the time."

"Hmm . . ."

"But," Friedman added, "the bullet found inside the body was intact, and it definitely came from the Llama. So, forensically, we're in good shape."

"What I want," Hastings said, "is to get samples of Teresa Bell's fingerprints."

Having allowed his cigar to go out, Friedman tossed the stub in Hastings's wastebasket. "You still think she did it, eh?"

"I think she's our best shot. Anyhow, I want to know more about her. I want to know *all* about her."

"What about a warrant?"

"I'd rather wait until you've talked to her. Or at least until we get some real evidence. All I've got now is a feeling. A very strong feeling."

"So when should we talk to her?"

"How about eight-thirty tonight? Her husband works nights, and I want to wait until he's out of the house."

"Do you think she'll let us in?"

"I think she will," Hastings answered. "I think she's a talker. I don't think she can stop herself from talking."

"Sounds good." Friedman heaved himself to his feet and began collecting his printouts. "I'll meet you at the Bell place at eight-thirty. Meanwhile, hopefully, I'll have something on the gun. Hopefully."

"Hopefully."

1:15 PM

"You know, Lieutenant—" Brow earnestly furrowed, plainly struggling to frame the thought, Canelli shook his head. "You know, there's something screwy about this Hanchett thing. Know what I mean?"

Hastings took off his reading glasses, put them on a stack of interrogation reports, and rubbed his eyes. The glasses were new, a reluctant concession to the aging process. The optometrist had suggested bifocals, with plain glass on top. Friedman, too, had recommended bifocals. But Friedman, Hastings had observed, continued to struggle with reading glasses. Ann had been noncommittal. After more than a month of delay, Hastings made his decision: when Friedman got bifocals, so would he.

"Screwy?"

"Yeah. Screwy. I mean, things just seem to be—things seem to be just—just sort of coasting. In neutral. Nothing's adding up."

Hastings smiled. "That's why they're called mysteries, Canelli."

"Hmmm . . ."

"Personally," Hastings said, "I think the Bells did it—the mother, maybe with support from her husband. She's wacko enough to have done it. And, God knows, wacko or not, she's got a motive. Or at least a perceived motive. From all I can get on Hanchett, he probably didn't bother to give the Bells much sympathy when he told them their son wouldn't be getting a liver. And that kind of thing can fester. If she started thinking that Hanchett was responsible for her son's death, and if she started to brood about it, and if she wasn't too stable to begin with, then she could've gone over the edge."

"Yeah . . ." Canelli nodded dubiously. Then, tentatively: "It sounds like we shouldn't have much trouble getting prints from her. I mean, if she's a loony and everything, then you could probably get her prints on something without her ever suspecting. Except that—" As if he were vexed with his own reasoning, he interrupted himself, and began again. "Except that some of those goddamn loonies, I've found, they're cagey. It's paranoia, that's the way it was explained to me. They—

you know—they're always suspecting people're out to get them. Which, of course"—he shrugged—"some people are. Like us."

"What about the ones you interrogated?" Hastings asked. "Paula Gregg and her father. What's his name?"

"It's Edward, Edward Gregg. He's a big-shot lawyer. Plenty of money, like that. A real asshole, in my opinion. Lawyers, you know, a lot of times they look down their noses at cops, have you ever noticed that, Lieutenant?"

Hastings nodded. Lawyers, doctors, psychiatrists, successful executives—all of them patronized the cops. The more taxes they paid, the higher the angle of their noses.

"So what about Paula?" Hastings asked. "I understand she hated Hanchett because he molested her."

"Boy," Canelli said fervently, "you got that right, Lieutenant. She hated him, no question."

"So could she've killed him, would you say?"

Once more furrowing his brow, Canelli considered this, then said, "I could see her killing him—you know, on the spur of the moment, like that. But planning it—lying in wait for him—" He shook his head. "I don't see it."

"Her father? Edward Gregg. Anything there?"

"You mean him killing the guy who wronged his daughter, that kind of thing?"

Hastings shrugged. "Stranger things have happened. Besides, Hanchett took Gregg's wife away from him. Hanchett took his wife and then screwed his daughter."

"Yeah—well—if Gregg was a wacko, like the Bell woman, maybe I could see it, Lieutenant. But this guy, he's thinking about his stocks and bonds and what he's going to wear to the opera, seems like to me."

"Well, it won't hurt to—" Hastings's phone warbled, the interoffice line.

"It's Pete, Frank." From the particular inflection in Friedman's voice, it was subtly apparent that he'd discovered something significant.

Which was Hastings's cue to respond with a disinterested "Hi." Playing the hard-to-get game.

"I got a name from Floyd Palmer. I'm disinclined to boast, as you know. But I have to say, as soon as I brought Florence Ettinger downtown and made sure that Floyd knew about it, why, Floyd rolled over, no sweat."

"And?"

"And it's Charlie Ross. Good old Charlie Ross. How about that?"

Charlie Ross—a slim, vain, dapper little man, sixty at least, who talked like a racetrack tout and preened himself like a pint-sized peacock. An impeccably garish dresser who'd worn toupees as long as Hastings had known him, Ross was San Francisco's most prosperous, most reliable fence, specializing in big-ticket items. During the brief time Hastings had worked the pawnshop detail, Charlie Ross was reputed to have successfully fenced a Renaissance painting and two Rollses, a package deal.

"If Charlie had that Llama," Hastings said, "then he sold it. No way did he kill anyone."

"Agreed."

"Have you got an address for Charlie?"

"Definitely." Friedman read off an address in Dolores Heights.

"I'll go talk to him," Hastings said. "I'll take Canelli."

"Right. Say hello to Charlie. Remind him that, the last time I busted him, when I was in Safes and Lofts, I gave him four cigars to smoke until his lawyer sprung him. *Loaned* him four cigars."

"Hmmm . . ."

"Hello, Charlie." Smiling, Hastings offered his badge. "Remember me?"

Squinting myopically, Charlie Ross looked first at Hastings, then at Canelli, then back to Hastings. "The face is familiar, but—" Apologetically shaking his head, he shrugged. "But I can't place you. Sorry."

"No problem, Charlie. I'm Frank Hastings. *Lieutenant* Frank Hastings." He paused to let the significance of his rank register. "I worked the pawnshop detail years ago, and we talked a few times. This is Inspector Canelli." Hastings introduced the two men with a wave. "I'm in Homicide now. Lieutenant Friedman and I are co-commanders. Lieutenant Friedman sends his best regards, by the way."

"Ah." As if he were recalling fond memories of happier days, Ross smiled. He was dressed in a gleaming white shirt with long collar points, knife-pleated gray polyester trousers, and a matching vest. His blue-on-blue tie was impeccably knotted; his tasseled loafers gleamed. His dark, lusterless toupee and pencil-thin matching mustache contrasted vividly with the pallor of his sallow, pinched face. His lips were heart-patient pale. "Ah, Inspector Friedman. That's how I always think of him." The small smile softened appreciatively. "Nice man, very fair, very smart. And funny, too. Dry, and funny. I always figured his humor went right over most people's heads. You know?"

"Listen"—Hastings's gesture requested admittance to Ross's apartment—"I'd like to talk to you, Charlie. I think you can help us with a case we're working on." Holding the other man's eye, he let a carefully calculated moment pass before he said, "It's a murder case."

Ross's expression went blank, a conditioned response. But the small, carefully drawn mustache twitched, an involuntary reaction. As Friedman had observed, the word *homicide* had near-magical power. Now the tip of Ross's pink tongue moistened thin, pale lips.

"Yeah . . ." Ross nodded. "You did say you're in Homicide now, didn't you? By the way, I'm sorry I couldn't place you, Lieutenant, from Pawnshops. The fact is, lately I've been having health problems."

"Maybe you should think about retiring. You're a celebrity. Quit while you're ahead."

"Yeah, sometimes I think about it. But then I think, what'd I do all day long?"

Hastings nodded sympathetically. The silence that followed signified that the preliminaries had been concluded. Whereupon Ross stepped back, allowing the two detectives to enter without further formalities—and without warrants. Appreciatively, Canelli's gaze swept the large, extravagantly furnished living room. "Very nice, Charlie," he said affably. Then, grinning: "I suppose you kept the receipts."

Ross's pained expression registered prim disapproval. His hospitality, his willingness to waive the matter of a warrant, had been affronted. Correcting the lapse, Hastings said, "Yeah, very nice, Charlie. Good neighborhood, too. And according to City Hall, you own the building."

"Yeah, well . . ." Pointedly ignoring Canelli, Ross delicately spread his small, manicured hands. "Well, I'm not getting any younger, Lieutenant. Like we said. And I don't collect Social Security."

Hastings nodded again. Then, signifying an end to the pleasantries, he dropped his voice to a lower, more businesslike register. "What we're looking for, Charlie—what we've got to have—is information on a Llama automatic." As he spoke, he took from his pocket a slip of paper on which he'd written the missing guns' serial numbers and the name of the original owner—only to realize that he'd left his reading glasses on his desk. He held the paper at arm's length, frowned, finally made out the name. "The original owner," he said, "was a Beverly Hills gun collector named Crowe. Fourteen of his guns were stolen, but eventually ten were recovered. That leaves four. Two of those four went through Floyd Palmer. We're trying to trace those two guns now. But whether or not we find them, they're accounted for. That leaves two guns. One of them is a Colt forty-five automatic—a presentation model, embossed, nickel-plated, very fancy. And the other gun—" Hastings paused and leaned forward, verifying that Ross realized they'd come to the essence. "The other gun is the Llama automatic. That's the one we're interested in."

"You mean you're looking for it?" Ross's expression registered nothing more than objective interest.

"No," Hastings answered. "We've got it. And we've got a bullet from it."

"A bullet, eh?" The question suggested only mild interest.

"The bullet killed a very prominent doctor named Brice Hanchett, two nights ago." Hastings's voice, too, expressed nothing beyond the academic. He and Charlie Ross were playing an intricate game: two professionals, maneuvering for position.

"So what we're looking for," Hastings continued, "is the owner of the Llama."

"Yeah." Ross nodded judiciously. "Yeah, I can see that, all right." Thoughtfully, he let his eyes wander to a Spanish-style window that overlooked Dolores Park, a prime view. Hastings had counted four apartments on the building's roster of tenants. Plainly, Charlie had saved his money.

"It's murder, Charlie," Hastings said softly. "Homicide. A rich, famous doctor. I guess you've seen it on TV, read about it."

"Oh, yeah . . ." Reflectively, Ross continued to gaze out on his premium view. "Yeah, sure, I read about it."

"And in Homicide," Hastings said, "in these murder investigations, everything is on the line. It's make-or-break time. You understand what I'm saying?"

Ross nodded. "Oh, yeah. Sure. I understand."

"What the lieutenant means," Canelli said, "is that a guy can store up lots of brownie points downtown. A *lot* of brownie points. In your business, I guess those points never hurt, Charlie. I mean"—Canelli smiled—"I mean, what the hell, there's no such thing as too many brownie points. Right?"

Ross nodded absently, but made no reply. Plainly he was calculating odds, weighing alternatives. Finally, speaking to Hastings, one prime player to another, he said, "Let me think about this. I, uh, I think maybe I can help you, but I've got to make a couple of calls."

Nodding, Hastings laid a card on a lamp table and rose. "Call me tomorrow, by ten o'clock. One way or the other, call me by ten. Clear?"

"Clear."

4:40 PM

Muttering darkly, Canelli braked the cruiser as he balefully turned his head to track an old, dented sedan as it careened through the intersection ahead, trailing earsplitting rock music, and ran a red light. The driver was a white male, unshaven, dark hair long and unkempt, wearing a Giants baseball cap with the visor reversed. The driver sat low behind the steering wheel, his eyes hardly higher than the dashboard.

"We should bust that bastard," Canelli said. Then, looking hopefully at Hastings: "Should we bust him?"

Hastings glanced at his wristwatch, then shook his head. "I want to be downtown by five o'clock."

"Shall I drop you?"

"Please. It's, uh, personal business. Why don't you take the car home, and stay on call? Lieutenant Friedman and I are going to talk to Teresa Bell at eight-thirty tonight."

"Are you going to try for a warrant?"

"Not now. Not without physical evidence. But if she should confess, we might need you. I know you're off the desk tonight, because of the extra hours on the Hanchett thing. Have you got plans for tonight?"

"Gracie's bowling tonight. She's in the semifinals, if you can believe that. And I was going to root for her. Where do the Bells live?"

"In the Sunset. Moraga."

"Ah." Canelli brightened. "The bowling alley's out on Geary. I can just take my beeper, no sweat."

"Fine."

5:10 PM

"Sir?" The parking attendant was advancing purposefully. "Ticket?"

Prepared, Hastings palmed his shield. "I don't have a car here. I'm waiting for someone."

"What?" The attendant frowned.

"Never mind." Hastings waved the attendant away, turned his back, and walked to the rear of the lot, where Victor Haywood's Porsche was parked. A van was parked beside the Porsche. He turned, stared the attendant down, then stepped behind the van. Ah, yes, Victor Haywood appeared at the parking lot's shack, waiting for the keys to his car. Moving to keep the bulk of the van between them, Hastings waited for Haywood to open the Porsche's driver's door before he showed himself. Startled from his stooping posture, Haywood suddenly straightened.

"What th—"

"Sorry," Hastings said. "I didn't mean to scare you."

Instantly taking the offensive, Haywood snapped, "I'm not scared." A trim, trendy man in his mid-forties, his face bronzed on the ski slopes and his body hardened by tennis and daily

Nautilus workouts, Victor Haywood was a psychiatrist who, Ann always said, specialized in the emotional problems of recently divorced women whose ex-husbands were rich and whose lapdog lovers were poor.

"What I wanted to tell you—what I wanted to say"—Hastings began, "is that Ann was pretty upset yesterday, when you called her. She said that you were bothered, apparently, by the fact that we're living together. So I—"

Still on the offensive, elaborately condescending, the elitist patronizing a civil servant, Haywood twisted his thin lips derisively as he said, "Do you think this is the time or the place to discuss it, Lieutenant?"

As if he were considering the question, Hastings looked around the parking lot. He shrugged. "It's as good a place as any."

"For you, perhaps. Not for me." Haywood turned to his car. "I'm afraid I've got to—"

"The thing is," Hastings said, "I want to talk to you about this. I don't care where, but I want to talk. Just the two of us."

Still half turned away, with his hand on the Porsche's door handle, Haywood remained motionless for a moment, holding the pose. His gleaming white cuffs with their golden cuff links, Hastings noticed, were an elegant contrast to his impeccably cut dark blue blazer.

Now, very deliberately, Haywood straightened, turning to face Hastings squarely.

"I don't know what you think we have to discuss, Lieutenant." Haywood spoke softly, in precise Ivy League cadence. "Because, for my part, I don't think we've got anything to discuss. Nothing."

"What about Ann?"

Projecting long-suffering forbearance compounded by barely suppressed anger, Haywood sighed. "What's between me and Ann, Lieutenant—and what's between me and my sons, particularly—is no concern of yours. None. Absolutely none."

"And what's between Ann and me, that's no concern of yours, either."

"Not so long as you do your screwing on your own time—on your own money—it's no concern of mine. Unfortunately, though, that's not the case. Unfortunately, you've chosen to—"

"I don't touch a dime of your money, Haywood. Not a dime. And you know it."

"If you and Ann want to be together, then get married."

"When we're ready to get married, we'll get married."

"Fine. But in the meantime, let my family alone."

"They're your sons. They're not your family. Not anymore."

Haywood snorted contemptuously. "I don't think you want to get into an existential argument with me, Lieutenant. I don't think you're equipped."

Hastings stood silently for a moment, thoughtfully eyeing the other man. Then, measuring the words, he said, "You're probably right. On the other hand, though, I don't think you're equipped to insult someone you can't bully. What do you think?"

"I think," Haywood said, "that this is making me late for a squash game. Excuse me." He opened the door and slid into the Porsche. Hastings stepped forward, blocking the door as Haywood was about to close it. Hastings put both hands on the door, shifted his feet for better leverage, and threw his full weight against the door, breaking its stop lever so that the door slammed flat against the Porsche's left front fender.

"Excuse me," Hastings said, then stepped clear, gently closed the door, turned, and left the parking lot.

7:45 PM

It was important, she knew, to remain utterly quiet, remain perfectly still. Because even the slightest movement, even the shifting of feet on the floor, even flesh moving inside clothing, the scraping, the rustling, it could do her harm, even more harm, she knew that now. So silence, just silence, was all that remained. Because only then, only in the silence, could she hear what must be heard, the echoes of the past mingling with the sounds of the present, voices returned from beyond, voices fading away.

At first she'd feared the final sound, the explosion that ended everything. At first she'd feared that the surreal eruption of orange fireblossoms in the dark would overlay the sound of the voice that began it all: a child, so softly crying. And then the last sound: the soft, eternal sigh that ended it all.

Until now, the final sound.

Until now, these minutes and the minutes to come, when he would come.

Would the world come alive when she saw him? Or would—?

The chimes.

Beginning and ending, the chimes.

Church bells, chiming both the beginning and the ending. Wedding bells.

And now the chimes that warned he was coming. The man with no name.

8:35 PM

As they walked together toward the short walkway that led to the Bell house, Hastings said, "I grew up near here. Our house was on Thirty-ninth."

"I guess I knew that," Friedman answered. "Somehow, though, I always associate you with Detroit."

If they'd been across a dinner table from each other, or across a desk, with Friedman's lazy-lidded eyes on him, the eyes that saw everything, revealing nothing, Hastings knew the observation would cost him. Whenever he talked about his years in Detroit, he was unable to keep the pain of memory from showing. But here in the darkness, both of them walking anonymously side by side, duty-bound, he could answer calmly, casually, "Actually, I was in Detroit for only a few years."

A few years. Yes. Add them up, take the total, admit to the terrible toll: Two good seasons with the Lions. His name in the paper, first for football, then, far bigger spreads, the stories of his marriage to Carolyn Ralston, socialite. Followed by the third season of football, in which Claudia was born—and his knee was ruined. Followed by a job working for his father-in-law, the PR job he could never define, but which included a corner office and a secretary who'd graduated from Swarthmore—a job involving too many drinks with too many clients: visiting VIPs, most of them football fans, all of them horny.

Followed by Darrell's birth.

Followed by more drinking—a lot more drinking, on the job and off.

Job?

Followed by the divorce.

Followed by the final trip to the airport, his last ride with his father-in-law's driver. At the airport, the driver hadn't even bothered to help him with his bags.

Inside the Bell house, lights were burning brightly. The house was built on a narrow lot, over the garage. Moving quietly, the two men ascended the short flight of Spanish-tile steps to the front door. Out of long habit they opened their jackets, each man loosening his revolver in its holster.

Hastings pressed the doorbell button, stepped back. Since he'd already spoken to the suspect, he would take the lead.

But, inside, there was no sound of movement, no sign of life. Another press of the button—and another. Nothing. Hastings stepped forward, held his breath, pressed his ear to the door. Still nothing. He tested the door, which was solidly locked. In the door's peephole prism, no movement was refracted. Hastings stepped back, returned his shield case to his pocket, stood staring at the door.

"At times like this," Friedman observed, "I can't help taking the cost accountant's view. I mean, here we are, two lieutenants, making pretty good money. What's it cost the taxpayers, portal-to-portal, for us to be here, shooting this blank?"

"Except that we don't get overtime. Only the troops. Or have you forgotten?"

"Except that we get to take time off. Unofficial time off, in the field. Or didn't you know?"

"Maybe we should find a phone and call. Her husband works nights. Maybe she doesn't answer the doorbell when he's gone."

"From the number of lights she's got on," Friedman said, "and from the feeling I get, I think she's in there." He stepped forward, made a ham-handed fist, and banged on the door, calling out, "Mrs. Bell!" He knocked again, harder. "It's the police, Mrs. Bell. Open the door, please." He stepped to the door, ear against the panel, listening. Finally he stepped back. "Maybe we should've covered the back. After all, she's a suspect, at least in your opinion."

"Is that a dig?" Hastings asked sourly.

"No."

"Anyway, these houses are all attached. So there's no way we can cover the back unless we climb fences. That means dogs."

"Let's call her, what the hell. Maybe she—"

"The police, did you say?"

It was a man's voice, behind them. Startled, both men turned. A man stood at the bottom of the stairs. Light falling on him from the Bells' brightly lit front window revealed a paunchy, balding man wearing a "Go '49ers" sweatshirt.

"Can we help you?" Friedman asked.

"I live next door." The stranger pointed. "I heard you say you're from the police."

"That's right." Palming his shield case, Friedman led the way down the narrow stairs. "We're looking for Teresa Bell. Have you seen her tonight?"

With the three of them standing beside the driveway, the man was studying Friedman's badge with great interest. Finally he said, "God, that's pretty impressive. Gold, eh?"

"Gold-plated," Friedman answered dryly. "It's your tax dollars, remember."

"Hmmm . . ."

"May I have your name, sir?"

"Sure. It's Penziner. Bernard Penziner. I live next door." He pointed again. "And I was working in the garage, on my car. There's an alternator problem, I think. It's cranking out the volts, but not enough amps. And I heard you pounding, and hollering 'police.' So, naturally"—as if to apologize for his curiosity, Penziner spread his pudgy palms—"naturally, I thought I'd take a look, see what it was."

"And have you seen Mrs. Bell?" Friedman persisted patiently.

"Tonight, you mean? Now?"

"Right."

"Well, no, I haven't. But she never goes out at night. Almost never, anyhow. At least not since—" He frowned, broke off, began again: "So it wouldn't mean much that I haven't seen her. What's it all about?"

"We're conducting an investigation, and we think she might be able to help us. This is Lieutenant Hastings. I'm Lieutenant Friedman."

"Huh." Speculatively, Penziner looked from one man to the other. "Two lieutenants. Big deal, eh?"

"I notice," Friedman said, "that she has a lot of lights on. Do you think she might be in there, and not answering the door?"

Looking up at the windows, Penziner was frowning thoughtfully. "Well, I was just going to say . . ." His voice trailed off. Then, clearing his throat and turning to face Friedman squarely, raising his chin and standing straighter, as if he were a private reporting to a superior officer, Penziner said, "I don't know what it is that you're investigating, Lieutenant. But the truth is—the fact is—maybe about a half hour ago, maybe a little longer, I heard a real loud noise over here."

"What kind of a noise?"

"Well . . ." Penziner elevated his chin again, cleared his throat again. "Well, at the time, I thought it could've been a shot."

The two detectives exchanged a quick, meaningful look. Hastings turned away, walked quickly to his cruiser, raised the trunk lid. The service light inside the trunk was inoperative, but he found the pry bar. He closed the trunk and began walking back to the Bell house, pry bar concealed, as Friedman finally succeeded in persuading Penziner to return to his garage and close the door.

"Okay," Friedman said. "Let's do it. Ring first. Right?"

"Right." Hastings pressed the bell button again, listened carefully, then inserted the pry bar between the door and the jamb. He braced himself, then began increasing the pressure until the door suddenly snapped and swung open. Hastings laid the bar on the small tiled porch, drew his revolver, and stepped into the interior hallway.

Yes, he could smell it: the stench of excrement and urine and blood, overlaid with a lingering tang of cordite. This was the odor that defined the homicide detective's job, the smell of violent death.

She lay in the entry hall, less than ten feet from the front door. She lay on her back, one arm flung wide, one arm folded across her stomach. Her eyes were half open, as if she were staring sidelong at something she found distasteful. Her mouth was agape. She wore a plain cotton housedress, the kind that Hastings's mother used to wear, he suddenly remembered. Her skirt was slightly raised, her feet slightly spread. Her entire torso, shoulders to stomach, was blood-soaked. The blood that had pooled on the hardwood floor was still fresh, still glistening.

Guns drawn, the two detectives went from room to room, checking out the closets and the shower stall, looking under the beds, verifying that the door to the rear garden was securely bolted from the inside. Except for the two bedrooms and the one bathroom, all the rooms were lighted. Nothing had been disturbed: drawers were in order, a woman's purse on one of the beds was intact. As the two men returned to the body, Friedman holstered his revolver and said, "He probably rang the front doorbell, got admitted, and killed her immediately, as soon as he closed the door. Then he left."

With his handkerchief covering the interior knob, Hastings was experimenting with the front-door latch. "It has a spring lock."

"Rats. I was hoping he'd used a key to lock up."

"The husband, you mean."

"You know the first rule—if a woman's killed, it's probably the husband. And vice versa." Friedman took out his own handkerchief, went to a telephone attached to the hallway wall, and put in calls to the coroner and the police lab. Then he returned to the hallway, where Hastings was studying the body.

"With all this blood," Friedman said, "it looks like the bullet hit a main artery."

"Or the heart."

"Yeah—the heart."

In silence, the two men stood motionless, side by side, looking down at the body. Finally, Friedman drew a long, deep breath. "Well, so much for the theory that Teresa Bell killed Hanchett." His voice was hushed, an involuntary response to the specter of death.

"They're connected, though. They've got to be connected. Whoever killed Hanchett had to've killed her. It's the only thing that makes sense."

"Sense?" Friedman snorted. "You want sense, in this business?"

"So what's the plan?" Hastings asked. "You're the senior officer."

"First," Friedman answered, "we get Canelli, or some other underling, to come and take charge, so we aren't stuck here all night. That's first. Command officers need their sleep, remember. Then, obviously, one of us talks to that guy next door—Penziner—while the other one of us makes sure the husband—Fred Bell—reported for work tonight. And then we wait for the prelims, tomorrow morning. Especially, we wait for the word from Ballistics."

"Why especially Ballistics?"

"Because," Friedman pronounced, "I have a feeling that the murder weapon was a forty-five Colt automatic. Presentation model."

9:30 PM

It was beginning again: the trembling, deep within. Even here, safe in his own living room. Even now, long after it was over.

The flash of memory that caused the trembling—what had triggered it? Was it her eyes? Those round, manic eyes, the eyes that first turned surprised, then turned anxious—

—and then turned to stone.

Or was it her voice? The last of her voice, rattling in her throat?

Or was it the twitching? The fingers and the feet: busy, fretful little movements, as if she sought to pluck at his sleeve, like a beggar on the street.

Had he drawn the drapes? It was essential, he knew, to draw the drapes. Yet it was an effort to raise his eyes to the window. And only then did he remember: he'd drawn the drapes before he left. First he'd drawn the drapes. All the drapes. And then he'd dressed. It had all been carefully planned: the dark jacket, the jeans, the wide leather belt for the gun. Then the cap. And, finally, the surgical gloves. And then he'd taken the pistol from under the mattress—the pistol and the clip, fully loaded. And then he'd—

The pistol.

He still had the pistol. Incredibly, the pistol was still thrust in his belt. He'd meant to throw the pistol in the sewer, only a block from her house. One particular sewer, its grating large enough to accept the pistol. But he hadn't done it, hadn't gotten rid of the pistol.

And therefore he was trembling.

So it wasn't her eyes, remembered, that made him tremble. It was the pistol thrust in his belt, flesh of his flesh, a cold steel tumor.

A cancer that could kill again.

11:15 PM

Sitting at the kitchen table, Hastings broke off a piece of French bread and dipped it into the thick, fragrant split-pea soup. Two days ago, a cause for celebration, Ann had made a large potful of the split-pea soup with ham hocks. The jumbo-sized bowl before him, she'd announced, was the last of the batch, defended from Billy and Dan by heroic means. Sitting across the kitchen table, sipping herb tea, Ann was looking gravely at him over the rim of the teacup. Hastings knew that look. Ann had something on her mind.

Had Victor Haywood called?

Yes, almost certainly, Victor had called. It was that kind of a look.

She would, he knew, wait until he'd finished eating. It was part of their unspoken agreement: never begin an argument while either partner was eating.

So, when he'd appreciatively cleaned the bowl with a last

scrap of French bread, and had drunk some of his milk, Hastings said, "Let me guess. It's about Victor."

She sighed, a ragged, tremulous exhalation. Was her hand unsteady as she placed her teacup in its saucer? He couldn't be sure.

"Isn't it always about Victor?"

He decided to make no reply.

"He says you did eight hundred dollars' damage to his car."

"That's bullshit. That's utter bullshit. A hundred, maybe. Not eight hundred."

"The door is creased, he says. And the whole side of the car has to be painted."

Creased? Could the door have been creased? Had he looked for a crease, looked for damage?

No, he hadn't looked, not really.

He drained the glass of milk. "It was a dumb thing to do. I—Christ, it's been a long time since I've done something like that, lost my temper. I wonder what his deductible is. Two hundred?"

"He wasn't talking about deductibles." Ann spoke in a low, tight voice. Her blue eyes had darkened, a sure sign of her distress. When he'd first known her, it was the eyes he'd always remembered whenever they were apart and he was thinking of her. And the line of her jaw, too. And her just-right nose, and the particular curve of her lips. And the sweep of her tawny blond hair as she moved her head.

"I'm sorry." He reached across the table, touched her hand. "I should've known he wasn't talking about deductibles."

She made no response to the touch of his hand. Her eyes were growing darker, not lighter.

"He's talking about court," she said. "About going to court."

He snorted. "For a dented door? I thought Victor was smarter than that."

"He *is* smarter than that." She drew a deep breath, looked at him squarely, with deep, reluctant gravity. "He isn't talking about deductibles. He's talking about custody."

"*Custody?*"

"You don't know him, Frank. Once he says he'll do something—once he makes a threat—he goes through with it. Always. It—it's part of his personality."

"He won't get custody of the kids after five years of divorce."

"He's married. He has a stable home. He makes lots of money. If he gets the right judge—a dinosaur . . ." She let it go bleakly unfinished. Now her eyes were downcast, dispirited. Ann hated controversy, hated the prospect of confrontation.

"I'll talk to him, Ann. I—I'll apologize. Swear to God."

"It won't help. I know what happened. Just listening to him, I know what happened. You threatened his masculinity. Victor can't stand that. Physically, he's a coward. When you threatened him physically, you—" She broke off, searching for the phrase. "You exposed him, brought the whole house of cards—his pasted-up public persona—tumbling down." She smiled ruefully. "That's a pretty labored metaphor, but . . ." On the Formica table, her forefinger began moving, as if she were drawing random designs in sand.

"What actually happened," he said, "was that he got the best of me. I know better than to lose my temper. But he got to me with his goddamn"—he opened his hand, closed it to make a fist, struck the table with rigidly suppressed fury—"his goddamn superiority. If I—if I hadn't hit his goddamn door, I'd've hit him." He tried to smile, to reassure her. "And then we'd really be in trouble."

"He hates you, Frank. He's always hated you, I suppose, because you're soiling goods that once belonged to him. That's how he thinks, you know."

"He's sick. He's supposed to treat people's neuroses. But, Christ, he's—he's—" Angrily, he broke off. Releasing energy, he rose, put his dishes in the sink, ran water into them. She hadn't risen with him. Instead, she sat as before, shoulders slumped, staring down at the table, still tracing random designs on the Formica. He went to her, took her shoulders, gently raised her to her feet, and turned her to face him. Then he drew her close, held her steady. When he felt her respond, felt her arms come around him at the waist, that one particular touch, he whispered into the hollow of her neck, "Let's go to bed. Okay?"

He felt her nod, felt her arms come closer around him. She'd forgiven him, then. For causing them trouble—serious trouble, maybe—she'd forgiven him.

Thursday, September 13

9:20 AM

As Hastings entered the squad room, he saw Friedman waving from behind the glass walls of his office. Good. From the particular pitch and arc of his arm motion, Hastings knew that Friedman had news.

Hastings picked up his messages and incoming files, opened his office door, and dropped the folders and printouts on his desk. Then he strode down the short, glass-walled hallway to Friedman's office. He took a seat, said good morning—and waited.

"As I predicted," Friedman said, "it was a forty-five Colt automatic that killed her."

"I don't remember your predicting that."

Instead of countering, Friedman said, "The bullet went right through her and was embedded in the wall, so it's not in very good shape. But Ballistics says that, for sure, it came from a Colt forty-five automatic."

Hastings was aware of a visceral lift. "So it starts with Charlie Ross," he said.

"Let's hope it doesn't end with Charlie Ross."

"I think he'll come around," Hastings said. "He's just giving himself room to maneuver."

"So when'll you see him?"

"Today. This morning. What about Fred Bell? Anything?"

"He's apparently clean. His time card says he was at work promptly at eight o'clock. And that's downtown. He's a printer at the *Sentinel.* So that's a half-hour drive, minimum. I checked back with Penziner, the next-door neighbor. He puts the sound of the shot at just a little after eight o'clock, absolutely. That's because he finished watching 'The Price Is Right,' one of those game shows, at eight o'clock. Then he went right down to the garage to do some work on his car. That's when he heard the shot. His wife backs him up."

"So Teresa Bell was dead for what? About a half hour, when we got there?"

Friedman nodded. "Something like that."

"And she was probably killed with a gun that Charlie Ross fenced."

"Odds on, I'd say."

"So someone wanted both Hanchett and Teresa Bell dead. He bought two guns, one for each job. He intended to ditch both guns, probably. But the Llama turned up."

Once more, Friedman nodded.

"If someone wanted both of them dead," Hastings mused, "then it's got to have something to do with BMC—with the death of the Bell child. That's the only connection between Hanchett and Bell."

"I wonder," Friedman said, "whether it could have something to do with a frustrated liver recipient, something like that." Speculating, he settled more deeply in his chair, let his eyes wander away.

Hastings frowned. "That'd only make sense if the Bell child got an organ that otherwise would've gone to another child, and that child's parents bore a grudge against both Hanchett and the Bells. But that's not what happened. The Bell child didn't get the liver. And he died. Which would have made Teresa Bell the perfect suspect. Grief drove her bonkers, and she exorcised her demons by killing Hanchett. Which, in fact, is exactly what I thought happened."

"Which, in fact, is what could've happened," Friedman said. "It's still a good theory. Except that now we've got to account for Teresa's murder. Which brings us back to Fred. Suppose Fred knew that Teresa killed Hanchett. Suppose he figured she'd talk. Which it sounds like she would've. And suppose Fred's a little bonkers, too. Or maybe he isn't bonkers, not like his wife was. Suppose he just can't bear to think of his wife behind bars. He knows she'll go crazy. So he puts her out of her misery. A mercy killing, in other words."

Hastings shook his head. "If he'd killed her out of love, he would've done it when she was sleeping. Or when she was watching TV, turned away from him. Besides, Bell has an alibi."

"He's got a punched-in time card," Friedman countered. "Time cards can be falsified."

"Have you got someone checking at the *Sentinel?*"

"No. But I will. Definitely."

"If we assume that the two guns came from Charlie Ross," Hastings said, "then both murders were planned well in advance."

"So maybe Bell planned them. Planned them, and committed them."

"If Bell killed Hanchett, why would he kill his wife?"

"Maybe because he knew she'd talk," Friedman suggested mildly. "If he didn't shut her up, she'd incriminate him. You said yourself that she's a talker."

"Hmmm . . ."

"Or maybe it was a suicide pact," Friedman said.

"Hmmm . . ."

"In any case, the game plan seems clear. You should take Canelli, and you should talk to Charlie Ross. I have an idea he'll go along. With his real-estate holdings, he's got a lot to lose."

Hastings nodded agreement.

"And then, no matter what Charlie says, you've obviously got to talk to Fred Bell."

"Where'll you be?"

"I'll be here, until I hear from you."

"Right."

10:30 AM

"Oh—hi, Lieutenant." Ross's welcoming hand gesture was uneven. His smile was ragged. His eyes moved fretfully. "Hi. Come in. Hi, there, Inspector." Ross stepped back from the door, making room for the two detectives. "I was just thinking about you guys when the doorbell rang. I really was."

Without comment, his expression grave, Hastings nodded heavily and entered the apartment. Canelli had been coached, and his manner was equally solemn.

When they were seated, Hastings said, "You didn't call, Charlie. I told you to call by ten o'clock. You didn't."

"Lieutenant, Jesus, I been waiting for a call myself, about—about this thing. And all I'm getting is promises. You know—'I'll get right back to you, Charlie. Be patient, Charlie.' " Dispiritedly, he shook his head. In the harsh morning light streaming through the huge window that overlooked Dolores Park, the skin of Ross's face was as pale as a corpse's. When he gestured, his hands trembled slightly.

Staring at the other man, Hastings let his eyes go stone cold. Then, pretending a regret so completely synthesized that it felt genuine, Hastings shook his head as he said, "Actually, Charlie, the way things've turned out, it's not really important now. Not after what happened last night."

Involuntarily, Ross blinked. His thin mustache began to twitch. But it was a cautious twitch, not a worried twitch. In the interrogation game, Charlie knew all the moves. Therefore he simply waited for Hastings to speak.

"There's another murder, Charlie." Hastings spoke with great gravity, as if he were breaking the bad news to a member of the deceased's family. "And it looks like it was done with that forty-five-caliber automatic, the one that disappeared along with the Llama, from the Foster Crowe collection."

"Yeah." Canelli shook his head lugubriously. "That's two for you, you might say, Charlie. Two strikes, put it another way. It begins to look like you're in deep shit."

Ross decided to register a puzzled frown. "Wait." He shook his head, raised a narrow, liver-spotted hand. "Wait. Hold it. Lemme understand this. You guys got a couple of murders to solve, and you're saying I'm it. Is that what you're saying?"

Mock-sympathetically, Hastings shook his head. "We don't have much choice, Charlie. See, Homicide's different from Pawnshops. In Pawnshops, there's an ebb and flow, you might say. We can't connect a guy to a few TVs, for instance, then we'll get him for a few computers, typewriters, whatever."

"Yeah," Canelli offered. "In Pawnshops, there's always another train coming along. But in Homicide, there's only one train. See?" Brow earnestly furrowed, Canelli asked the question solicitously, doing his best.

"And in Homicide," Hastings said, "it's all physical evidence. That's all the DA cares about. Confessions, eyewitnesses, that's fine—depending on the witness. But without physical evidence, nothing happens."

On cue, Canelli picked up the beat. "And, see, we've got the Llama tied tight to the Hanchett homicide, with ballistics. And we've got the Colt forty-five tied to the homicide last night. And we've got you tied to those two guns. So I have to tell you, Charlie"—Canelli shook his head mournfully—"I have to tell you, it don't look like the future's too bright for you." Canelli turned toward the sun-drenched view of Dolores Park, and the Bay Bridge beyond. "All this, Charlie, and you wind up standing trial for murder." Canelli shook his head again. "What a waste."

"Hey—*wait.*" Aggrieved, Ross held up both hands, palms out. Pointedly ignoring Canelli, speaking to Hastings, he said, "What you *really* got is Floyd Palmer, that's who you got. You got him connected to a few guns from this gun nut's collection, as I understand it, and then you got him saying he got the guns from me. Christ. What's that? Is the DA going to take that to the bank? Come on, gimme a break here."

Elaborately patient, Hastings leaned closer to Ross. "What I'm starting with, Charlie—what I'm assuming—is that Floyd Palmer is telling the truth. That's where I'm starting. And then—"

"Telling the *truth*? Christ, Lieutenant, the guy's waiting for a court date. He'd tell you his mother's an ape if he thought it'd help. He'd—"

"Charlie. Wait." Hastings shook his head sternly, raised his hand. "Wait. You interrupted me. We're doing business, you and I. And the rules are, you don't interrupt. I can interrupt you. But you don't interrupt me. That's because I've got a badge and you haven't."

Ross muttered something, shifted his bony body in his chair. One elbow cocked on the arm of the chair, he slammed his chin down in the palm of his hand as he looked peevishly away.

Continuing in the same patient voice, Hastings said, "I guess I didn't make this plain yesterday, Charlie. I guess I'll have to lay it out for you again, eh?"

Still sulking, Ross refused to respond.

"See, I'm starting with the supposition that Floyd Palmer is telling the truth, like I just finished explaining. And then I'm assuming, since you're basically a wholesaler—an operator—that you started with a big part of the action, and that you broke it down for retail distribution. I'm assuming that you started with maybe ten guns from the Crowe collection."

"Ten?" Ross frowned.

"I forget the exact tally. That's not important. What's important is that you sold two guns to someone who killed two people in this town the past week." Hastings let a definitive silence settle before he said, "I'm not saying you pulled the trigger, Charlie. I know better than that. But, like I say, I'm assuming that you've got information I need—material evidence in a homicide. That's my assumption. So then I assume that, since you're not willing to cooperate, you're obstructing justice. And that's a very, very serious business." As if the prospect of Ross's fate dispirited him, Hastings shook his head. "Someone who obstructs justice in a capital case, Charlie, especially someone with a record like yours, he's looking at some pretty heavy time. He's looking at probably—"

"Hey. Wait." As if he'd been touched by a hot wire, Ross's whole body jerked. *"Wait.* You—Jesus—you're trying to—"

At Ross's elbow, a high-tech phone warbled. As if he were reaching for a prize, Ross grabbed greedily for the telephone and pressed it furtively to his ear.

"Yeah?" A pause. Then: "About time." Exasperated, he tapped his teeth with a manicured thumbnail as he listened. Finally: "Where are you now?" A brief, impatient pause. "Okay. Stay there. Stay put. Do like I told you. This time, for Christ's sake, do like I told you." In one abrupt movement, suddenly all business, Ross cradled the phone, rose to his feet, and spoke briskly to Hastings. "Those two guns you're talking about, that was the call I was waiting for, see, before I called you."

Also on his feet, also all business, Hastings was ready with a notebook and a ballpoint pen as Ross recited, "Her name is

Dolores Chavez. She's a bartender at a place called The Haven, out on Church Street. Church and Twenty-eighth, Twenty-ninth, you can't miss it. The place is probably closed, door locked. But knock, and she'll open the door for you. Don't waste any time, though. Dolores, she's still a little green. And she's stubborn, too. She can be very hard to handle. But she's got what you want. We talked last night, me and Dolores. It'll take a hundred, though."

"A hundred, Charlie?" Pocketing the notebook, Hastings shook his head and spoke reproachfully. "A hundred, did you say?"

"Oh—*Jesus.*" Ross crossed quickly to a cabinet, pulled open a drawer, produced two fifty-dollar bills. "Here. Take them. *Jesus.* Just *get* there, if you want anything from Dolores."

"Thanks, Charlie. We'll be in touch." Quickly, the two detectives strode toward the door.

"And don't forget those goddamn brownie points," Ross called out after them. "Pass the word downtown."

"Gotcha."

11:30 AM

The Haven was a workingman's bar that had been upgraded when the yuppies with their briefcases and BMWs began infiltrating the Mission District, San Francisco's traditional blue-collar bastion. Budweiser signs had been taken out of The Haven's plate-glass window, random shake shingles had been nailed to the front façade, and the door now featured a small stained-glass window that was protected by clear plastic. A check with Mission Station suggested that The Haven's record was good: no drug dealing, no pimping, few fights—and no known fencing of stolen property on the premises.

"Why don't you stay in the car," Hastings said. "I'll see which way she jumps."

"A lady fence." Marveling, Canelli cocked his head."I don't think I've ever heard of a lady fence. I bet she wrestles on the side."

Hastings smiled. "You don't think bartending and fencing keeps her busy enough?" He got out of the cruiser, walked to the door of The Haven, tested it, knocked. When the door opened a crack, he was ready with the badge. Immediately, a small, quick-moving, dark-eyed woman opened the door wider. A moment later he was inside, with the door bolted, facing her. She was about thirty, short but robustly built, a full-breasted Latino beauty. Her dark, snapping eyes were bold, her body language strong-minded. Standing just inside the door, Hastings surveyed The Haven's interior. With the chairs stacked on the tables and open cartons littering the mahogany bar, the place was lifeless, depressing, without purpose. In the rear, wearing Walkman earphones, a black man was leisurely mopping the floor, his slow strokes synchronized to some inaudible rhythm.

"Back here . . ." The woman turned away, began walking purposefully toward an Exit sign at the end of a short back corridor with His and Hers on either side. Like her manner, the movement of Dolores Chavez's buttocks and thighs was purposeful, straightforward, assertive. Some women walked to please men. Dolores walked to cover ground. In cadence, her thick black hair, earlobe length, swung rhythmically.

She lifted a two-by-four that barred the metal-clad rear door, drew back two large bolts, swung open the heavy door, and walked into a small, paved areaway stacked with garbage cans and trash bags. As he pulled the door shut behind them, Hastings glimpsed a furtive, furry movement between two garbage cans. Good. If Dolores caused trouble, a call to the health department would be Hastings's first move.

She turned to face him, saying, "I talked to Charlie."

Hastings nodded. "I was there when you called."

"Charlie says you're okay, don't screw people over." As she said it, her dark, quick eyes boldly assessed him.

"Charlie's right." He let a beat pass. Then, meaningfully: "People like us—you and I—we've got to keep our word, keep our promises. Otherwise it all comes apart."

Plainly still suspicious, she nevertheless inclined her head slightly. "Yeah . . ." Her voice was only lightly accented. Contradicting her exterior self, there was a softness to her face, a harmony of ovals, gently joined. But her dark, vivid eyes remained hard. Legs braced wide, fists propped on her hips, her body language was still uncompromising. Plainly, butting heads with Dolores would yield nothing more than a headache.

So, relaxing his own body, Hastings waited for her to speak.

"This is the first time I've ever done this. Talked to a cop, I mean," she said.

Hastings nodded.

"I've got a kid. A son. You understand?"

"I understand." Why was he tempted to say, *I've got a son, too. And a daughter*?

"My arrangement with Charlie's nothing, really. I used to date a guy, one of Charlie's guys. He introduced me to Charlie. Then we broke up, this guy and me. So then, a couple of times, I hear about someone's looking for something, I give Charlie a call, turn a couple of bucks. Mostly TVs, a couple of CD players, like that. I never held the stuff, not really. I just took a cut. A little cut."

Hastings nodded again.

"Guns, though . . ." Mouth set firmly, eyes still hard, she shook her head. Was she about to deny that she'd done it, dealt the Llama and the .45? Charlie Ross would pay, if she backed away. Charlie would pay and pay again, everything doubled.

"They were a mistake," she was saying. "Those guns, they were a mistake."

Suppressing a grateful exhalation, Hastings nodded again. The areaway where they stood was bordered by the air shafts of two small apartment buildings, each three stories high. A narrow blind alley led from the areaway to the street. Hastings stepped a companionable foot closer and said quietly, "Tell me, Dolores. Just tell me how it went. Don't try to second-guess yourself. Just tell me."

"Yeah . . ." She nodded. She was softening. But only a little.

Hastings took the two folded fifties from his pocket, palmed them, passed them to her as he held her eyes with his. "Here—this is from Charlie."

She took the bills, slid them smoothly into the hip pocket of her designer jeans. Yes, Dolores knew her way around. All the moves were right.

"Let's get this over with, Dolores. Let's cut it short."

She drew a deep breath. The fabric of her "San Francisco Quake of '89" sweatshirt drew taut across her breasts. Her body, Hastings realized, was exciting—vital, expressive, compelling. Now she lowered her chin. It was a definitive mannerism, the street fighter digging in, psyching up. Then she began:

"There was this guy came in the bar. Call him Bob. He said he had a customer looking for a gun, maybe a couple of guns. Well . . ." She shrugged. "That's nothing new. Everyone's looking for guns. But this guy—Bob—was talking about some big bucks, it sounded like. His customer was . . ." She shrugged again, hesitating, this time searching for a word, a phrase. "He was an uptown type, the way it sounded. I mean, it didn't sound like he was going to rob a liquor store or anything. So I made a couple of calls, checked around, found a couple of guns. So then I got in touch with Bob. I said I had two guns, and he said okay, he'd be in touch. But then Bob started to feel some kind of heat from his probation officer. So he said he was out. Fifty dollars, and he's out. Meaning that I'd do business directly with his customer. Which was fine with me. So then I picked up the guns. And that was it. The guy came in, had a drink, said he was a friend of Bob's, like we'd arranged. I handed the guy a paper sack with the guns in it, and he handed me a sack with the money. No problem."

"You got the two guns from Charlie Ross."

Deliberately, she looked him over. Then, coolly: "I didn't say that."

He set his jaw, hardened his gaze. Translation: this evasion he would allow. Only this one.

"Describe the guns."

She frowned. "What d'you mean?"

"I mean what I say, Dolores. I mean describe them. Were they automatics? Revolvers? Uzis? What?"

"I . . ." She hesitated. "I don't know from guns. They—" Ruefully now, she hesitated. Then, admitting: "They scare me, you want to know the truth."

Was it the truth? He must know.

He turned to the narrow alleyway. "Does that lead to the street?"

Puzzled—wary now—she nodded. "Yes. But—"

"Is it locked?"

"Bolted."

"All right. Wait here. Right here." Without waiting for a reply, he turned, walked quickly to the access door, unbolted it, and strode to the cruiser, parked a hundred feet from The Haven. As Hastings swung the door open, Canelli started.

"Sorry." Hastings looked up and down the deserted sidewalk. "Give me your piece. Not your service revolver. Your backup."

Without comment, Canelli took a Walther semiautomatic from the holster at the base of his spine and handed it over. Yes, the hammer was on half-cock, the safety set. Still leaning into the cruiser, Hastings surreptitiously slipped the Walther into his waistband, buttoned his jacket. "Back in a minute." He retraced his steps, walked down the strong-smelling alley to the air shaft where Dolores waited. He raised his head, scanned the windows above. Nothing. Using his left hand, he took Canelli's Walther from his waistband, held it flat in his palm. With his right hand he drew his service revolver, a Smith & Wesson with a four-inch barrel.

He raised the Walther. "This is an automatic. The cartridges are in the handle. So it's flat. See?"

Unwillingly, she studied the pistol, then nodded hesitantly.

"And this"—he raised the Smith and Wesson—"this is a revolver. The cartridges are in a round cylinder. You can see them in there. Right?"

She nodded again.

"Okay. So between these two guns, which were the ones you sold this guy? This?" He raised the automatic. "Or this?" He raised the revolver.

"That." She pointed to the automatic.

"Both of them. Both guns?"

"Both of them."

"You're sure? Absolutely sure?"

"Absolutely."

"Both of these guns have what's called a blued finish. Right?"

She nodded.

"The guns you sold. Were they both this blued finish?"

"No. One of them—the big one—it was all chrome, or silver, something like that. And it had pearl handles, too. I remember that."

"Okay." Concealing the surge of relief and excitement he felt, he nodded, put the two pistols away, buttoned his jacket. Then, speaking quietly, flatly, in his voice of departmental command, he said, "Okay—give me a description of the customer."

"A description?" As if she were puzzled, she frowned.

"Yes, Dolores." The two words were weighted acidly. "A description. You know—is he old? Young? Hair? No hair? That's what this little talk is all about. We're looking for this guy. We're looking for him because we think he committed two murders. Understand?"

"Well, yeah. But—" She broke off, shook her head. "But what're you saying? You saying court? The witness stand? Like that?"

"I'm saying we want to find this guy. I'm saying that we've got two people dead. They were killed by these two guns we're talking about, Dolores. Do you understand that?"

"Yeah. But—"

"There's no 'buts,' Dolores. Right now, the trail leads from a man named Crowe in L.A., to Charlie—to you. So, right now, you're it, Dolores." Then, softly: "That isn't the way you want to leave it—" A moment passed. "Is it?"

No response. Only a hard look from her dark, snapping eyes.

"You say you've got a child. What'd happen to him if we had to lock you up, Dolores?"

"Hey, what're you trying to—"

He silenced her with a curt gesture that cut toward The Haven. "What's your work schedule?"

She frowned. "Work schedule?"

"What hours do you work?"

"It changes. This week I come in at ten, a little before, open at noon. I work till six. Then I work nights, sometimes. We change off. Why?" It was a wary question. Her eyes were very still.

"Because I want you to look at a couple of people. Maybe we can run them by here, maybe not. We'll see."

"You mean guys who—?" She let it go apprehensively unfinished.

"Obviously, we'll want you to identify the guy who bought the guns. I'm not talking about a lineup, downtown. I'm talking about you probably sitting in an unmarked car, looking at someone walking by, like that. He doesn't need to see you. That's up to you. And we won't bring him by The Haven, if that's the way you want it."

"Hmmm . . ." It was an uneasy monosyllable.

"But first I need a description, Dolores." Feigning elaborate caution, he scanned the windows above them. "I want it now. Right now. Don't stall, it won't do you any good. And the longer we're here, you know, the more chances you're taking, being seen talking to a cop. You understand that, don't you?"

For a long, smoldering moment her dark Inca eyes held his. Then she muttered an obscenity. Ignoring it, Hastings waited silently. Finally she spat out, "He's maybe forty, I'd say, around there. Maybe thirty-five, I don't know. Almost as tall as you, but not as husky. He was dressed just ordinary—slacks, an old leather jacket. And a stocking cap, I remember that. Dark blue, pulled down around his ears, reminded me of a sailor, a little. And, yeah, sunglasses. Dark sunglasses. And it was night, you know, when he came. Dim lights in the bar. So I didn't get much of a look at him."

"He was disguised, it sounds like."

She nodded. "Yeah, that's the way I figured. Disguised."

"What about his voice?"

She shrugged, spread her hands. "Who knows? All he said was, 'Are you Dolores?' Then he said maybe a couple more sentences, that was it."

"How'd he talk? Uptown? Latino? Tenderloin? What?"

"Uptown, I'd say. No accent, that's for sure."

"I gather he was white."

"Yeah—white."

"Dark complexion? Light?"

She shrugged. "He wore a mustache. Dark. His hair was dark, too, what I could see of it."

"Was it a fake?" he asked. "The mustache—could it've been a fake?"

"I guess so," she answered indifferently. "Like I say, I wasn't trying to memorize his face, nothing like that. I just—you know—took the money and said good-bye. Most of what I saw of him, I saw in the mirror back of the bar."

"How much did he pay for the two guns?"

She hesitated momentarily, then admitted, "It was a lot. Eight hundred."

He nodded, studied her thoughtfully for a moment. Then, signifying that for now their business was concluded, he stepped back.

But there was still something to say—another question to ask. "How many children do you have? Just the one?"

Instantly her dark eyes flashed angrily, defensively. "Why're you asking?"

Impassively holding her gaze, he made no reply. Finally she muttered, "Yeah. Just one. A boy. Nine years old."

"Have you got a man? A husband?"

Her baleful stare was the answer. Hastings studied her for a moment before he decided to ask, "How old's your car, Dolores?"

Surprise momentarily straightened the defiant curl of her lips. "It's new." Then, puzzled, she asked grudgingly, "Why you asking?"

"I'm asking," he said, "because I've got some advice for you."

Contemptuously, she nodded. "You going to tell me how to raise my kid, eh? You jerk me around, you and Charlie Ross. Then you're going to start preaching. Right?"

"You're right, Dolores. You're absolutely right. I'm going to start preaching. I'm going to tell you to wise up and start living within your means, without breaking the law. You're smart, and you're ambitious. You're good-looking, too. Bartenders can make good money. But what I hear you saying is that you want more. You're greedy, Dolores—going for the flash. And I'm telling you—I'm promising you—that if you keep on fencing, handling hot merchandise, you're going to fall. You're going to do time—

and your son's going to be on the streets, or else in an institution. Do you have any idea what can happen to a kid in juvie? Any idea at all?"

She made no response. But, almost imperceptibly, her body was slackening, no longer drawn taut by defiance.

"Think it over, Dolores. You've got brains. Use them. Meanwhile, don't leave town. Because you're going to be hearing from us." He turned abruptly and walked down the foul-smelling alley to the street.

11:45 AM

He switched off the engine, shifted the gearshift lever to Park. The Twin Peaks observation area was populated by a dozen-odd sightseers and their cars, just as he'd calculated. Drawing a long, deep breath, he made himself focus on the vista before him: the San Francisco cityscape seen from the heights of Twin Peaks, one of the world's premium views.

Was it wise for them to meet so soon?

She hadn't wanted them to meet. From the sound of her voice, from the cautious cadence of her speech, he'd heard her reluctance. Yet, when he'd insisted, she knew she must agree.

Meaning that murder made the difference.

Flesh was flesh and money was money. But murder made the difference.

Almost fourteen hours now . . .

Time . . .

Time could conceal.

But time could corrode. Time could tear open the wound, make memory the barb, make the terror of night the dark secret of the day.

Corrode . . . conceal . . . congeal. Time, ticking away, measuring the moments.

One minute alive . . .

One minute dead.

Where was he now, this moment? The big man with the quiet eyes—Hastings. Where was he now? Which trail was he following?

In the mirror he saw her car turning into the observation area. Swinging open the door, he stepped out of the car and walked to the low concrete parapet, pretending to fix his gaze on the view, one tourist among many.

A minute—and another minute.

Time . . .

Then he was aware of her beside him. Like him, she kept her eyes focused forward. Two tourists. Two strangers, exchanging casual comments.

"How are you?" she asked.

Suddenly he laughed, a spontaneous eruption. Or was it a giggle?

A giggle?

"How would you expect me to be? I've never done this before. Never killed anyone. Ring the bell, say hello, then kill someone."

"You shouldn't talk like that. Please don't talk like that."

"You didn't want to come."

"It's dangerous, being here."

"Dangerous for me?" he asked. "Or dangerous for you?"

"For us," she answered, her voice very low, almost inaudible. "Dangerous for us."

1:15 PM

"This business is no different from atom smashing," Friedman pronounced. "You've got to develop a theory, and then you've got to stick with it. And my theory is that these two murders are connected."

"I think it's probably eighty percent," Hastings answered.

"But don't forget, we assume they're connected because Hanchett was shot with the Llama, and Teresa Bell was shot with a forty-five. Which is to say we're assuming that the forty-five was the one Charlie and Dolores fenced. But that could be wrong. Teresa Bell could've been killed by a burglar who panicked—and who just happened to have a forty-five automatic, of which there're hundreds in San Francisco. And not all automatics, either. It could've been a revolver."

Friedman shook his head. "Wrong. The bullet came from an automatic. Ballistics can tell that much, apparently. It's something to do with the jacketing. But they'll never be able to tie the gun to the bullet. It went right through, you know. It's totally mangled."

"Okay—so it was an automatic. How many of those are around?"

"Not many, in fact. Don't forget, Colt is the only manufacturer who ever made a forty-five automatic. Most automatics are thirty-eights, or nine-millimeters, or seven-point-six-five-millimeters."

"I *know* that." Hastings's voice rose irritably. At this point in a homicide investigation, stalled, groping, Friedman's imitation of a squad-room Socrates often rankled. "What I'm saying is, there's no real basis for—"

"I already told you," Friedman said, "it's theoretical. I'm *assuming* that the forty-five is the one Charlie fenced. Which is why I assume the two murders are connected. It's a percentage play."

"Okay, let's say they're related. So tell me *how* they're related—*why* they're related."

"I was afraid you were going to ask that."

In spite of himself, Hastings smiled. "Motive." He pronounced the word solemnly, himself the moment's Socrates. "That's what we need for the Bell murder. For the Hanchett murder, we've got nothing *but* motives. For the Bell murder . . ." He shrugged, spread his hands, and asked, "Have *you* got a motive?"

"The only thing that makes sense," Friedman said, "assuming they *are* connected, is that someone thought Teresa Bell killed Hanchett, and wanted to wreak vengeance." He smiled: his pixieish, playful smile superimposed on his broad, swarthy Buddha-face. "How about that?"

"Except," Hastings pointed out, "no one cared, apparently, whether Hanchett lived or died. His own flesh and blood didn't even care."

"How about Carla Pfiefer? Maybe she cared."

"Maybe."

"And, speaking of flesh and blood, what about—" Friedman consulted his notes. "What about Hanchett's son? John. Have you talked to him?"

"Briefly. Very briefly."

"And?"

"He's pretty screwed up, I'd say. Very hostile. Very . . ." Hastings searched for the word. "Very scattered. Unfocused. All over the place. But if you're asking whether he killed Teresa Bell because she killed his father, then I'd say the chances are about zero. I could see him killing Hanchett for all the damage Hanchett did to his mother. Or maybe because he wanted his inheritance. But vengeance for his father's death?" Hastings shook his head. "No way."

"So far," Friedman pronounced, "Fred Bell's our best bet."

Hastings snorted. "If Fred Bell's the most viable suspect we've got, then I'd say we're in deep, deep shit."

"That's negative thinking."

"That's a carefully considered opinion. I've seen them together, Fred and Teresa. And I can tell you, he wasn't about to murder his wife. Not when I saw them. Besides, he was at work when it happened."

"Ah." Friedman raised a professorial forefinger. Hastings

knew that mannerism. Friedman had a surprise for him—a carefully timed surprise. "Ah, but I spent some time checking into that one. Fred Bell is an ink mixer at the *Sentinel*'s printing plant. And ink mixing, as it turns out, is a very solitary occupation. Typically, Bell arrives on the job at eight, punches in, goes to his ink mixing room, and begins mixing. Then, at about nine o'clock, he begins his rounds, feeding the presses, getting ready for the first printing. So, if he got someone to punch in for him, at eight, then he could easily have killed the missus, right around eight o'clock, and been at his ink-mixing post by eight-thirty. No sweat."

"What about eyewitnesses at the *Sentinel*?"

"So far, none. I've done all this by phone. I'm going to send someone out there, but not till the night shift arrives, obviously."

"So what now?"

"I'd say collect Canelli and Dolores, and start making the rounds of every guy connected with the case who fits Dolores's description of the guy who bought the two guns."

"Considering that the guy was obviously disguised—dark glasses, maybe even a false mustache, I suspect—her description'll fit almost all of them."

"Well," Friedman observed equably, "it won't do any harm to plow another furrow, so to speak. By the way, how do you rate Dolores?"

Hastings considered. "I think she's okay. I kind of like her, in fact. She's . . ." He hesitated. "She's spunky."

"Is she smart? Observant?"

"Very."

"Well, then . . ." Friedman waved him on his way. "You'd better get to it. Where'll you start?"

Hastings knew the approved answer. "With Fred Bell, of course."

Gratified, Friedman nodded. "Of course."

2:30 PM

"Listen, Dolores . . ." Exasperated, Canelli turned to face the woman sitting beside him in the unmarked car. "Listen, this'll be a whole lot easier on both of us if you'll just relax and enjoy it, know what I mean?"

"No," she answered, her voice icy, her dark eyes flashing Latino fire. "No, Inspector—what *do* you mean, exactly? Tell me what it is you mean."

Belatedly conscious of his remark's sexual innuendo, Canelli could feel his face growing hot. How long had it been since he'd blushed? During all the years they'd been engaged, had Gracie ever made him blush?

"What I meant was . . ." But why was he explaining? He was a policeman—a detective, with a gold shield. She was a self-admitted fence, a hustler.

But she was a hustler with a small, compact body, rounded to perfection.

Making love, she could send a man sky high, light him off like a Roman candle, take him soaring.

Had he ever had a Latino girl?

Had he ever—?

Ahead, Lieutenant Hastings's brown Honda station wagon was turning the corner, pulling to the curb. Time to go to work.

"What I meant was, you got to do this, do this stakeout number for us. So why make it harder for yourself?" As he spoke, Canelli was conscious that, yes, he had a partial erection. What was it about Dolores? He cleared his throat, saying, "You've got to—"

"What I got to do," she said, "is work so I can get money so I can raise my kid, buy him clothes, pay the rent. I spend all day doing this for you guys, I lose a day's pay. It's not fair."

"It's not fair that a couple people were killed with guns you fenced, either, Dolores. You got to think about that."

"I said okay, I'd do the stakeout thing. But not when I'm supposed to work. Nobody told me about that—about taking time from work."

"In this business it's pretty tough to make plans, Dolores." He tripped the door handle, swung the driver's door open. "I got to talk to the lieutenant. Wait here." As he strode toward Hastings, he surreptitiously dropped his hands to his crotch, arranging himself.

What *would* she be like in bed? He could imagine her dark, vivid eyes gone wild with passion, her breasts alive to his touch.

He strode to meet Hastings, who had already locked his car.

"Is he in there, do you know?" Hastings moved his head toward the Bell house. In the double front windows, the venetian blinds were blanked out.

"I don't know, Lieutenant. Me and Dolores, we just got here."

Hastings smiled. " 'Me and Dolores,' eh? What's that mean?"

"Huh?" As if he were puzzled, Canelli frowned. But, once more, he felt his face grow warm.

What was happening to him?

Even as a boy, a teenager, he'd never—

"Is she giving you any trouble?" Hastings asked. "She's a hothead, I imagine, if she gets you going."

Gets you going . . .

Yes, oh, yes—get him going. All the way home, he and Dolores.

"No—no—" He waved a deprecating hand. "No problem, Lieutenant."

"Good. Well . . ." Once more, Hastings gestured toward the Bell house. "Here I go. Keep your radio on. I told Dispatch you'd be catching for me."

"Oh. Right. Sure." Canelli nodded, watching Hastings stride toward the small stucco house—the house that probably still had blood on the floor.

2:40 PM

Carefully, Hastings stepped around the edges of the opaque plastic sheeting that covered the hallway floor and concealed the bloodstains and the chalked outline of Teresa Bell's body.

Had it only been yesterday—last night—that he'd entered this same hallway, to find himself staring into Teresa Bell's dead eyes?

"I'm sorry to bother you, Mr. Bell, at a time like this. But there're a few things I've got to clear up. It shouldn't take long."

Bell had turned his back and was already in the living room, sitting on a lumpy sofa. His eyes were blank, his face expressionless. He sat slumped on his spine, his body slack.

"I've just come from the morgue," Bell said. "I had to—to identify her."

"Ah." Hastings nodded. "Yes. Did one of our people take you down, bring you back?"

Bell nodded.

"Is there anything else we can do for you? Anything at all?"

"No. Nothing. The funeral home, they're taking care of it. There's—" Bell swallowed painfully. "There's an autopsy first."

"I know."

"It's hard to think of it—think of them . . ." Bell shook his head sharply.

"I'm glad you have a good funeral home. That means a lot at a time like this."

The other man gave no sign that he'd heard. Hastings let a moment pass, then began, "The first thing I want to ask you, Mr. Bell, is whether you have any idea who killed her—*why* someone killed her."

For a long, inert moment, Bell made no response. His deeply etched face was hollow-eyed, ravaged by constant psychic pain. A son who'd died a lingering death—a half-demented wife who'd died in a pool of blood in the house they'd shared—all of it, and something more, was tearing at the tortured face.

Finally Bell shrugged, a meaningless movement, without definition or hope. "No," he answered, "I can't—I don't—" As if confused, he frowned, shook his head.

"It wasn't robbery," Hastings prompted. "And since the door wasn't forced, we have to assume the murderer was known to her."

With great effort, Bell raised his eyes, focused on the detective's face. "Known to her?"

"Sure. She wouldn't've opened the door to a stranger. Would she?"

"No . . ."

"Was she careful about the door—about keeping it locked, using the peephole?"

"Yes." As he said it, Bell lapsed into his previous posture, his body slack, nervelessly slumped on the ragtag sofa, legs spread, heels on the floor. It was the posture of a man without hope, without the will to live.

A homicide and a suicide? A death pact?

Had Bell lost his nerve last night? Had he killed her and then been unable to kill himself?

"Mr. Bell." Deliberately, Hastings put an edge on the question. "This isn't getting us anywhere. Someone murdered your wife last night. And it's up to us—you and me—to find whoever did it, and put him in jail. Isn't that what you want?"

"I—I don't know anymore. I just—" Helpless, exhausted, Bell broke off.

"Mr. Bell—" The edge in Hastings's voice was sharper now. "You'll have to answer these questions. Now or later, you're going to have to answer. I realize that you've had a terrible shock. But I've got a job to do. And I want to do it."

A *job to do*—God, how empty it sounded, how self-serving.

No response.

Sighing deeply, regretfully, Hastings said, "Your wife hated Dr. Hanchett because of—of your son. Isn't that so?" As he spoke, Hastings's eyes were drawn involuntarily to the small onyx urn in its pine-bough niche atop the fireplace mantel. Then he continued doggedly, "It became an obsession with her, isn't that what happened? She couldn't go on—not when your son was dead, and Hanchett was still alive. So—" Looking for some reaction, some sign, he stopped. Then, very softly: "So she killed Hanchett. That's all she could do. There wasn't anything left for her, except to kill Hanchett. Because he'd taken her sanity."

At the final words, as if he were coming faintly awake after a deep sleep, Bell began to stir, to blink, to half-flex his fingers.

"You bought the guns," Hastings said, feeling his way. "You gave one to her, and you kept one for yourself. You had to keep one for yourself, because you didn't know whether your wife would—"

"Guns?" Bell drew his feet inward, drew himself straighter on the sofa. In response, instinctively, Hastings gathered himself, surreptitiously shifting in his chair to make his revolver more accessible.

"Guns?"

"The Llama and the nickel-plated Colt automatic. You bought them from the woman at the bar. Dolores, the Latino woman."

As if he were perplexed—genuinely perplexed—Bell frowned. Assessing the frown, Hastings felt his conviction draining away as Bell shook his head, saying, "I didn't buy any guns."

"Two pistols. Two automatics. One with pearl grips."

Causing Bell simply to frown again, shake his head again. With his eyes fixed on Hastings, Bell was more alert now, more responsive. "But I—I don't know what you're talking about."

"Mr. Bell, when I was here on Tuesday—the day after Hanchett was killed—when I talked to your wife, I had the very strong feeling that she'd killed Doctor Hanchett. And I think *you* suspected she did it, too. Isn't that so?"

"I . . ." Bell shook his head again. But now the gesture signified both desperation and despair, no longer denial. Yes, Bell suspected his wife had killed Hanchett, perhaps even knew she'd done it. But, no, he hadn't bought the two automatics.

Was there another link in the chain? Had the two guns gone from Charlie Ross to Dolores to another fence, who'd then sold the Llama to Teresa Bell, and the .45 to someone else, to the person who'd murdered Teresa Bell two days after she'd murdered Hanchett?

It was the kind of puzzle that endlessly intrigued Friedman—and endlessly frustrated Hastings.

But the guns were secondary. First the murderers, then their tools.

"She killed Hanchett." Hastings spoke softly, simulating a sympathy that, yes, he felt for this sad, cowed man who'd lost his son to disease and his wife to a murderer. "Didn't she?"

"I—" Bell nodded once. Then, as if it had suddenly grown too heavy to support, Bell's head dropped until, once again, his chin rested on his chest.

"Didn't she?"

"I—yes—I think she did. I—I'm afraid she did it."

"Where did she get the gun—the pistol she tried to ditch?"

"I—I have no idea." Bell's voice was hardly audible.

"Did you know she had a gun?"

"No." With great effort, he shook his head, repeating, "No." Then, after a moment, speaking in a low, bemused monotone, he said, "We haven't had guns in the house for a long time. I used to have a rifle—a twenty-two that my father gave me, kind of a keepsake. But when we had Timmy, Teresa insisted that—" Suddenly, as if his throat had convulsed, he broke off. Then, mumbling, he began shaking his head.

"But she knew how to shoot," Hastings pressed. "Handling an automatic takes practice. It's not like a revolver. You don't just pull the trigger. Even after an automatic is loaded—the clip in the handle—you've got to pull back the slide, jack a cartridge into the chamber. Then you've got to set the safety, and lower the hammer when you carry it. Otherwise, it could discharge accidentally. And you've got to take the safety off and cock the gun before you can fire. It's not simple. It takes instruction to fire a gun like the one that killed Hanchett."

During the time Hastings had been speaking, Bell had remained motionless, eyes fixed on the floor, the incarnation of despair. With an effort, Hastings dropped his voice to an authoritative, uncompromising note as he said, "Did you teach your wife to shoot, Mr. Bell?"

No response.

"Mr. Bell." Hastings moved forward in his chair, spoke sternly: "Answer the question."

Finally, Bell shook his head. "No." His voice was a whisper. "No. I've already told you, I never—" His voice died.

"Someone taught her. Who?"

Bell shook his head. Letting his exasperation show, his body still angled forward, a confrontation, Hastings drew a long, deep breath. "Why do you think she was killed, Mr. Bell? Who do you think killed her?"

"I—I don't know."

"Was it the same person who taught her to shoot a Llama semiautomatic pistol?"

"I—" Bell raised his eyes, haunted eyes, shadowed by a vision of endless pain. "I—I can't tell you, Lieutenant. There's—there's nothing I can tell you. Nothing more."

After a long, inscrutable moment, studying the other man, Hastings finally nodded, rose to his feet, and crossed the room. Walking carefully around the plastic sheeting, he opened the front door, stepped out on the tiny porch, and beckoned to Canelli, who pointed inquiringly to Dolores. When Hastings nodded, Canelli and Dolores left Canelli's cruiser and came up the front steps. With the three of them standing crowded together on the porch, Hastings was about to instruct Dolores when he sensed movement behind him. Turning, he saw Bell standing in the interior hallway, with the plastic sheeting between them. Hastings turned to Dolores, nodding covertly. She nodded in return—

Then she shook her head.

4:15 PM

"What's a house like that sell for, anyhow?" Dolores pointed to the three-story house with its carefully tended hedges and the Japanese maples growing in a small front garden. "A million dollars, maybe?"

"More," Canelli said. "San Francisco real estate—" In wonderment, he shook his head. "It's out of sight."

"Earthquakes, taxes, drugs—nothing keeps it down, they say."

"It's space," Canelli said. "There's no more space. San Francisco's like New York—Manhattan, anyhow. A friend of mine went to real-estate school, and that's what they told him. There's the harbor. That's how it started, with the harbor. But then San Francisco's so small—just a peninsula, like Manhattan's an island, you know. So that's why all the lots in San Francisco are so small. Ninety-five percent of them, the residential lots, anyhow, they're only twenty-five feet wide. So that's why property values keep going up." He spread his hands. "It's supply and demand. Everyone wants to be here, and there's no more land. So real estate goes up."

"You lived here all your life, it sounds like."

Canelli turned to face her. She kept her eyes forward, staring moodily through the cruiser's windshield at Fiona Hanchett's million-dollar town house with its view of San Francisco Bay. "Why do you say that?" he asked.

She shrugged. "You just talk like you were born here—just a feeling."

"Well, you're right. I was born out in the Sunset. In fact, Lieutenant Hastings and me, we grew up not so far from each other. Except that he's older."

"Lieutenant Hastings . . ." Thoughtfully she touched the tip of a small pink tongue to her upper lip. Still staring straight ahead, her eyes narrowed slightly, she said, "He's a—" She hesitated. "He's a formidable man, I think."

"Formidable?" Canelli smiled. "That's not the word I'd pick, I don't think."

She shrugged. "Everybody's different, sees things different. But Hastings—he's one of those big, quiet men. Get on the wrong side of him, you'd have a problem."

"Well . . ." Judiciously, Canelli nodded. "Well, that's certainly so, come to think about it."

"My mother lived with a man who reminded me of Hastings. God, he was tough, that one. Didn't say much—never, you know, threw his weight around. But get him mad . . ." Remembering, she shook her head. "Get him mad, watch out."

"Where'd you grow up?"

"Mexico City." Saying it, her voice dropped, her eyes hardened, her mouth tightened.

"How was it? Pretty tough?"

She glanced at him. It was a brief look, plainly touched with the half-concealed hostility the underclass reserves for its masters. "Yeah," she answered, once more staring straight ahead. "Yeah, pretty tough." Her voice was bitter.

"Your mother was—what—divorced?"

She laughed—a brief, harsh laugh. "My mother was never married. She had five kids. All by different men. She—"

Across the street, a latticed gate beside the house swung open to reveal Hastings and a younger, slimmer man: John

Hanchett, dressed in jeans and a loose-hanging shirt. His face was drawn and pale, his dark hair in disarray, his eyes haggard—or haunted.

Canelli waited until the two men came closer, then spoke to the woman beside him. "Well, what do you think?"

Frowning, she was studying John Hanchett as Hastings maneuvered him to stand immediately in front of the cruiser, his face profiled.

"I . . ." She hesitated. Then, annoyed, she shook her head, gestured impatiently. "This is hard, like this. I mean, sit him on a goddamn bar stool, put a stocking cap on him, dark glasses, lights down low . . ." She shrugged. "Who knows?"

"Yeah. Well . . ." Canelli caught Hastings's eye and moved his head to signify that Dolores had seen enough—and not enough. As Hastings nodded in response and turned away, Canelli said heavily, "Yeah, I know what you mean. If these guys were actually suspects—if they were in custody—we could put them in a lineup with caps and glasses all around, whatever. This way"—he shook his head—"it's a goddamn crap shoot."

"Jesus." She looked at him, an expression that might be equal parts of amusement and puzzlement. "Jesus, no wonder there're so many crooks running around, the way you guys operate."

4:45 PM

She filled the wineglass, eyed the bottle. Almost half gone. Already, almost half gone. Was this the first sign of weakness, the first suggestion of guilt, therefore, of vulnerability? Should she return the bottle to the cupboard—conceal the evidence?

Evidence?

Evidence of what?

Concealed from whom? Why?

Only a few days ago the calculations would have been meaningless, a muddled jumble of mere mumblings, scraps from the subconscious, fragments of coherence, shards of a life left over from the time before Monday night.

Monday night, and last night: two mute, mangled corpses.

No, not mangled.

Punctured, not mangled: tiny holes, surgical holes.

Would Brice have approved?

In those last moments, would Brice have appreciated the intricacy of her plan? Would he have approved its precision, admired its two-plus-two logic?

Nothing plus nothing equaled nothing. Logic.

She took the wine into the living room, placed the glass on the coffee table, sat on the sofa. Solemnly, she stared into the amber depths of the wine.

Was it possible to conjure up his thoughts as he felt life slipping away? Was it necessary that she try?

In the question, the answer was self-evident: yes, it was necessary that she try. It was essential that she try.

Two instruments—two imperfect instruments, he and Teresa Bell. One instrument flawed by insanity, one flawed by—

By what?

Did she know? Really know?

This question—this dilemma—must now be addressed. Urgently addressed.

First, she knew, the police looked for motive. Just as she, too, must now decide on his motive. His real motive, not his pretended motive.

His motive—and her motive.

How had it begun? Surely that was the essential starting point: that tiny seed, germinating so slowly, beginning to grow, first in her subconscious, inexorably spreading its tendrils until, finally, it penetrated her consciousness: the vision of Brice Hanchett, dead.

It could have begun with a look: no words, just one of Brice's looks, eloquent with a calm, calculated contempt.

One moment she'd been able to tolerate that contemptuous look from him; the next moment she hadn't. It was as if she'd stepped through an invisible wall. On one side, she'd accepted her humiliation, the ruin he'd left behind, herself contemptuous of herself.

On the other side, the far side of the invisible wall, she'd known that he must die. If she were to live—survive—then he must die. It was a simple equation, cause and effect. One of them would die.

And if she survived—accepted the risk, and prevailed—then she would prosper. Risk must be rewarded; he'd taught her that.

And so the thought had surfaced; the unthinkable had become real.

She'd never thought of it as murder. Execution, yes. Retribution, yes. Punishment, certainly. Sometimes she thought of a balance scale, the scales of justice, good on one side, evil on the other. Overload one side, and the beam tilts. Verdict rendered. Sentence pronounced.

So she'd begun to make her plans. Beginning with Teresa Bell, fatally flawed, that demented woman who'd known she must die.

Beginning with Teresa Bell—

And ending where?

7:15 PM

"But what's the big *deal?*" Across the dinner table, Billy's voice rose an aggrieved half-octave—and cracked into a twelve-year-old's falsetto. Exasperated by his younger brother's protestations, Dan elaborately raised his eyes, then concentrated on his plateful of fettuccine and white clam sauce.

At the head of the table, Ann calmly chewed her own fettuccine, swallowed, sipped her tea. Then she said, "The big deal, Billy, is there isn't a hundred dollars in the budget to buy you a pair of Air-Flex running shoes. Especially since the shoes you've got are perfectly—"

In the hallway, the telephone warbled.

"I'll get it." Hastings wiped his mouth, put down his napkin, gulped his tea, and left the dining room as, behind him, Billy's voice rose another half-octave, while Ann's voice, replying, dropped an ominous half-octave. If the call was for him, Hastings decided, even if it was an aluminum-siding salesman, he would prolong the conversation until the sounds of combat from the dining room subsided.

"You're probably right in the middle of dinner." It was Friedman's voice.

"It's okay." Untangling the cord as he went, Hastings carried the phone into the living room. He sat on the sofa, took the TV wand from the coffee table, and began running through the channels, volume off. "What's doing?"

"I just had a thought."

"A thought?"

"A theory on the Hanchett-Bell thing."

"Okay . . ." On the TV screen, wearing a trench coat and a slouch hat, Robert Mitchum was holding an automatic on a woman wearing a low-cut evening gown. The woman's breasts were superb. Mitchum looked incredibly young. The gun was a Colt .45 automatic.

"I think," Friedman said, "that Teresa Bell was set up as a hit person."

"Hmm . . ."

Behind Mitchum, a door was slowly, ominously opening.

"What's that mean? 'Hmm.' What's that?"

"It means I'm thinking."

"It's the only thing that makes sense. Let's say, for instance, that Carla Pfiefer's husband—what's his name?"

"Jason Pfiefer."

"Right. Jason. Let's say he's insanely jealous of his wife and Hanchett. He decides to kill Hanchett. But he's too smart to do the job himself. He's too smart, and he's got too much to lose. Let's say he knows about Teresa Bell—which he would, since he works at BMC. He figures he can put a bug in her ear, tip her over the edge, get her to kill Hanchett out of vengeance. He'll even give her the game plan. It figures, when you think about it. After all, who better than Pfiefer, the proud, insanely jealous husband, to know that Hanchett would be with his estranged wife at a particular time and place? He probably had PIs spying on them.

"But, of course, he's got to supply a gun—a gun that can't be traced to either him or Teresa. So he contacts Dolores. He gets one gun for Teresa—and one gun for himself, just in case. Maybe he figured he might have to kill Teresa before she talked to the police and incriminated him. Which, in fact, probably would've happened if Teresa hadn't been dead when we got there last night. You said so yourself. You figured she'd talk her head off, if her husband wasn't there to shut her up."

"It's a good theory. All we need now is proof."

"True. How's Dolores Chavez working out?"

"I doubt that she'll be much help."

"Has she seen Pfiefer?"

"No. She's seen Bell and John Hanchett."

"And?"

"Either she isn't willing to cooperate or she's getting confused. I can't decide which."

"What we need," Friedman said, "is sufficient grounds to bring one of these guys in for a lineup, put a blue stocking cap and dark glasses on him."

"And a mustache."

"Right."

"Speaking of a mustache," Hastings said, "Pfiefer wears a

beard. If he had the beard before Dolores sold the two guns, that eliminates Pfiefer."

"But if, on the other hand, he grew the beard after Dolores sold the gun," Friedman countered quickly, "then the ball is in his court."

"It's easy enough to check."

"Are you going to do anything on the case tonight?"

"I want to talk to Paula Gregg, Hanchett's stepdaughter."

"The one he's supposed to have molested when she was young?"

"The one who hates him, apparently. Still."

"I wonder whether she and John Hanchett could have cooked this up," Friedman mused.

"I wonder whether John and his mother—Fiona Hanchett—could've done it. They both hated Hanchett. And John'll undoubtedly profit, get an inheritance."

"What about Barbara Hanchett? Not only was she the wronged wife, the classic motive, but she'll certainly profit, too. Which reminds me, Hanchett's will has probably been submitted for probate by now. It'll be interesting to see who gets what from the estate."

"What about Barbara and Clayton Vance?" Hastings said. "According to Fiona Hanchett, they're lovers. So suppose they decided they'd get rid of Hanchett, get Barbara's slice of the inheritance, and live happily ever after."

"Another classic motive," Friedman answered, adding judiciously, "I like it. Lust and greed." Hastings could imagine him nodding elaborately. "Good. Very good."

"Barbara could've known about Teresa Bell. She could've planned it." Warming to his subject, Hastings spoke more rapidly now, more avidly. "Vance got the guns. Then one of them—Vance or Barbara—contacted Teresa Bell. They planned the whole thing, in detail. Vance gave Teresa the gun, told her how to use it, gave her the game plan. But when we started questioning Teresa, they spooked. They knew she'd talk. So one of them killed her, to keep her quiet."

"It's actually all the same theory," Friedman said. "Just different characters. My theory, don't forget."

"How could I forget?"

"So what now?"

"First, I'm going to finish dinner. Then I'm going to interrogate Paula Gregg. Then I'll find out how long Pfiefer's been wearing a beard."

"Good man."

9:15 PM

"Miss Gregg? Paula Gregg?"

She was tall and vivid, a lean, restless-moving blonde with bold eyes. Legs braced, one fist propped on an outthrust hip, the other hand on the doorknob. She wore a man's large, long-tailed white dress shirt—and probably nothing else.

Looking down at the gold shield, frowning, she said, "More police. I already talked to someone. An Italian. And I've got . . . company." She said it defiantly, challenging him.

"Do you have a bedroom?"

The frown deepened as she raised her eyes to meet his. She was a brown-eyed blonde, an unusual type, if the blond hair was real.

"Yes, I've got a bedroom. Why?"

"Tell him to stay in the bedroom and close the door. I'm not interested in your sex life. But I'm investigating the Hanchett murder—and, now, another murder. And I want to talk with you. It won't take long. But it's got to be done. Now. Right now."

"Don't you need a warrant before I have to let you in?"

He nodded. "You're right, I do. And I don't have a warrant. So if you don't let me in, that's it. You close the door and I walk away. But I don't think that's a game you want to get into, Miss Gregg."

"Oh? Why's that?"

"Because it all goes on your tab, that's why. You can cause me trouble tonight. But I can cause you a lot more trouble down the line. Believe me."

For a long, furious moment she defied him with smoldering eyes. But finally: "Fuck it." She whirled, strode down the short hallway and across a huge, dimly lit room to a half-open door. She said something to someone inside, said "Fuck it" again, slammed the door, and strode to a leather sling chair. As she threw herself into the chair, Hastings caught a glimpse of pale thighs and red panties beneath the white shirt.

The apartment occupied the top floor of a waterfront loft building that had originally been a loading shed built on one of the city's turn-of-the-century deep-water wharfs. But as real-estate speculators had dumped fill into San Francisco Bay and then built high-rise buildings on the fill, the bay had grown smaller. The wharves that had once served square-riggers now offered high-cost housing to trend-conscious San Franciscans.

"Interesting place." Hastings surveyed the outsize room. Its rough wood walls and lofty roof cross-bracing were white-washed; its ancient planked floor was oiled. Half of one wall was glass, and looked directly out on San Francisco Bay, with the jewel-lit hills of Berkeley and Oakland in the background and the slow-moving red running lights of an inbound freighter animating the vista in the foreground. The whitewashed walls featured more than a dozen huge blowups of Paula Gregg, some of them nudes.

"Jungle Passion," Canelli had said, marveling as he remembered interrogating Paula Gregg.

Her leather sling chair was one of three companion chairs placed close beside the large, free-standing, black iron fireplace that dominated the room. Without ceremony, Hastings hooked the frame of one of the chairs with his toe, turning it to face the woman.

"Since you're tight on time," Hastings said, glancing pointedly toward the closed bedroom door, "I'll come right to the point."

"Good."

"At eight o'clock last night—Wednesday night—where were you?"

She shrugged. It was a slow, languid gesture. The brown eyes were brooding now, more speculative than hostile. She was changing tactics: the female of the species, sizing up a new male.

"I was out. Somewhere." She shrugged. "Anywhere."

Watching her, listening to her, Hastings decided that she was probably on a recreational drug—cocaine, possibly. When he'd knocked on the door, she'd been up, manic. Now she was coming down. Slowly, sensuously coming down. Looking him over. Had she ever had a cop? Was she trying to remember?

"Who were you with last night?"

She shrugged again. Her back was arched, her neck curved. Her whole body came together, tight as a drawn bow, registering haughty disdain. If she'd ever had a cop, it had been a disappointment. "I was with different people. It was a party."

"You'll have to do better than that, Paula. A lot better."

"Oh? Why?"

"I've already told you. There're two murders. Brice Hanchett was shot and killed Monday night, on Green Street. Teresa Bell was shot and killed last night at her home in the Sunset. These murders were connected."

"And you think I killed them." It was a flat, hostile statement. Her eyes, too, had gone flat and hostile.

Yes, "Jungle Passion." A steamy thirty-second TV commercial: the wild, predatory female with hair like a lion's mane, a body that promised everything, and eyes that smoked, devouring the camera.

"I think you had a motive. And in my business, motive is what it's all about."

"What motive are you talking about?"

He'd been expecting the question; he was prepared. Even before she'd come on so strong, the aggressor, he'd decided on his reply. "I'm told that when you were young, living with Hanchett and your mother, Hanchett molested you." Holding her gaze, he spoke quietly, evenly.

The reaction began down deep: a tightening of her mouth, a shifting of her long, lean legs, an inward contraction of the torso, as if she were shrinking away from him. Finally the dusky brown eyes faltered, flinched, revealing a crevice of hidden pain.

"Who told you that?" Her voice was low and harsh; her eyes turned hot and hostile, masking the pain.

"It doesn't matter. What I—"

"It *does* matter, goddamn you." She sprang out of the chair, strode to the plate-glass window, turned to face him. The anger had returned, touching her magnificent body with sexual magic.

The body was her fortune—and the anger was her shield.

Twenty years old, Canelli had said. Marveling.

"It was my mother. Wasn't it? She told you."

"No," he answered, "it wasn't your mother. That much I'll tell you. That much, but no more."

"Fiona?" It was a hard, bitter demand. "That drunk?"

Watching her, he made no response. The long, hostile moment held.

"Shit." She shook her tawny mane sharply, then strode to the chair. This time the flash of her legs revealed more. He recognized the display for its true meaning: a statement of contempt, not enticement. Bred-in-the-bone contempt. Paula's way.

If she was on drugs, then she'd come back from the downer. Paula's high.

"You know John Hanchett?" Hastings asked. "Right?"

"Is *he* the one?"

"Listen, Paula—forget it. I'm not going to tell you who told me. Period. Have you got that?"

No reply. No quarter. Just the eyes, boring in.

"*Do* you know John Hanchett?"

As if she were making an effort to control herself, she drew a long, harsh breath. Then: "Everyone's entitled to a mistake. John was a mistake, put it that way."

"Are you lovers, you and John?"

"We're back to my sex life, are we?"

"We're back to murder." He decided to gamble, therefore to lie: "We've got information that John Hanchett might've brought the two guns that killed both Brice Hanchett and Teresa Bell. So if I were you, Paula, I'd stop and think. I'd think very carefully. Because if we connect John to the murder weapons, and if you're connected to John, then that connects both of you to murder." He watched her for a moment before he said, "Have you got that?"

She made no reply. But her eyes were losing focus. His words were sinking in. Slowly sinking in. Signifying a shift of emphasis that would allow the question of her connection with John to simmer.

Signifying that he should soften his manner as he said, "Last night"—he took out his notebook—"you say you were on the town. Which means that—"

"I *was* on the town. And I wasn't keeping track of—"

"Which means," he continued, "that you were with people. So if you'll just give me a few names, so I can—"

"So you can *what?*" She demanded.

"So I can verify that—"

"Forget it."

He looked up from the notebook. "I'm investigating a homicide, Paula. A capital crime. And you're giving me a hard time. That's called obstruction of justice. And that's a felony. Now—" He let a beat pass. "Now I'm going to ask the question again. And if you duck it again, then I'm going to haul your beautifully shaped ass downtown. I'll book you. Then I'll turn you over to a matron. She'll take you to a holding cell, where you'll spend the night. Maybe you can find a lawyer who'll get you released tomorrow morning, when a judge is available. I expect you probably can. But I can guarantee, Paula—I can absolutely guarantee you—that your ass is never going to feel quite the same to you again, after a night in a holding cell with maybe a dozen hookers and druggies." He let her think about it. Then: "A lot of those hookers, you know, swing either way. They swing with men for the money—and women for the kicks."

"You're bluffing."

"Try me."

For a long, decisive moment their eyes locked. She muttered a single heartfelt obscenity, then capitulated. The four names she gave him were all men.

After verifying the spellings, Hastings thanked her, returned his notebook to his pocket, and rose.

"I don't want you to leave town, Paula. Not unless you check with me." He stepped close, dropped his card in her lap, then walked to the door and let himself out. As he walked the half-block to his car, he committed firmly to memory the single essential question the interrogation had developed: Why hadn't Paula Gregg asked about the connection between Teresa Bell and Brice Hanchett?

Was the obvious answer the right one? Had she already known the connection?

11:30 PM

Carefully closing the bedroom door, Hastings put his holstered revolver and shield case and handcuffs in the top dresser drawer, put his billfold, keys, paper, and small change on "his" end of the big double dresser. He draped his robe over "his" chair, verified that the window was open about six inches at the top, the way Ann liked it, and closed the lower sash—the way he liked it. Then, noiselessly, he moved to his side of the bed, drew back the covers, and slipped into bed. Careful not to wake her, he settled himself, sighed, pushed at his pillow, sighed again. Now he turned on his left side, to face her. She was turned toward him. Her dark blond hair, shoulder-length, fell softly on the pillow, a halo of gold. Some of the hair fell across her face. Delicately he lifted the fine-spun strand, moved it away from her face.

Should he awaken her?

Would she like to talk?

When he'd left, she and Billy had still been at the dinner table, still arguing about the running shoes that "all the guys, every single one," were wearing. When Hastings had clipped on his gun and pocketed his shield case and checked his pager and announced that he had to go out for an hour or two, and kissed Ann on top of the head as she sat at the table, her look had been skeptical. Did he really have to leave? Couldn't he stay, and lend her moral support?

Last night it had been the ex-husband, Victor Haywood, and his constant threats of harassment. Compounded, last night, by Victor Haywood's beloved Porsche, with its broken door.

Last night, Ann's ex-husband.

Tonight it had been Billy, twelve years old, feeling his way. Tomorrow it could be Dan, sixteen. Billy was the extrovert, the activist, the squeaky wheel that got the grease. Dan was the quiet one. Billy inflicted pain on others; Dan, brooding, punished himself.

Yet they were good, sound, generous kids who loved their mother. Neither of them lied, neither of them cheated. And neither played Hastings off against Ann. Billy and Dan fought fair. In appreciation, he'd done what surrogate fathers were supposed to do: He'd taken them to ball games and put up a basketball hoop in the driveway. He'd also taken them to the police range and, despite Ann's misgivings, taught them to shoot.

Yawning, Hastings turned, lay on his back, let his eyes close.

Fighting fair . . .

Was that the essence of family life? If you fought fair, you might survive. Was that what marriage meant?

Had they ever fought, he and Carolyn? Screamed at each other? Laid hands on each other? No. In more than five years of marriage, they'd almost never shouted. They'd once cared enough to produce two children. But they'd never cared enough to fight. Carolyn was too cool to fight, too calculating, too busy playing the socialite about to have her picture taken. And he'd been too—too—

Was there a word for it?

What was the word for him?

He was in his forties, and he still hadn't discovered the word. There were images—snapshots in the album of his memories—but no single, definitive word. There was an image of his boyhood home: a cookie-cutter stucco row house, like the Bells' house. There was his father, the small-time real-estate broker, a big, talkative, vain man who always wore ties and drove big cars he couldn't afford. There was his mother, a thin, discouraged woman with wounded eyes who'd had to go to work at Sears, selling better dresses, after his father had left.

There were other images: The first day of tryouts for freshman football in high school. Later, there were the newspaper clippings when he'd made all-city, then all-state, in his senior year. But by that time his father was dead. So, with only his mother to read them, the clippings had lost much of their meaning.

Then there was the letter from Stanford, his scholarship acceptance: four full years, as long as he remained eligible for football.

It had all started, really, with the letter from Stanford. That night, lying in bed, the fantasies had begun. Most of the fantasies began with football—and ended with football. The Stanford frosh team, a first-stringer from the start. Second-string varsity in his sophomore year, first-string in his junior year. As college graduation came close, the scouts from the pros would begin to call. Finally the deal: a hundred-thousand-dollar bonus, a fortune, he'd thought, in his twenties. Of course, his mother would witness the contract. It would be signed in her living room, her proudest hour.

There'd been other fantasies: the girls in their tight jeans and twitching skirts, hair bobbing as they walked across the sunny Stanford campus, books cradled beneath their swelling breasts. Girls from places far from the Sunset District of San Francisco, girls whose fathers were wealthy enough to send them to Stanford. Girls who were meant to ride in convertibles and swim in private pools, girls who kissed in the shadows of fraternity-house parties, girls whose bodies promised ecstasy.

But there were two classes of students at Stanford: the rich students and the scholarship students.

So he'd watched them pair off, the girls and the boys who dressed with the same particular casual flair, who spent their vacations in the same large, comfortable homes, and who talked about the same movies and books and plays. While he played football on Saturday afternoons and practiced football every day during the week and memorized plays and collected his clippings and tried desperately to stay eligible for football, the girls with their golden smiles and the boys with their gift of privileged nonchalance had driven away in their convertibles, trailing laughter.

When the scouts had finally called, the offer had been twelve thousand, not a hundred thousand. Included in the same envelope with the contract had been a one-way ticket to Detroit and a form letter from the Lions' chief trainer. One paragraph contained two blanks, each with handwritten numbers. The first number had been his authorized weight when he reported to training camp. The second number had been the fine for arriving overweight.

Once a year, at the start of the season, Carolyn's father gave a party for the Lions. Charles Ralston manufactured automobile radiators. Many times a millionaire, Ralston's passion was the Lions. Ralston acquired players new to the Lions like some men collected stamps, or coins. The rookies were Ralston's only hobby.

At the first party of the season, it had been Ralston who introduced them:

"Frank, this is my daughter Carolyn. She likes tennis more than football. Maybe you can help me change her mind."

From the first, that very first moment, that very first hour—from their very first night together—Carolyn had set the pace. Blond, beautiful, willful, supremely self-confident, she'd acquired him as effortlessly as she'd acquired her first car, or her first lover.

At the wedding, Carolyn had hardly spoken to his mother. When Claudia was born, and his mother had offered to come to Detroit, Carolyn had laughed. When his mother had died, Carolyn had been three months pregnant with Darrell, and had decided not to attend the funeral.

At the start of his third season with the Lions, still a second-string back, he'd been clipped on a draw play. The Rams had received a fifteen-yard penalty; he'd been carried off the field on a stretcher. When he'd seen his leg, bent the wrong way at the knee, he'd known his playing days were over.

His father-in-law had given him a corner office and a secretary. The title was Public Relations V.P.; the job was entertaining important visitors. Which translated into drinking and partying and talking football and women and golf. Endlessly drinking. Endlessly partying.

Two years later, one cold, bleak afternoon in February, he'd gone to his office window and looked out over the Detroit River, frozen solid. His customary early-morning hangover had lingered, souring his stomach. As he stood in front of the window, his hands braced wide apart on the windowsill, he'd felt some essential essence began to drain away, leaving an emptiness at his center. In that moment he'd known that, somehow, he'd lost his way. It was a moment he knew he'd never forget—and he never had. Time had sharpened that moment, not softened it.

And so he'd finally faced it: yes, he had a drinking problem. And, yes, in the depths of Carolyn's cool gray eyes, he could see a change beginning.

A few months later, on a sunny Sunday morning while he was nursing a hangover and Carolyn was off playing country-club tennis in a foursome with the man she would later marry, her lawyer had served the divorce papers.

The next morning he'd found the lock changed on his office door.

The next week, on another sunny day, he'd left Detroit. There were four large suitcases and a large box: the sum total of a lifetime. As he helped his father-in-law's driver stow the box that contained his football trophies, he'd felt a lump rise in his throat. When he'd looked up and seen Claudia, so tiny, looking down at him from her bedroom window, her expression grave, he'd choked back a sob. When he'd waved to her, she'd turned away.

It was another moment that time had seared into his memory: the little girl in a fluffy white sweater, turning away from the window.

11:40 PM

How long had he been lying here, staring up at the ceiling? How long had he been listening to the sounds of the night, an airplane rumbling across the sky, traffic muttering on the street beneath his window?

Somewhere a siren was wailing.

Had Teresa Bell heard the sound of sirens as she'd walked down Hyde Street?

Over the banshee wail of her own demons, could she have heard the siren sounds?

Had he heard sirens when he'd driven down Judah Street away from Moraga, following the plan he'd so carefully prepared? Had his own banshees been wailing, blocking out the sound?

Judah . . . Judas . . .

No, there was no connection; the doggerel lines didn't scan. There was no treachery, no betrayal. There was only expediency, only necessity. Kill or be killed.

No fault, therefore no guilt.

But when would the images begin to fade? Teresa Bell, her eyes so wide and querulous, her mouth pursed so primly as she saw the gun—how soon would that picture fade? And the blossom of blood on the breast of the dowdy housedress she wore, itself printed with blossoms of flowers—when would that image fade?

The answer, he knew, was never.

The images, he knew, would surely sharpen as the minutes and the hours and the days and the years passed.

When had it started?

Suddenly it was important that he remember. As scientists searched for the Big Bang, the beginning of everything, he must fix in his mind the time and the place. He must isolate the first sentence, then the first word.

Or had it been only a look?

If love affairs could begin with only a look, then so could murder.

But they hadn't been looking at each other, when it had

happened. They'd been in a North Beach coffee house, both of them drinking espresso. She'd been sugaring her espresso, staring down into her cup as she stirred the coffee. She'd spoken very softly, with great precision:

"There's the money. Without him, there'd be the money."

Then, very deliberately, she'd placed the small espresso spoon in her saucer. She'd raised her eyes to meet his.

Just as deliberately, he'd met her gaze. In that moment of silence—and the moment that followed—they'd made the pact, taken the final step.

Then, as if the decision had left them drained, they hadn't spoken, had hardly looked at each other as they gravely finished their espresso and collected their things and left the coffee house. In silence, they'd walked to his car, which he'd parked illegally.

When he'd seen the ticket tucked under the windshield wiper, he'd experienced the first small stab of fear. The ticket placed him in this particular place, at this particular time——the time and the place where they'd agreed that, yes, they wanted Brice Hanchett dead.

Friday, September 14

9:15 AM

"It's occurring to me that maybe we're letting our imaginations run away with us in this Hanchett thing." As Friedman spoke, he began unwrapping a cigar, his first of the day.

Riffling through the paper in his In basket, the stack that never quite disappeared, Hastings decided not to comment. When Friedman had gotten the cigar lit to his satisfaction, and sailed the smoking match into Hastings's wastebasket, and blown a series of smoke rings on a quartering angle across Hastings's desk, he would elaborate.

"We talk about revenge and insanity," Friedman intoned, "and jealousy in high places, all that fancy stuff. But we haven't paid much attention to greed. And greed, after all, is behind most murders. Or, at least, most premeditated murders."

"Has the DA requested the probate court to supply a digest of the will?"

Friedman nodded, blew another series of smoke rings. "But, as of yesterday, the will hadn't been submitted for probate."

"Can't you get the name of his lawyer?"

"I've got it, and I called him. But he hasn't called back."

"When'd you call him?"

"The day after the murder. Tuesday."

"Well, this is only Friday."

"True. I'll call him later today." Friedman sighed, yawned, flicked his cigar ash into Hastings's wastebasket. Then: "What about you?"

"I'm going to see a man about his beard."

"Jason Pfiefer."

"Right. Jason Pfiefer."

10:40 AM

Hastings shifted in the chair, glanced at his watch, tried unsuccessfully to catch the nurse's eye as she stood at the reception desk studying a computer monitor. In the past fifteen minutes she'd seemed to tantalize him, sending her cool, practiced glance within inches of his own. It was, Hastings realized, an expertise that receptionists and maître d's and department-store clerks must either cultivate or else change jobs. But the realization did nothing to ease his impatience.

"Dr. Pfiefer says to tell you he's got five minutes at about ten-thirty," the nurse had said, elaborately loading the statement with weary condescension. Clearly, to her, Hastings was nothing more than a common nuisance. Only the gold badge had saved him from an instant brush-off.

Across the vast lobby of the Barrington Medical Center, a marvel of modern architecture, Canelli and Dolores Chavez sat in adjoining chairs. Plainly irritated, Dolores was flipping through the pages of a woman's magazine. From a distance of thirty-five feet, Hastings could hear the magazine pages crack as Dolores's quick-moving fingers snapped them open. Beside her, Canelli shrugged sheepishly as he met Hastings's gaze. Did Canelli realize that the bold, sexy, willful Chicano with the close-cut back hair and the flashing black eyes and the small, exciting body was systematically pussy-whipping him? To what purpose? Would she use her body to make a fool of a cop—any cop? Or was she drawn to Canelli? Did the big, amiable, cheerfully innocent detective have something she needed—or wanted—or thought she could use? For as long as squad-room memory went back, Canelli had been engaged to Gracie, the X-ray technician who was Canelli's mirror image. Gracie, too, was overweight and amiable and anxious to please. Both Canelli and Gracie, in their late twenties or early thirties, still lived at home. They—

Seeing Canelli's eyes sharpen and shift, Hastings turned, saw Jason Pfiefer striding purposefully toward him. Pfiefer wore green "scrubs," the enveloping green plastic gown that was the surgeon's operating-room uniform. As Hastings rose to his feet, Canelli touched Dolores's forearm.

"I don't have much time, Lieutenant." Pfiefer made it sound like a warning.

As he took a deliberate moment to look the man over, Hastings realized that Pfiefer and John Hanchett and Clayton Vance—and, yes, Fred Bell—all fitted one catch-all description: about five foot ten or eleven, about a hundred seventy pounds, with a full head of hair. Put the four men in a lineup, dress them in dark watch caps and fake mustaches, dye Vance's hair darker, and a witness could flip a coin.

"Well?" Pfiefer demanded. "What's the problem this time?"

"There's no problem, Doctor." Aware of the satisfaction it gave him, Hastings allowed himself a small, false smile of bogus reassurance. Then, quietly: "It's just that there's been another murder, Wednesday night. We think it's connected to the Hanchett murder."

"And so?"

"And so we're wondering whether you could help us?"

"Help you? How?" The dark, remorseless eyes bored in.

Somehow, Hastings realized, he'd been put on the defensive. It was one of Pfiefer's talents—one of his many talents.

"Well," Hastings said, "you could start by telling me where you were the night before last—Wednesday night—at about eight o'clock."

"I can't tell you, Lieutenant. At least not with any precision."

"Were you here? Working?"

"No." Pfiefer raised his wrist, frowned as he worked at the elastic that secured the surgical gown's cuff, finally succeeded in exposing his wristwatch. "No," he repeated. "I wasn't here. Now you'll have to excuse me." He turned abruptly and walked to the reception desk, where he talked briefly with the nurse on duty. As they talked, the nurse stole a significant look at Hastings. Then, obviously having received a curt order, she nodded.

Hastings rose, caught Canelli's eye, then turned and walked to the bank of doors that opened onto the street. They would talk outside.

10:57 AM

"With that beard," Dolores complained, "what can I tell you?"

"You can imagine how he'd look without it," Hastings said.

She shrugged. "I tried that. I came up with a blank. You want the truth, that's the truth. Listen"—she tapped her wristwatch—"I've got to go. It's an appointment, at eleven-thirty. I've got to—"

Annoyed, Hastings interrupted, "I told you we've got to do this. There's still one more guy. He sells Jaguars. The showroom's ten minutes from here. We can—"

"But I *can't.*" Her voice was plaintive, thinned by something that could be anxiety. As if to confirm it, her eyes widened.

Was it anxiety or a different, subtler con? She was resourceful, Hastings had decided. And smart.

Determined, she began again: "I've got to—"

Implacable now, remorseless, Hastings cut in again: "I told you to make arrangements at the bar where you work. I warned you."

"It's not the bar." As she spoke, she dropped her eyes, shook her head. Watching her, Hastings realized that today Dolores was wearing high heels, a skirt, a white blouse, and a light jumper that complemented the skirt. Her jewelry was understated. She was telling the truth, then; it wasn't the bar. In these clothes, she would never tend bar.

Now her manner was subdued as she repeated, "It's not the bar." As she spoke, she met Hastings's gaze squarely. She wanted something from him—something different, something she didn't know how to ask for.

Or was it a new game? Dolores, experimenting with the oldest con of all: sex.

Jeans and a leather jacket and tough talk had worked on Canelli. Did she think a skirt and heels would tempt Hastings?

"I'm sorry, Dolores. But this is homicide we're talking about. I'm not going to—"

Suddenly she flared: "It's my kid, goddamn you. He—they've got him in juvie, the fuckers." Back arched, fists clenched, eyes bright with a sudden rage she couldn't control, she faced him like an angered animal: the elemental mother, ready to do battle.

Then, just as suddenly, she began to sob. Stricken, Canelli looked to Hastings for guidance. Taken aback, Hastings blinked, shrugged, helplessly spread his hands. Canelli turned to the woman, moved a single step closer. Her body rigid, arms locked straight down at her sides, fists still tightly clenched, she stood with her chin defiantly raised, tears streaking her face. Mascara was beginning to dissolve beneath her eyes. Tentatively, Canelli touched her shoulder.

"Hey, Dolores, come on . . ." Awkwardly, Canelli patted her upper arm. "Hey—what'd you mean, 'juvie'?"

"I mean that his prick of a father deals drugs, that's what I mean. And the—goddamn sonofabitching fucker, he used my kid to carry, that's what I mean." She turned to confront Canelli, the swell of her breasts inches from Canelli's chest. "What'd you *think* I mean? I mean he's in jail, you—you—" Now she shook her head sharply, dug angry fists into both eyes. The mascara was badly smeared. Hastings realized she would be furious at them for seeing the mess the makeup had made of her face. Especially, she would be furious with Canelli. It was Canelli's fate. During the confrontation, a dozen passersby had skirted them, most with their eyes studiously averted. A few, however, frowned at Canelli—and a few more muttered disapprovingly.

"Well—jeez . . . " Canelli spread his hands. "Jeez, juvie's not exactly jail, Dolores. I mean, kids go to juvie for all kinds of—"

"There're perverts in there." As she spoke, her voice choked with anger, she rose on her toes, forced Canelli to step back. "One night in that hole, and a kid is ruined. *Ruined.* For life. They're—"

"Is his father in custody?" Asking the question, Hastings carefully pitched his voice to a neutral, disinterested tone.

She turned away from Canelli to face Hastings. But Canelli had taken a hankerchief from his pocket. Hesitantly he touched her arm again. "Listen, Dolores, your, uh, your makeup, it's—it's kind of smeared. Why don't you—?"

She snatched the handkerchief, wiped at her face, stared balefully at the stained handkerchief. She refolded the handkerchief, vigorously blew her nose. Then she turned toward a nearby trash receptacle, cocking her arm to throw. Surprised and aggrieved, Canelli raised a hand in protest. But, unaware of the gesture, she hesitated, set her jaw, angrily thrust the bedraggled handkerchief into a side pocket of her purse.

"*Is* he in custody?" Hastings asked.

"No. his pusher, he was busted. And Oscar, too."

"Oscar?" Puzzled, Canelli frowned. "Who's Oscar?"

"He's my kid," she flared. "My *kid.* Who'd you think?"

"Ah." Placating her with his sheepish smile, Canelli nodded. "Oscar." He shrugged. "Nice name."

"What's the *matter* with Oscar? What're you, some kind of an authority or something?"

"What's the pusher's name?" Hastings asked. "The one that got busted. What's his name?"

"His name's Santos. Raúl Santos." Once more, she rounded on Canelli. "I suppose you don't like that, either," she said bitterly. "Raúl. I suppose you think *that's* funny too."

"What's your kid's last name?" Hastings asked.

"It's Chavez," she said defiantly. "Just like mine."

"How old is he?"

"He's nine." As she said it her voice fell, her body began to slacken. Sadness was smothering her rush of anger. "Only nine. Jesus . . ." She took out Canelli's handkerchief, found a fresh spot, blew her nose again. As she replaced the handkerchief she looked defiantly at Canelli—who smiled uncertainly.

"What're the particulars?" Hastings asked.

"Particulars?"

"How'd the arrest come down? What actually happened?"

"It happened about seven-thirty this morning."

"Seven-thirty in the *morning?*" Canelli was incredulous.

Her first response was instinctive anger. But, as if she'd lost the will to make the effort, she let her head drop as she nodded, saying, "The son of a bitch, he was parked on the street, waiting for Oscar. He was walking to school. Oscar, I mean. And Freddy was parked a couple of blocks from the school. He told Oscar to—"

"Freddy's Oscar's father," Hastings interrupted.

"Yeah." Deeply resigned, she nodded. "Yeah—his father. The prick."

"What's his full name?"

"Alfredo Fernandez."

"Okay. Go ahead."

"Well, Freddy gave Oscar a paper sack. Like it was his lunch, you know—with an apple and a sandwich and everything. And he told Oscar that a guy in a black Corvette—Raúl Santos—would be parked a block away. And when Oscar gave Santos the sack—just tossed it through the window, onto the seat—then he'd get a dollar. But they were following Santos, I guess. The narcs. Because about eight-thirty, something like that, my doorbell rings, and it's two narcs. And they tell me Oscar's on his way to juvie."

"Why didn't you mention this to us before?" Hastings asked.

For the first time she answered him fully, without anger or calculation—only exhaustion, and visibly deepening despair. "I didn't see any point. How would it help to tell you? I figured . . ." Dispiritedly, she let it go unfinished. Hastings allowed a long, speculative moment to pass as he stared at her. Was her story true? Was she faking her hatred of Alfredo Fernandez, protecting herself? Could she be the dealer, using Oscar to carry for her? How far gone was Dolores? How far had she overstepped the line? Did she love her child more than she hated Alfredo Fernandez?

Hastings pointed to his cruiser, parked across the street in a red zone. "Wait for us in the car, Dolores."

"But"—she looked at her watch—"but I got to—"

"It'll just take a minute." His eyes expressionless, Hastings moved his head toward the car. As she walked grudgingly away, Hastings studied the determined set of her head and shoulders—and the provocative movement of her buttocks and thighs, doubtless enhanced by the high heels she wore. From Canelli, Hastings heard a soft, wistful sigh.

"Beautiful sight," Hastings observed.

"Yeah . . ." Followed by another sigh.

"So what d'you think?"

"About her story, you mean?"

Hastings nodded.

"It seems pretty straight to me."

"Does she love her kid, do you think?"

"Oh, yeah." Canelli nodded decisively. "No question, she loves that kid. She lives with two other women. They're all mothers—unwed mothers. They live in the Mission—nice house, nice block, I was surprised. And they got their day figured so they all take turns baby-sitting. They seem to have everything covered."

"But she also does a little fencing? Maybe a lot of fencing."

"She swears she only did it a couple of times. She says Charlie Ross conned her."

"What would you expect her to say?"

"Yeah . . ." Eyeing the woman, who now sat in the cruiser, Canelli nodded ruefully.

"Would you say she's being cooperative with these identifications? All she seems to say is that she can't be sure."

"I just don't know, Lieutenant. It's one of those heads-or-tails things, if you know what I mean."

"You've never seen her kid—talked to him?"

"No. But I've seen the house, like I say. And it's nice. Very clean, very cheerful." As he spoke, Canelli still stared at the woman. Now, incredulously, he shook his head. "Oscar, Jeez, what a name. I can't get over it."

"So you believe her story about Fernandez and the drugs."

"Yeah, I guess I do."

Hastings considered, then finally said, "Tell her that if she'll tell us where to find Alfredo Fernandez, and if Narco's interested in him, getting him set up, then tell her you'll get Oscar out of juvie, if she'll turn Fernandez. You handle it with Narco. Then, if she cooperates, you go with her to juvie."

Canelli shrugged, then nodded—then smiled. "Fine. Good. What about you? What're you going to do?"

"I'm going to find out when Pfiefer grew that beard."

"Ah." Canelli said it approvingly. "Gotcha."

"Then I'm going to talk to Clayton Vance. So when you

spring Oscar and get him home, you tell Dolores she's got a date with me. Clear?"

"That's clear. Jesus . . ." Marveling, Canelli shook his head. "Oscar."

11:25 AM

Shrugging, Susan Parrish spread her hands. "I'd say it's about a month since he started to grow the beard. Maybe two months. No more."

"Listen, Susan, I know you're busy, and I hate to ask you, but could you get a little closer than that? It's important."

Across her desk, looking wholesome and starched in her white uniform, Susan's gaze quickened. "What's it all about, Frank?" Even though the thick, solid wooden door of her office was closed, she dropped her voice a conspiratorial half-note as she asked, "Do you think Pfiefer killed Hanchett and the Bell woman? Is that it?"

"Jesus, Susan, come on. Do you expect me to answer a question like that? Cops can get sued for libel too, you know."

"No," she answered. Then quizzically: "Really?"

"Sure."

"Hmmm . . ." Thoughtfully, she leaned back in her chair, let her eyes wander. "That's interesting. That's very interesting. The public, you know—we think cops are above the law."

"It depends on the situation, if you want the truth. Mostly we're chasing guys without much clout—and not many brains, either. We've got it pretty much our own way, chasing guys like that. But people like Pfiefer—the upper crust—that's different. They hire lawyers."

"So what about parking tickets, free apples from fruit stands, dinner on the house, things like that?"

"No comment."

"I'll feel silly, asking around about Jason Pfiefer's beard."

"For a lunch? An expensive lunch?"
"Hmmm . . ."

12:40 PM

In the 1930s, the building at 795 Van Ness had been a bank, with four fluted Grecian columns in front and pink marble in the foyer. By the fifties, Van Ness Avenue had turned most of its banks and many of its storefronts into auto showrooms, hi-fi shops, and steak houses. In the early fifties, Hastings remembered, before the Japanese learned how to make automobiles, the Jaguar showroom at 795 Van Ness, with its lofty ceilings and Grecian decor, had been a mecca for the affluent and the low-budget snobs who mimicked them. A profusion of potted palms had adorned the marble parquet floors, and all the salesmen spoke with British accents and wore blazers and, invariably, button-down oxford shirts.

Now, struggling, Jaguar shared half of the cavernous showroom with Alfa-Romeo, Fiat, and Ferrari. The other half was a used-car salesroom.

Wearing a navy blue blazer, a pale blue button-down shirt, and a regimental striped tie that complemented his guardsman's mustache, Clayton Vance was seated at a small desk in a plate-glass cubicle. As their eyes met through the glass partition, Hastings saw Vance's male-model face go momentarily rigid. Then, looking impassively away, Vance lifted a telephone from its cradle on the otherwise uncluttered desktop. He touched the buttons, waited, spoke briefly into the phone. Then he put the phone in its cradle and rose to his feet. Without meeting Hastings's glance, Vance buttoned the blazer, touched the knot of his tie, squared his shoulders, then raised one hand in a small gesture directed to an older, paunchier man who occupied a large office at the rear of the showroom. Responding to the gesture, the paunchy man nodded briefly, then turned his attention to a stack of papers on his desk. Vance walked down the short corridor between the salesmen's cubicles and went directly to Hastings.

"Something in a Jaguar, Lieutenant? Maybe a Ferrari?" Beneath the mustache, Vance's lips were twitching urbanely at the corners.

Of the four men whose lives touched Hanchett's, only Vance had a mustache. Dress Vance in dark glasses, a stocking cap, and a nondescript jacket, put him in a lineup, and what would Dolores Chavez say?

Deciding not to answer the smile, Hastings spoke brusquely: "I hate to bother you at work, Mr. Vance, but there're a couple of questions."

Still smiling, gesturing smoothly, Vance turned and led the way to the showroom's front door. "I was just going out for a snack. Join me?"

"I'll have some coffee, maybe."

"Fine."

12:55 PM

"Only coffee?" Vance asked. "You're sure?"

Hastings nodded. "I'm sure."

Vance ordered two coffees and one quiche, bestowed an automatic smile on the young black waitress who wore an African tribal necklace and carried herself like a Bantu princess, head held high, hips swinging rhythmically. As Hastings followed the waitress with his eyes, Vance said, "She's a folksinger. Very good. If she gets the right agent, a friend of mine says, she could be somebody."

"I can believe it."

Once more appreciatively watching the waitress move, Hastings waited for her to serve their coffee. Then, deciding on a low-key opening, he said, "What I'm doing is investigating the murder of Teresa Bell, night before last."

Vance's handsome eyebrows drew together in a studied frown. "Teresa Bell?" He shook his head, sipped his coffee. "Sorry. It doesn't register."

"She lived out in the Sunset." A pause. Then: "We think it's possible that she killed Brice Hanchett. So we think her murder might be connected to the Hanchett homicide."

"Wait a minute." As if he were puzzled and signaling that he needed time to think through the riddle Hastings had just presented, Vance raised a graceful hand. "Wait—am I missing something here?"

"I don't understand."

"Why are you telling me all this?"

Now it was Hastings who pretended puzzlement. "I laid it out for you. Hanchett was having an affair with Carla Pfiefer. Which, according to the percentages, makes Jason Pfiefer an automatic suspect. Also according to the percentages, Barbara Hanchett is a suspect—the wronged, jealous wife. And since you're involved with Barbara . . ." Meaningfully, Hastings let it go unfinished.

Vance nodded impatiently, "I understand all that. And if you'll recall, I was playing racquetball the night Hanchett was killed."

Hastings nodded. "Right."

"So what's all this got to—" Vance broke off, considered, began again: "What's this about—" He broke off again. Then, vexed: "What's her name again?"

"Teresa Bell."

Vance nodded. "Right. What's her murder got to do with me? I—Christ—I never even heard the name Bell before this minute."

"We're trying to cover all the bases, Mr. Vance—all the possibilities, the combinations. So we're checking out everyone connected with Hanchett."

"Checking out? What's that mean?"

"It means," Hastings said, "that I'd like to know where you were the night before last. Wednesday night. Between, say, seven o'clock and ten o'clock."

"What happened then?"

Hastings waited for the waitress to serve Vance's quiche before he said, "Teresa Bell was murdered about eight o'clock on Wednesday night." His voice was patient, but his eyes were hardening.

Vance carefully cut off the triangular end of his quiche, raised it to his mouth, and began chewing methodically as he studied Hastings. When he finally spoke, Vance's voice thinned as if he were aggrieved, pleading his case: "So are you saying—are you telling me—that I'm a suspect, that you think I killed this woman? Is that what you're saying?"

"If I thought you'd killed her, Mr. Vance, I'd have to charge you, and give you your rights. You've seen the movies. You know how it goes."

"Then why're you asking all these questions, if I'm not a suspect?" The quiche forgotten, Vance laid his fork aside. His eyes were beginning to move restlessly, uneasily. His hands, too, were in uneasy motion, fingers indecisively clenching and unclenching. Apart from the eyes, Friedman had always said, the hands were the most revealing.

Hastings sighed, pitched his voice to an ironic note. "It's called the process of elimination. We start with a motive. Then comes opportunity. Then we need evidence. Of those three, opportunity is the easiest to establish. Teresa Bell was murdered about eight o'clock on Wednesday night. That we know. So if you were playing racquetball, say, between seven and nine, then I can be on my way." As if to establish the point, Hastings drained his coffee cup, pushed it away.

"The problem is, I wasn't playing racquetball. Right now, right this minute, I can't remember where I was Wednesday at eight o'clock."

Hastings made no reply. As he studied the other man, he saw the telltale signs of tension surfacing: the thinning of the nostrils, the constriction of the throat, the uncertainty around the mouth, the narrowing of the eyes. Now Vance's right hand moved toward his coffee cup—and then hesitated. Was he afraid Hastings would see his hand tremble as he raised the cup to his mouth?

With the game in the balance now, perhaps tilting in his favor, Hastings decided to lean back in his chair, fold his arms—and wait impassively. Watch, and wait.

"You talk about—" As if his throat had suddenly closed, Vance broke off, quickly licked his lips, and began again: "You talk about motive. Why the hell would I murder someone I don't even know?"

As if he agreed, Hastings nodded. "That's what we're trying to figure out." He spoke amiably, one-on-one, a standard interrogating maneuver calculated to lull the suspect into the belief that they were sharing a confidence.

A suspect? Vance?

Once an officer suspects a given subject of a crime, the law reads, then that officer must advise the subject—now a suspect—of his constitutional rights.

But not yet. Not quite yet.

Instead, in the same amiable voice, tactically, Hastings said, "We've got physical evidence that suggests the two murders were connected. But so far we—" As a second thought suddenly surfaced, a companion to the first, Hastings let it go unfinished. As if afraid that Vance might see too much in his eyes, Hastings frowned, shifted in his chair, looked away. How would Friedman react to this new idea—to these new ideas? Would Friedman listen, nod, then claim that—

"—at home, Wednesday night at eight o'clock," Vance was saying. "I was home, on my exercise bike, watching TV."

"Ah." As if he were relieved, Hastings nodded. "TV. Yes. Thank you."

1:30 PM

Friedman leaned back in Hastings's visitor's chair, laced his fingers over the mound of his stomach, allowed his heavily lidded brown eyes to half-close, and nodded judiciously. "I like it. Maybe it's a little fancy. But I've got to admit it accounts for everything, ties up a lot of loose ends, gives us motives for both the murders. You realize, of course, that it's essentially a refinement of the idea I got last night, when I called you."

"I realize that."

"And, of course, work yet remains."

"I realize that, too."

"So how do you want to handle it?"

"What's Dolores say? Anything there?"

Dubiously, Hastings shook his head. "That's a dark horse. Either she's conning us, or—" His phone warbled, an outside line.

"Frank, this is Susan Parrish."

"Hi, Susan."

"About that expensive lunch . . ."

He smiled. "About that beard . . ."

"It's what I said originally." As he listened, Hastings could imagine Susan Parrish sitting at her half-cluttered desk, a wholesome, comfortable, conscientious person, the same person he'd known in high school, all those years ago, give or take thirty pounds and a few gray hairs.

"It was just about two months ago," she was saying, "that he started to grow it."

"Was he clean-shaven before that? Or did he have a mustache?"

A pause. Then: "That wasn't part of the original deal."

"I know."

"He was clean-shaven." Another pause. "I think."

"Think?"

"I can check that easily enough. But I'm almost sure he was clean-shaven. Let's say that's the answer. Otherwise, I'll call you back. Right away."

"Fine. Thanks, Susan. I'll get back to you about that lunch. Maybe the three of us can do it—you and me and Arnie."

"Great. Gotta go."

Hastings broke the connection and relayed the information to Friedman, who nodded complacently, as if he'd already known what Susan Parrish would say.

"Mustaches and beards and sexy Chicano gun fences . . ." Marveling, Friedman shook his head. "This case has it all."

"Don't forget the rich and famous society surgeon and the beautiful stepdaughter who's a high-fashion model and the neurotic, disaffected son and assorted wives and lovers."

"So if we go on this new theory of yours," Friedman said, "it comes back to the guns. Specifically, the Colt forty-five."

Without comment, Hastings nodded. Friedman, he knew, was about to develop a game plan.

"Which is to say," Friedman said, "that, according to your theory, a man who maybe wore a false mustache decided he wanted Brice Hanchett dead. He found out how to get a couple of guns, which is a significant point, it seems to me. I mean, not everyone knows how to buy an illegal gun. Or, more accurately, not everyone has the stones, since the transaction is usually concluded in some dark alley, somewhere. But, anyhow, he gets the two guns from the glamorous Dolores. That was about—what—three months ago?"

Hastings nodded. "I think that's right. Maybe four months."

"Of course," Friedman continued, "it's significant, it seems to me, that he bought two guns, wouldn't you say?"

Hastings decided not to respond.

"And it could be significant that they were collector's guns."

Hastings considered. "Significant how?"

"He probably paid a premium for guns like that. Meaning

that either he had money to burn, or else he was a novice in the hot-gun market."

"Or else he wanted to get in and get out. He wasn't about to shop around."

Friedman nodded. "An amateur."

"An amateur. Like all our suspects."

Friedman nodded thoughtfully. "How long ago did the Bell child die?"

"About six months ago, I think."

"So we're assuming that sometime between six months ago and, say, three weeks ago, give or take, our suspect made contact with Teresa Bell, and began indoctrinating her—infecting her—with the idea that she should kill Hanchett because he was responsible for the death of her son. Right?"

Hastings nodded. "Right."

"That's a long time to keep something like a blueprint for murder secret, it seems to me."

Hastings made no response.

"In order to make the plan work," Friedman went on, "the murderer had to know three things. First, he had to know about the Bell child's death. Then he had to know the circumstances surrounding the child's death. And, finally, he had to know that Hanchett and Carla Pfiefer were lovers."

"Right."

"How long've they been lovers, do you suppose?"

"I don't know. I can check, though, probably."

Friedman waved a negligent hand. "That part doesn't matter. The rest of the time frame—when the guns were bought, and when Pfiefer grew his beard—they're important. But how long Hanchett and Carla Pfiefer were screwing each other, that's immaterial. The point is, our murderer knew Hanchett would be leaving Carla's place on Green Street, Monday night."

"The way I figure it," Hastings offered, "our boy gave Teresa

Bell the whole plan—showed her where Carla lived, told her how to shoot the Llama, told her what route to take leaving the scene, told her to ditch the Llama—all those things. Everything. He programmed her. Then, when everything was set, all he had to do was activate the plan—give her a call and tell her that Hanchett was at Carla's place and would probably be leaving at ten or eleven, something like that. And that's what happened Monday night."

"And then," Friedman said, picking up the narrative, "on Wednesday night our boy knocks on Teresa Bell's door. She opens the door, invites him in—and gets shot with the forty-five our boy got from Dolores."

Hastings nodded.

"Do you happen to have a theory as to why our boy killed Teresa Bell?"

"He wanted to shut her up. What else could it be?"

"Except that if he was willing to murder her—to expose himself to the risk of being caught—why didn't he just kill Hanchett himself, in the first place?"

"Obviously because he was hoping we wouldn't figure that Teresa killed Hanchett. It was a calculated risk. But then, when he realized Teresa was a suspect and was being questioned, and would probably talk, he knew he had to kill her to cover his trail."

"And he used the forty-five to do the job."

"Right."

"Are we assuming that this guy had enough foresight to buy a second gun, just in case he had to silence Teresa Bell?" Friedman asked.

Hastings gestured impatiently. "Come on, Pete—next you'll be asking me what he likes for dessert."

Having anticipated the complaint, Friedman shifted his ground: "So who doesn't have an alibi for Wednesday night, and knew Hanchett and Carla were lovers and also knew Teresa Bell was bonkers?"

"Pfiefer," Hastings answered promptly. "He's the most obvious. Then there's Clayton Vance."

"Who has a mustache," Friedman observed. "But no visible motive."

"Except that Barbara Hanchett has two first-class motives: jealousy and money. And she and Vance are lovers. With Hanchett dead, Barbara and Vance could live happily ever after."

"That's assuming Barbara wasn't cut out of Hanchett's will."

"Even if she *is* cut out," Hastings said, "a wife can always fight it. And win, usually. So can natural children. That's the kind of case any lawyer in town will take on contingency."

"Hmmm . . ." Tapping a forefinger on his stomach as he lolled belly-up in his chair, Friedman considered, his heavily lidded eyes veiled, his face impassive. Finally: "Circumstantially, it's got to be Jason Pfiefer. From what you say, he sounds like an arrogant bastard, just the type who couldn't handle being cuckolded. Plus he could still be crazy about his wife, which could send him right over the edge. And obviously he knew about Teresa Bell, and would've known how to get in touch with her, known how to prey on her obsession, and . . ." Friedman's voice trailed off into silence; his eyes lost their focus. His voice was soft and reflective as he said, "God, that poor woman. She loses her son, loses her sanity, loses her life. And, Jesus, her husband—he's the one who's got to go on living."

"Except," Hastings said, "that her grudge against Hanchett was groundless. There was only one liver available, and there were several candidates. It was a pure medical decision. Hanchett didn't deserve to die for that. He was just doing his job—and doing it well, apparently. For other reasons, sure, he might've deserved what he got. But not for the death of the Bell child. Teresa Bell was just bonkers, that's all. Thousands of mothers lose their children. But they don't commit murder because of it."

"All that probably doesn't help Fred Bell sleep."

"Well," Hastings answered wryly, "he's only got himself to blame. He never should've married the girl."

Friedman snorted, blinked, roused himself to say, "We've talked about Pfiefer, and we've talked about Vance and Barbara Hanchett. But what about John Hanchett, the screwed-up son? And what about his neurotic, alcoholic mother? Both of them hated Hanchett. And John stands to inherit. Couldn't his mother have put John up to it?"

Hastings nodded. "Absolutely."

"Then there's Paula Gregg, the beautiful stepdaughter who everyone says Hanchett molested, and who's apparently running wild, and who could've been screwing John. Why couldn't Paula and John have planned to kill Hanchett? It sounds like Paula would've known where to buy illegal guns. Then she got John into bed, maybe got him doing a little cocaine, whatever, got him all psyched up. She could've done it just for the thrills, it seems to me. Just for the kicks—the satisfaction of having Hanchett killed, the satisfaction of manipulating John. Or maybe she just used John to buy the guns. Given her personality, I think it's a real possibility. Maybe she actually pulled the trigger on Teresa Bell."

"You're right about her personality. She's . . ." He searched for the word. "She's awesome. Beautiful, but awesome. She's capable of anything, I think. Anything at all."

Intrigued, Friedman spoke softly, speculatively: "Interesting cast of suspects."

"Hmmm."

"I still think Pfiefer's the only one who makes sense," Friedman mused. "Especially if we factor in your theory about the murderer using Teresa Bell. It's hard for me to believe that Paula, for instance, knew about Teresa Bell's child."

"Except that we don't have any evidence against Pfiefer. None."

"The guns," Friedman said. "They're our only hope. If our boy has the forty-five, and we tie him to it, then we'd have him, especially if his fingerprints show up on the Llama's shell casings. Incidentally, the lab finally got around to lifting Teresa's prints at the morgue. And her prints don't show on either the Llama or the Llama's cartridges. Signifying that she probably wore gloves when she fired the gun."

"Thanks for telling me." Hastings's voice was heavily ironic.

"It just came down."

"Hmmm."

"Cheer up. It corroborates your theory that some mastermind was pulling Teresa's strings. Ergo, your mastermind loaded the gun, gave it to Teresa, and told her to shoot Hanchett."

"What about prints on the forty-five shell casing found at the scene of Teresa's murder?"

Regretfully, Friedman shrugged. "No prints. In fact, no shell casing."

"No shell casing? How come?"

Friedman shrugged. "The murderer must've taken the casing with him. Or her, as the case may be."

"Shit."

"Exactly."

"And the prints on both the fired and the unfired Llama cartridges match, you say," Hastings mused.

Friedman nodded. "So if your theory proves out—if Pfiefer, or whoever, programmed Teresa, gave her the game plan, showed her how to use a gun, gave her the loaded gun—then there's a good chance that his prints'll match the prints on the Llama's cartridges." Plainly pleased at the prospect, Friedman nodded again.

"Except that if you're talking about Pfiefer, I have a lot of trouble believing that he's going to let us take his prints. A *lot* of trouble."

"There's always a way . . ." As he said it, Friedman's gaze wandered speculatively to Hastings's window, with its view of the East Bay hills in the background and a sliver of the Bay in the foreground. Hastings knew that look, knew that particular mannerism.

"I know what you're thinking."

"Alan Bernhardt," Friedman intoned. "It so happens he owes me back-to-back favors."

Alan Bernhardt, Friedman's favorite PI, the actor who also wrote plays and directed little theater. To support his habit, as he wryly called his addiction to the theater, Bernhardt hired out as a free-lance investigator.

"What we'll do," Friedman said, "is put tails on Pfiefer and Vance—and maybe John Hanchett, too. When they're out of the house—safely out of the house, under surveillance—Bernhardt can get inside, hopefully, and lift some fingerprints, or maybe swipe a glass, whatever. If we get a match with the Llama's cartridges, we'll go for a search warrant."

"You're kidding."

"Kidding?"

"What if the judge asks us how we got the prints? Christ, Bernhardt could be jailed for breaking and entering."

"We get a broad-minded judge."

"Bullshit."

"Okay." Airily, Friedman waved. "We'll go to plan B." His expression turned crafty. "As I understand it, even as we speak, Canelli and Dolores are down at juvie, where her kid is being held. Right?"

Warily, Hastings nodded. "Right."

"Well, then, our game plan is obvious. We contact Canelli. He gets it across to Dolores that, in exchange for springing her kid, she's got to make at least a tentative identification of whoever we say."

"Are you serious?"

"Actually, I'm not serious," Friedman answered blandly. "Not totally. But, what the hell, it's worth a shot. She gives us enough to get a search warrant. We pick up a glass, or whatever, and we're in business. Maybe we'll even find a Colt forty-five, who knows?"

"What if Dolores refuses to go along?"

"Then we let Canelli play the white knight who virtuously defies his superiors to save Dolores's child—who, obviously, we plan to get released no matter what. But Dolores, of course, won't know that. So maybe she'll be so grateful that Canelli'll get himself laid."

Hastings shook his head incredulously. "You're really something, you know that?"

Modestly, Friedman cast his eyes downward. "I try."

"Of the two, I'd rather go with Bernhardt. Forget about Dolores. Christ, we'd *really* be in trouble if she told the judge we conned her. Think about it."

"Fine. We go with Bernhardt. I'll set it up. Meanwhile, though, let's tell Canelli to put some pressure on Dolores. What can it hurt? He tells her he'll spring her kid and we'll drop the receiving-stolen-goods charge. All she has to do is go along. If she does, then we've got two ways to go. We've got Bernhardt *and* Dolores. That's called insurance."

"Hmmm."

2:15 PM

"Wait a minute," Dolores demanded. "Let me get this straight." She stood truculently before Canelli, hands propped on her hips, dark eyes snapping furiously. Giving way a half step,

Canelli was conscious of her breasts, so close to his chest. They stood in the large reception room of the youth guidance center. The windows were screened with heavy steel mesh, the linoleum floor was cracked, the chairs and tables and walls were covered with graffiti. Most of the bedraggled chrome-and-orange-plastic chairs were occupied by grieving adults, almost all of them minorities. For a terrified child and his despairing parents, Canelli knew, this was the anteroom of hell, the first way station on a long, sad journey to nowhere.

"Wait a minute," she said again, each word sharply bitten, "are you telling me this is a setup—a deal? A ransom, for God's sake, my kid for your murder case, is that what you're telling me?"

"Aw, jeez, Dolores, that's not it. You're—jeez—you're exaggerating. All I'm saying is—"

"You want me to lie. You want me to—"

"Not lie. It's just—just—" Lowering his voice, he glanced at the couple closest to them: two blacks, both of them gray-haired, both of them crying, tears streaking their worn, seamed faces as they touched each other awkwardly, seeking comfort. "It's just that the lieutenant needs a little room to maneuver, that's all. See, he wants to—"

"Yeah, he gets room to maneuver, and I get the shaft, same old story. I've got a choice: fall for fencing, or fall for perjury. And I'll tell you right now, Canelli, I'll take the fencing fall. My record's clean. There's no way I'll do time for fencing. Probation, sure. But there's no way—"

"Dolores. Wait. You're—jeez, you got it all wrong. All you gotta do is go along, do like you're told, just this once. Your kid gets sprung, and we drop the fencing thing. So you'll be clean, nothing on your record. All you gotta do is have a little, you know, a little flexibility. A little faith. All you gotta do is—"

"*Faith?* Christ, faith in what? In who? You? The cops? You're all—all *crooks*. You—" Suddenly her knees buckled, and she sank into a nearby chair. She opened her purse, began furiously looking for a handkerchief.

"Aw, jeez . . ." Canelli drew another chair close to her, produced a handkerchief, handed it over. As she snatched it out of his hand and began blowing her nose, he ventured a smile. "That's two that you owe me. Handkerchiefs, I mean."

The handkerchief muffled her monosyllabic response. Tentatively he touched her knee. She moved sharply away, blew her nose with a note of finality, dropped the handkerchief in her purse, and turned to face him.

"I trusted you," she said. "I—" As if it were painful to say, she winced, shook her head, finally confessed: "I liked you. And now you—you're doing a number on me. You're—"

"Dolores. Please. Jeez, I—"

"What you're doing—really doing—is holding him hostage."

"Holding—?"

"Oscar. He's your—your goddamn captive, that's what he is."

"Wait." Firmly, he raised his hand. "*Wait*. Back up, here. *I* didn't fence those two guns. *You* did that, Dolores. Don't forget that. And I didn't give Oscar a sack of dope to deliver. Your ex-husband, or whoever he is—he did that, not me. So don't start doing a number on me, Dolores. Don't try to run over me, because it won't work. I—I'm glad you like me. I like you, too. You probably know that. Girls know those things, I finally figured that one out. But let's keep the record straight here. Nobody ever said cops don't cut corners. But—"

"Half the people I know, the cops've got them by the throats. They want something hot, maybe girls, dope, TVs, whatever it is, the cops always get a deal. They don't pay full fare for anything. They snap their fingers, and—" She sniffled, blinked, pressed the handkerchief to her nose.

"Listen—" Uneasily, Canelli pointed. "Your, uh, mascara, or whatever it is, it's—"

"*Ah!*" Furiously she turned her back on him, dug into her purse for a mirror and compact. "You always get me crying. I don't cry, except when you make me. You know that?"

"No fooling?" Speculatively, Canelli frowned. Then, puzzled: "Really?"

"Oh—fuck off, will you?" With her back still turned, she squared her shoulders, lifted her chin, crossed her legs. "Just fuck off."

"Ah, jeez . . ." He put his hand on her shoulder. "Don't be like that, Dolores."

She drew away from his touch.

"Listen," he said, "don't sweat it, okay? Just cool it, hold on to that goddamn temper. And I'll—" He rose, touched her shoulder again. "I'll give the lieutenant a call, set him straight."

"Oh, yeah?"

"Yeah."

2:30 PM

He stared at the telephone as if it were an icon. It sat on its own stand beside the window. It was as if the table were a pedestal, and the window a celestial backdrop: shape and shadow and substance, one fateful composition.

He'd once read that the telephone was the ultimate twentieth-century power symbol. In medieval times it had been the lance and the sword. Whoever commanded the most swords wielded the most power.

Now it was the telephone: life or death at the sound of the dial tone. The red phone sat on the President's desk. Lift the receiver, say a few words, and millions would die, vaporized.

Lift this phone—his phone—and two had died. Hanchett,

sated with sex, blinded by his own ego, had died in the gutter. Teresa Bell, haunted by her demons, had gotten his call, opened her door, smiled her madwoman's smile—and died.

He got to his feet, walked a dozen steps to the far side of the room, turned, fixed his gaze on the telephone.

Two calls made . . .

One call remaining.

Before the police came again, there was one call yet to make.

But not here. Not yet. Not from this phone.

Even though it was a local call, it would doubtless be logged. Somewhere, on some phone company tape, the record would exist.

And yet, if they went back over the phone company records, the police would discover that, until Hanchett had died, they'd talked almost daily. So now it would be suspicious that they didn't call each other, didn't talk almost every day.

He realized that he was still standing staring at the phone, his back braced against the wall.

Back against the wall . . .

Was his back against the wall?

A prisoner, awaiting death by firing squad, that was the meaning of the phrase. All pleas exhausted, all hope gone, the prisoner stood with his back to the wall, blindfolded.

As he stared at the phone, his eyes lost focus; the image of the phone blurred.

To call, or not to call . . .

Hamlet's lament. Laurence Olivier with bleached blond hair, weighing his options, life or death.

Just as now—here—he was weighing his own options, calculating his chances, life or death.

No, not death. In California, only the indigent went to the gas chamber. Thank you, Governor Jerry Brown. Thank you, Justice Rose Bird.

Moving slowly, conscious that an effort of the will was required, he pushed himself away from the wall, returned to the chair beside the telephone, lowered himself into the chair.

Before he called her, he must first bring it all into focus. Sometimes it was essential that the chronology be complete.

He could vividly remember the words that had first touched fire to the fuse: "There's the money," she'd said, sugaring her espresso. That had been the beginning.

But where would it end?

In death?

Yes, surely in death.

After the first words spoken in the coffee shop, those words that seemed so innocuous now, it was then necessary that they speak of death. They'd been in bed. In the afterglow, he'd been lying on his back, fingers laced behind his head, staring up at the ceiling. She'd been lying on her side, turned away from him, aloof. Yet, making love, she'd been fierce, demanding everything, taking everything for herself.

Was that what had him hooked—that fierce, rapacious, headlong sexual greed? Or was it her utter ruthlessness, contemptuously undisguised?

Earlier in the evening, dressed in jeans and sweaters and running shoes, the uniform of the yuppie, they'd had pizza and gone to a movie on Union Street. Eating the pizza and drinking red wine, she'd been moody, preoccupied. After the movie, driving to her place, they'd hardly spoken. He'd debated the wisdom of questioning her. Would she flare up? The answer was inherent in the question: yes, she would flare up.

But perversely, he'd decided to test her. Speaking quietly, self-consciously casual, he'd said that he'd decided to go to Cancún for the skin diving. He'd be gone for a week or ten days. Could she come down for a weekend, at least?

Still turned away from him, she hadn't responded for a long, distancing moment. Then, her voice low and impersonal, she'd said, "What good would that do?"

He'd said that he didn't understand. What good did anything do?

Her response had been a low, vicious grunt, hardly a ladylike response.

Ladylike?

It was the last word he'd ever think of to describe her. Beautiful, yes. Irresistible, certainly. Fascinating, always.

But ladylike, never.

"That isn't in the rules," she'd finally said. "Going away isn't in the rules."

Then she should change the rules, he'd said. Immediately adding, "*We* should change the rules."

"How?" she'd retorted bitterly. "Kill him?"

One word—two words—and reality shifted. The past and the present and the future had tilted, fused, then separated, finally re-formed. All in seconds. Milliseconds, really.

If he'd chosen not to reply, it would have ended there. In the silence between them, the seconds would have elapsed: longer, more fateful seconds. Followed by minutes. Then hours. Finally days. Eventually—sooner, not later—she would have found someone to take his place. The same scenario would begin: the seduction, the exploration.

Kill him . . .

The words had lingered in the darkness, a palpable third presence. He'd never been able to remember the response he'd made. It could have been mere mumbling, inarticulate assent—wishful thinking.

But it had been enough.

Once the words were spoken, once the sounds of approval had been uttered, illusion changed shape and substance. Wishful thinking became commitment.

From the first, those first few seconds and minutes, the

pattern remained unchanged. Always she took the initiative. Driven by a hatred that had consumed her and a greed that never let her go, she began to make plans. Once more, a pattern emerged. Always, it began with the "what if" game, shades of earliest memory: children, fantasizing. The word *murder* was never spoken. Instead, it came as a "what if" question, at first so deliciously tantalizing: what if they could "arrange for him to die"?

Expertly, she'd begun by sketching in the images: the sunny beaches, villas in Spain or southern France. Exotic nights of love, love in the afternoon. Freedom. Complete, utter freedom. And, yes, money. Kill the king, snatch the key to the counting house.

And, yes, justice.

For what Hanchett had done, death was the due.

And all without risk.

Find Teresa Bell. Tip the fragile balance. Make the madwoman their executioner. The perfect plan, flawlessly executed.

Die, Brice Hanchett. Pay. Finally, pay.

And then the lieutenant had called.

Was it the title of a play—a movie? *The Inspector Calls.* Yes, certainly, the title of a movie.

From the first, he'd known that Hastings suspected them. Just as, from the first, he'd suspected that Teresa Bell might confess. It had always been a calculated risk, that she would confess: the madwoman in search of absolution.

Die, Teresa Bell, the lost soul, the madwoman wandering wild-eyed through the empty, echoing corridors of her mind.

Leaving the two of them, now. Once more, the two of them, planning, scheming. But now the visions of villas and sun-soaked beaches had faded, along with the imagined nights of magical love. So suddenly, gone.

Fear had done that: obliterated the fantasies, leaving only reality.

Followed, he knew, by the first nibbling of terror. Already he could feel it beginning, deep down in the center of himself.

With an effort, he extended his left arm, lifted the telephone, used his right hand to touch-tone her number.

"Hello?" She'd answered on the second ring.

"Hi."

"Ah—" He could hear her catch her breath. She'd been expecting him to call.

"Let's get together tonight."

"Yes—I guess we should."

"Nine o'clock?"

"Yes . . ." It was an uncharacteristically wan, indecisive monosyllable. She was feeling it too, then. The first nibbling of terror, like a rat chewing the border of a shroud.

"Okay—nine o'clock, then. I'll—"

"Are you all right?" Her voice was hushed.

"No, I don't think I'm all right. Not really all right."

"Are you—?" She broke off, cleared her throat. "Do you want to—to get out? Is that it?"

"We have to talk. See you at nine." He broke the connection, heard the dial tone begin.

2:40 PM

She replaced the telephone in its cradle, rose, went to the kitchen, selected a stem glass from the rack over the counter, took last night's half-finished bottle of Chardonnay from the refrigerator, and filled the glass. Appreciatively, she sipped the wine, just a little too cold.

Nine o'clock . . .

More than six hours . . .

Why had he said nine o'clock?

Like all conspirators, they'd fixed a secret meeting place: the yacht harbor, the slip that led to one row of berths. The slip was perhaps two hundred feet from the yacht club's main parking lot. He'd selected the place, a good choice, not too isolated, not too public. This would be their fourth meeting here. Twice, dressed in windbreakers and jeans and deck shoes, as if they were going sailing, they'd met during the day. Once—the first time—they'd met at night, a cold, foggy night. They'd planned that first meeting down to the minutest detail. It had been a Friday night, which meant there would be a crowd at the yacht club. So they'd dressed as if they were going to dinner, ostensibly part of the crowd.

Two days after they'd met at the yacht club that foggy Friday night, he'd given Teresa Bell the gun.

And the following Monday night, Brice Hanchett had died.

That's how she thought of it: died. Not murdered. Died.

She took the glass of Chardonnay from the table, raised the glass, sipped. Yes, the flavor was rising as the wine warmed.

How often in the past five days had she tried to recall the precise moment she first realized he must die? Sometimes it seemed that the decision had come in a dream. She'd been an executioner in the dream—a hangman's apprentice, the one charged with tying the black hood over the victim's head to spare the onlookers the sight of his dead face, contorted by death's final agony. But then she'd been instructed to kiss him good-bye before she pulled the hood down over his face. And then, violently protesting, she'd awakened, horrified. Because somehow he was already dead, before the hangman's trap had been sprung. His skin was cold and clammy, his eyes empty, his purple lips slack, his mouth idiotically gaping.

She'd gone back to sleep after the nightmare had released her. But the next morning, awakening, the horror had returned. The vision of his dead face, so cold and clammy to the touch, had persisted.

And then the phrase "hire a hangman" had begun to stir deep in her amorphous, awakening consciousness. If she could hire a hangman—an executioner, a killer—she would be rid of him. Finally rid of him. Finally free.

In the moments that followed, still lying in bed, still with her eyes closed, as if she were a child, afraid the vision would vanish if she opened her eyes, she lay motionless as, yes, the possibility congealed into certainty: an incredibly matter-of-fact necessity, a simple puzzle that required a solution no more complex than finding a mechanic or a gardener or someone to plan a party.

Yes, hire a hangman . . .

For days—weeks—she'd nurtured the vision, let it germinate, allowed the desire to solidify into the plan.

And then, deliberately, she'd waited patiently for her chance.

She'd only had to wait until the following Friday night, when they'd gone to the movie, then gone for pizza, then gone to her place. He'd told her he was going to Cancún. It was, she knew, a test, one of his little games, to test her. Instantly, she'd seen her chance.

She'd realized instinctively that it would first be necessary to pronounce the words. A few days before, over espresso, they'd signaled with a look, only a look, that murder might be the answer. But, the next step, words must be spoken. And, almost immediately, the opportunity had come. When he'd said that she should do something about Brice, anything, to ease her burden, she'd said, "How? Kill him?"

And, like the self-blinded fool he was, he'd swallowed the bait whole. So that the next time they saw each other, she had only to wait for him to create his own opening. She'd expected him to begin by repeating his wish that she come to Cancún with him. But, instead, he'd simply said he'd been thinking about what she'd said the other night—thinking about Brice Hanchett, dead.

The rest of it had followed the same script, line for line. There was a woman named Teresa Bell, whose son had died for want of a liver transplant, she'd told him. If he were to approach Teresa Bell, befriend her, sympathize with her, then Teresa Bell would do their work for them. Teresa Bell would be their instrument of vengeance—and, yes, of gain. Enormous gain, his hangman's bounty.

Magically, the scenario had once more played out according to the script. As if she were a robot, a marionette, Teresa Bell had taken the pistol and gone to the address on Green Street.

But then the waiting had begun, the agony of uncertainty. When would they know? Would the policeman's knock on the door be their first word?

Only later—only during their second meeting at the yacht harbor—had she learned that, incredibly, he'd been unable to stand the uncertainty. Late Monday night, he'd gotten in his car and gone to Russian Hill. He'd played the part of a spectator, gawking at the blood that still stained the pavement. It was a mad, senseless risk—a risk induced by fear.

But at least he'd known. His agony of waiting was over. Hers had only begun.

But finally the police had come. She'd prepared herself, so that it was only necessary to continue reading from the script.

But she couldn't prepare him. She couldn't know that already he was weakening.

Minutes after Hastings questioned him, he'd called her. They had to meet. It was on Tuesday, the day after the murder. Her first close look at his face confirmed her fears. Under questioning, he might tell the police everything. If his actual words didn't betray him, his actions would.

Betray himself . . .

Betray her.

Then he'd told her that the police had already questioned

Teresa Bell. How did he know? she'd asked. Because, he'd answered, he'd seen Hastings leaving Teresa Bell's house. His voice had been ragged, his eyes furtive with fear, his face pale and waxen. His telltale hands were in constant motion, twitching, plucking, fretting.

First he'd gone to Green Street.

Then he'd gone to the Bell house, come close enough to see Hastings—and be seen in turn.

Then he'd told her he had another gun. With that gun, he'd said, he would kill Teresa Bell, to protect them. There was no other way.

She'd planned the killing of one monster—and created a second monster. The first monster was crazed by greed and arrogance and ruthlessness. The second monster was crazed by fear.

The first monster, Brice Hanchett, had threatened to take her sanity. The second monster threatened her freedom, even her life.

After the second murder he'd called again. He'd told her they were safe, now they were safe. But they must meet again, he'd said. More than ever, he needed her. She'd refused. Yesterday, she'd refused.

Today, she knew she must accept. Even though it was dangerous to accept, it was more dangerous to refuse.

Nine o'clock, he'd said.

Less than six hours, now.

A lifetime less.

4:30 PM

Frowning, Canelli patted his pockets again. Finally he shook his head. "Sorry, no pen."

Without comment, the woman behind the counter took a pen

from a drawer beneath the counter and placed it on the clipboard. As Canelli signed, the attendant said, "Don't forget your badge number."

"Oh. Right." He printed the number, added "Homicide," and returned the clipboard and pen. The attendant nodded, yawned, and pressed a buzzer beneath the counter. Stepping back, Canelli moved to the door, looked through the small, wire-reinforced glass pane. In the waiting room, Dolores was pacing. In her establishment dress and high heels, hair carefully done, makeup meticulous, she was drawing the appreciative stares of a dozen males, some of them in handcuffs. But if she was aware of the attention, she gave no sign.

Behind him, another buzzer sounded; another door opened. Turning, Canelli saw him: a slim Chicano boy wearing jeans, sneakers, and a Giants T-shirt. He carried a small backpack by its shoulder straps. Fixed on Canelli, his eyes were large and dark and very still.

"Oscar?"

Standing just inside the inner door that led back to the detention section, the boy stood motionless, still staring.

"Come on, Oscar." Canelli opened the outer door, gesturing toward the visitor's section. "Your mother's here."

The boy remained motionless, his face revealing nothing.

"Come on." Canelli opened the door wider. "Your mother's waiting. She'll take you home."

Warily, keeping as far from Canelli as possible, the boy moved forward, began edging through the door. Now he held the backpack with both hands, waist-high, as if for protection. Like his mother, the boy was instinctively ready for trouble. Had he been mistreated while he was in custody? Slapped around? Even sodomized? It could have happened, Canelli knew. Even in the daylight hours, one of the older inmates, a teenager already gone bad, could have—

"Oscar." Suddenly Dolores was there, her arms wide, scooping the boy up, hugging him so hard that his feet left the floor. For a moment, still holding the backpack, the boy remained rigid in her arms. Then he dropped the pack, threw his arms around his mother's neck, and began to cry.

4:50 PM

"So—" Friedman tilted back in his swivel chair, propped his feet on the bottom drawer of his desk, and eyed Alan Bernhardt, seated in one of Friedman's two visitors' chairs. Bernhardt was a tall, lean man in his early forties. "Lived-in" was the phrase Friedman had privately ascribed to Bernhardt's appearance: thick, unruly salt-and-pepper hair that always needed trimming, slacks that needed pressing, loafers that needed shining. Plainly, the well-worn Harris tweed jacket was Bernhardt's very own, along with the open-collared button-down oxford-cloth shirt that Friedman suspected might have come from Brooks Brothers. Bernhardt's face matched his lived-in persona: a thoughtful, reflective, distinctly Semitic face. The nose was a little too long, the mouth a little too small, the cheeks a little too hollow. But the soft brown eyes were both watchful and knowing, and the deeply etched pattern of the face's lines and creases unified the whole. It was, Friedman had always thought, a rabbi's face. For better or worse.

"So how's it going, Alan? How long's it been since you cut loose from that snake Dancer?"

"A little more than a year." Bernhardt's voice matched his face: measured, modulated.

"You're doing all right free-lance," Friedman said. Then: "Aren't you?"

Bernhardt considered. "Yeah, I suppose I am. Everyone wants more business, I guess. But in my case . . ." He let it go unfinished.

"Meaning that, really, you'd rather write plays than surveillance reports."

"Except that if the plays don't get produced, then I've got to keep writing the reports."

"And you and that classy lady you saved from Hollywood, you're still an item?"

Bernhardt smiled. "You're an incorrigible busybody, you know that, Pete?"

"So I've been told." Friedman spoke complacently, then pointedly let a silence settle. He was expecting an answer.

Bernhardt's smile widened as he said, "Okay, the answer is yes, we're still an item."

"Good." With an air of finality, Friedman nodded. Having satisfied his curiosity, he was ready to proceed. "You'll recall that the last time we talked, you said you owed me a big one for that fingerprint search a month or so ago on the State of California's six-million-dollar Japanese fingerprint computer. Right?"

"Definitely."

"So how're you fixed for time, the next day or two?"

"I've got time." As he spoke, Bernhardt took out his notebook and pen. "What can I do for you?"

"What I need," Friedman said, "is a little illegal entry, maybe a little fingerprint lifting. Are you any good at fingerprints?"

Bernhardt shrugged. "I've done it. But I can't say I'm very proficient. What's the rundown?"

"There're three, maybe four guys I need fingerprints on. Do you know about the Hanchett murder case?"

"Sure. I read the papers."

"And the murder of Teresa Bell, two nights ago?"

Bernhardt frowned. "Teresa Bell?"

Friedman sighed. "Teresa Bell was neither rich nor famous, so she didn't make the front page. But she's dead. We think she killed Hanchett. Then we think she was killed to shut her up. If we're right, we may have the fingerprints of her murderer on some cartridges. But all we've got are suspicions, not nearly enough to get search warrants."

"So?"

"So I need you to get fingerprints from a list of suspects, like I said. We'll do a little on-the-spot fingerprint work. You get inside the guy's house, find something like a drinking glass, maybe unscrew a doorknob, whatever it takes. You bring the item out to our van, where we've got a fingerprint technician. He takes a couple of minutes to lift some prints. Then you return the glass, and we go on to the next suspect."

Bernhardt frowned. "But, Christ, what if—?"

"Wait." Friedman raised a peremptory hand. "I know what you're going to say, and I've got it covered. It'll be a team effort. I'll be the team captain." He smiled puckishly at the other man. "Does that reassure you?"

"Hmmm."

"You'll have a half-dozen guys backing you up. There'll be a guy tailing the suspect, naturally, so he won't walk in on you. Then one guy in front of the suspect's house, and another guy in back. Plus me and the fingerprint guy. A goddamn task force, in other words. How're you on locks?"

Bernhardt shrugged. "Sometimes I win, sometimes I lose. You know how it is with locks. If the technology is ahead of you, then you lose."

"Well, I'll get a locksmith. A private party. So all you have to do is go inside. You'll have a walkie-talkie, of course. And I'll be coordinating from the van. If the subject returns home, I'll give you fair warning. You'll have to bring your own car, though. We don't want anyone to connect us, naturally."

"What about the walkie-talkies? If they're police-issue, they'll connect us."

"I'll get a couple from the property room. Drug dealers are very big on walkie-talkies."

Bernhardt nodded, then shrugged, one gesture canceling the

other. "Sounds like it should work. But I don't understand what you'll gain by all this. Talk about illegally gathered evidence. The DA'll never touch it."

Always impatient whenever a pet project was questioned, Friedman dismissed the point with a wave of the hand. "You get the goods, I'll handle the details. And, meanwhile, you'll be back in the black, so far as our private tally is concerned. Okay?"

"Yes. Fine. When do we start?"

"How about now? This evening? I've got four subjects in mind, like I said. I'll put a stakeout on each one of them. The first one who leaves the house, gives us a shot, we'll go for it. Same thing applies to his place of business. I figure that, with luck and good communications, we'll have what we want in twenty-four hours. Okay?"

"Okay."

6:20 PM

Standing side by side in the archway of the small living room, they watched the boy as he sat absorbed before a small TV set. On the screen, cartoon characters chattered and shrieked. No matter what the characters did, the boy's face remained unchanged as he methodically ate a chili dog they'd picked up at Taco Bell. The archway was narrow. Canelli was conscious of Dolores standing close beside him, their thighs sometimes brushing. After she'd gotten Oscar settled, she'd gone into the bedroom and changed into jeans and a silky blouse that clung to her torso. Her feet were bare. Beneath the silken swell of her breasts, her arms were crossed.

"Television . . ." Resigned, she sighed. "What're you going to do?"

"He looks like he'll be okay, though," Canelli offered.

"Yeah, he'll be okay."

They remained silent for a moment, still companionably

close. On the TV screen, during a raucous commercial, a clown was pitching a computer war game; the sound effects might have come from a Vietnam film clip.

"Well," Canelli said finally, "I guess I better get back to the Hall." Unwilling to move away from her, he spoke softly, regretfully. On the TV screen, the pyrotechnics continued. He decided to take a tentative half-step backward, into the hallway. Moving with him, she led the way to the front door. Then, turning toward him, her back to the door, she stood motionless. As if she were determined to measure up to some distasteful task, she lowered her chin, bowed her neck, set her shoulders.

"Listen, Canelli, I, uh—" She frowned, broke off, began again, this time speaking in a rush: "I, uh, just wanted to thank you." Still she stood motionless, obviously struggling. Then, slowly, with grave determination, she raised her eyes to meet his. "I wanted to thank you a lot. I mean . . ." She shook her head sharply, as if to dispel some painful vision. "I mean, it would've been terrible, if Oscar had stayed in that hole." Deep in her dark eyes Canelli saw a softness. As if to deny it, her frown deepened. But, still, the softness remained.

"Ah, jeez, Dolores . . ." Canelli's head bobbed. "Jeez, it's okay. I'm just glad it worked out, is all. You know, sometimes you get tangled up in that bureaucracy, all that crap, it doesn't always work out. But this time it did. So . . ." In acknowledgment of their good fortune, he waved a hand. Then, because they were standing so close, he touched her shoulder, let his hand linger. "So I'm glad."

With his hand still on her shoulder, she suddenly smiled. Plainly, the smile surprised her. "You're a funny guy, you know that? Especially for a cop, you're a funny guy." As if they'd just been introduced, she studied him for a moment. Then, boldly: "Have you got a girl?"

"I, uh . . ." He squinted, frowned, shifted his feet, took back his hand. Visibly uncomfortable, he cleared his throat. "I, uh, yeah, I do, as a matter of fact. Gracie. We're . . . engaged, I guess you'd say."

"Ah . . ." Self-protectively, she nodded. Now she said something in Spanish, three short, wistful words. Then her eyes changed. Her voice was crisp as she said, "Listen, looking these guys over, there's one more to go. Right?" It was a businesslike question, asked with precision.

"Yeah. Right. At least I think that's what the lieutenant is saying. But—"

"Is this last guy the one you suspect most, or what?"

He snorted. "Who knows? You gotta talk to the lieutenant for that."

"But you want the guy eyeballed. Right?"

"Right. But I thought you—"

Impatiently, she shook her head. "I never said I wouldn't do the job. I just said I didn't want to lie. I mean, I've got problems enough without that."

"Well . . ." He grinned. "Well, let's do it, then." He checked the time. "Let's give it a shot, see what happens."

"Can I be back in time to put Oscar in bed? Eight-thirty?"

"No problem."

"Okay, I'll tell Oscar and make sure Maria can watch him. But it's gotta be eight-thirty, Canelli."

"Guaranteed."

In the narrow hallway, before she could pass, he was compelled to flatten himself against the wall. As he did, she came close, rose up on tiptoes, and kissed him full on the mouth. Once more, she said something in Spanish. Only a few wistful words.

6:25 PM

Hastings pressed the blinking plastic button and lifted the telephone to his ear.

"Hastings."

"This is Susan Parrish, Frank."

"Susan." He smiled. "You're my most faithful informant, you know that?"

"Is that good?"

"It proves you're on the side of the angels. What can I do for you?"

"Well, I feel kind of silly, telling you this. I mean, it's just gossip, that's all it is. But when you told me you wanted to know about Dr. Pfiefer's beard, the easiest thing to do was talk to his nurse. It was hard because I couldn't tell her why I was asking—except that, really, I think she figured it out. It's all over the hospital that Dr. Hanchett was murdered as he was leaving Carla Pfiefer's place. And then, of course, you've been here, questioning Dr. Pfiefer. And that's stirred up a lot of gossip, naturally. But anyhow—" In the background, a telephone warbled. "Oh, damn. Hold on a second, Frank." She clicked him on hold. A half-minute passed. Then, a little breathlessly: "Sorry, Frank. I think I need a vacation."

"I think you've earned one."

She laughed ruefully. "I just had one." They shared a short, companionable silence before she said, "Well, anyhow, the bottom line is that, just about an hour ago, I saw Dr. Pfiefer's nurse—Maggie Christian—in the cafeteria, on her break. She was pumping me about whether or not you thought Dr. Pfiefer was a suspect in the Hanchett murder. I said that if he was a suspect, he was one of several. Was that the right thing to say?"

"Perfect. You catch on quick. Always have, come to think about it."

"Thanks." Plainly pressed for time, she spoke briskly, anxious to finish her story. "Anyhow, according to Maggie—who, until now, I'd never really known, except to nod and say hello to—according to Maggie, Carla Pfiefer is one very kinky lady. Maggie thinks that, even though Carla had moved out on Pfiefer, and was going hot and heavy with Hanchett, she was also seeing Pfiefer—screwing him for old time's sake, whatever. Maggie thinks Carla is one of those women who get their kicks driving men mad, mostly by playing one against the other."

"How do you rate Maggie Christian as an observer? Do you think she knows what she's talking about? Some people, you know, just like to stir things up."

"As I said, I don't really know her. But I think she's very smart, and probably very observant. She's been here for about six months. So I think I'd've known if she liked to cause trouble. It's my business to know things like that."

"Is she well liked, would you say?"

"I'd say that—" Once more, Hastings heard another phone warble. "Listen, Susan, I'll let you go. And I'll tell you what happens."

"Promise?"

"Promise."

6:45 PM

"*Wait* a minute." As if she were releasing tightly coiled energy, Carla Pfiefer strode to the large plate-glass window that overlooked the street where Hanchett had died. She turned to face Hastings. Every line of her body registered outrage and defiance. She wore stone-washed blue jeans, a white cashmere sweater, and thong sandals. The skintight jeans revealed lean, provocative flanks; the sweater suggested small breasts and a supple torso. Her shoulder-length dark hair was thick and full. Her mouth was hard, her voice harsh.

"*Wait.*" She raised both hands, palms forward, as if to restrain Hastings, push him away. "I don't think I'm getting this. I don't think I understand what this is all about. What are you, a voyeur? Do you get off on hearing how people spend their time in bed? Is that what this is all about?"

"What this is all about," Hastings answered, his voice heavily measured, "is that I'm trying to get some feeling for your relationship with Brice Hanchett. Monday night—the night of the murder—it seemed likely that it was a street crime. A robbery, maybe, that went sour. So I wasn't especially interested in the details of your relationship with Hanchett. But that was Monday. Today's Friday. There's been another murder in the meantime, that we think is connected to the Hanchett murder. And we—"

She frowned. "Another murder?"

"Wednesday night. A woman named Teresa Bell." Looking for a reaction, Hastings let a moment of silence pass. But he saw nothing behind the defiant frown, now turned puzzled. "We think she killed Hanchett. We think it was premeditated murder—very carefully planned."

"And you think—you've come to tell me—that you think Jason is involved." Incredulously, she shook her head. "Jesus, you must be crazy. Really crazy. Have you talked to Jason, told him what you've been telling me, all this crap about him being a jealous husband?"

"Of course I've talked to him."

"And?"

"Look, Mrs. Pfiefer"—he hardened his voice—"I'm asking the questions. Okay?"

"Jealousy." It was a contemptuous epithet, contemptuously delivered. "Christ, you don't know how ridiculous you sound." As if she pitied him, she slowly shook her head.

"Premeditated murder means there was a motive. And jealousy is one of the best motives around."

"But Jason—" She dismissed her husband with a flick of her hand. "Jesus, he's a goddamn iceberg. When he's the maddest, he's the coldest. Jealousy—Christ, that's for ordinary mortals, people who feel things, who can't control their emotions. Jason's whole thing is control. If you knew him, you'd realize that."

"When people like that snap, though . . ." Hastings let it go provocatively unfinished.

She made no response. With her first flare of anger fading, she returned to her chair, began impatiently picking at the chair's arm with bright red fingernails. Her expression had turned sullen, moody.

"I gather control was Brice Hanchett's thing, too."

"Except that they were exact opposites. Compared to Jason, Brice was a volcano."

"But the result was the same. They called the tune, manipulated people."

Her eyes turned bitter. "Doctors are gods. Hadn't you heard?"

"That sounds like you aren't too fond of doctors."

Eyes gone cold, she was watching him as one duelist might watch another, anticipating the next thrust.

"You don't like doctors. But you were involved with two of them—two doctors who worked with each other."

She made no reply.

"I think," Hastings said, "that you were using your sexual relationship with Hanchett to taunt Pfiefer. And if—"

"That's none of your goddamn—"

"And if I'm right, then we're back to motives for murder. And it comes down to the oldest motive for bloodshed in the world—two men lusting after the same woman. You."

She sprang to her feet, flung out an arm, pointed a quivering forefinger at the door. "Get out, you son of a bitch. Get out, and don't come back."

Moving slowly, deliberately, Hastings rose, went to the door. With his hand on the doorknob he turned back. Saying: "You're a beautiful woman, Mrs. Pfiefer. You're beautiful—and you're trouble."

"What we'll do," Canelli said, "is I'll try to get him out of the building so you can get a look at him."

"What d'you mean, you'll try?" Dolores demanded. "How come you don't just tell him?"

Canelli sighed. "The guy isn't a suspect, Dolores. Not really. We're just—" He broke off, searching for the phrase. "We're just conducting an investigation, that's all. We're fishing. Like, I don't even know what the guy looks like."

"What?"

He shrugged. "You asked. I'm telling you. The lieutenant interrogated him. Not me."

"Don't you even have a picture?"

"No," he admitted.

"You guys aren't very well organized, are you?"

He pointed to a van parked in front of Vance's apartment building. "Why don't you stand behind that van, there? You can see him through the van windows, I think. Without him seeing you." As he spoke, he switched off the cruiser's engine, set the emergency brake.

"What's the difference if he sees me?"

"You're sure asking a lot of questions, you know that?"

Ignoring the point, she repeated the question. Finally, exasperated, Canelli said, "If he's the one, and if he recognizes you, then he could split before we get warrants. This isn't the wild west, you know. We do what the judge tells us to do."

"Ah." Satisfied, she nodded. Then, severely: "Remember, I've got to be home by eight-thirty, no matter what."

"Guaranteed." He turned toward her, felt the closeness, smiled into her eyes. Briefly the moment held between them. He touched her shoulder hesitantly. Then, about to speak, he saw her eyes move sharply, tracking something outside the car, over his shoulder. Was it alarm he saw in her eyes? Recognition? Speculation? Something else? He began to turn, but she gripped his forearm.

"Wait." Her voice was soft, her eyes cautious.

"What's wrong?"

"That looks like him."

Following her eyes, Canelli turned slowly to face the apartment building. A man was striding up the walkway that led to the building's lobby. Visible only from the back, the man wore jeans, a leather bomber jacket, and high-top Reeboks. He was of medium build and moved easily, athletically. His hair was dark blond, stylishly cut and shaped. In the crook of his left arm he carried a brown paper bag of groceries.

"Wait here." Canelli eased out of the car just as the man thrust a key into the glass and metal door of the small lobby, entered, and strode quickly to a flight of stairs adjoining an elevator. As the man's legs disappeared, climbing the stairs, Canelli lunged forward, his hand touching the door a moment after it clicked solidly closed.

Muttering a heartfelt obscenity, Canelli turned to the building's registry. There were four floors. "C. Vance" was listed in 305. Canelli considered a moment, then pressed the buzzer for 305. No response. He tried again. Still no response. Nodding to himself, he walked back to the cruiser, leaned down to the open driver's window. "I'm going to give him a couple of minutes, then try him again, see if he's up there."

"Remember. Eight-thirty."

"Relax." He returned to the apartment building's glass entry door just as the elevator doors opened to reveal a large, flamboyantly dressed woman cradling a small dog in her arms. The woman wore rings on her fingers and thumbs; the dog wore a red ribbon.

Canelli waited for the woman to pass through, then caught the open door.

"Just a moment, please." The woman's voice was deep and imperious.

"It's okay." He smiled affably. "Police business." Without waiting for a reply, Canelli began climbing the stairs, arriving at the third floor out of breath. As he walked to 305 he calculated the odds. What was the probability that the identification was accurate? Fifty percent? More? Less? What were the chances that Clayton Vance and the man in the bomber jacket were one and the same? Eighty percent? More?

At the door of 305, finger poised over the buzzer, Canelli hesitated. Would Hastings want him to actually talk to Vance, interrogate him? Or were his orders to simply collect data and pass it on? Did Hastings want Vance stirred up? Or did he want Vance lulled into a false sense of security? It was pick and choose time, the subordinate's constant lament.

He pressed the button, waited, pressed it again, longer this time. He looked up and down the empty corridor, then stepped closer. About to press his ear to the door, he heard the latch click. The door swung open, revealing, full face, the man Dolores identified.

Clayton Vance.

Frowning darkly, Canelli said, "I'm looking for Lester Parks, the guy that's working on your TV cable. I'm from Cablevision. Have I got the right apartment?" He looked over Vance's shoulder, as if he expected to see Lester Parks. Good old Lester; they'd known each other since childhood. Whenever Canelli needed a quick fake name, he was never at a loss.

7:50 PM

"So was that him?" Dolores asked.

"Yeah. At least that's what the name on the door says."

Canelli flicked on the radio, took the microphone from its hook.

"So now what?" she demanded. "Now can I go home?"

"In just a minute. First I gotta make a call."

"Well, just so you don't—"

"Wait," he interrupted sharply. "Shut up a minute, will you?" He called Police Communications, requested contact with Lieutenant Hastings, who was in the field. As he switched to a discreet channel and waited for the patch-through, he turned his gaze to the woman beside him. In apology for the harsh words, he smiled tentatively. Her response was a frown. Then she turned away, allowing Canelli to study the swell of her breasts and the graceful curve of her dusky throat and the surprisingly delicate line of her cheek and forehead. Had her ancestors been Mexican noblemen? Had—?

"Inspector Fifty-three?" It was Hastings.

"Roger. Fifty-three." Canelli responded.

"Go ahead."

"Clayton Vance," Canelli said. "I've got a tentative ID on the gun possession."

"Where is he?"

"At home."

"Where're you? There?"

"That's affirmative."

"What's the address?"

"Seven-fifty-one North Point."

A silence. Then: "Okay. You stay there. I'll come by in fifteen, twenty minutes. We'll see what we've got. You don't think he's running, do you?"

"I don't think so."

"Okay. Sit tight."

"Ah—sir?""What is it?"

"I, ah, I've got the informant here—the female informant." As he said it, Canelli saw Dolores stir, almost a flounce.

"And?"

"And she's, ah, got to be somewhere at eight-thirty."

"No problem. Cut her loose. I'll talk to her later."

"Well, ah, the thing is, if I don't take her—drive her—she won't make the appointment. And it's important. It's part of the deal."

Even over the static-sizzling radio, Hastings's irritation was clearly audible. Finally, testily: "Okay. Go ahead. When you're clear, go back to Vance's. I'll be there."

"Yessir. Thanks."

"Don't mention it," Hastings answered. Adding dryly: "Please."

8:20 PM

"Jeez, Dolores, all I'm asking you to do is give me a figure, so I can pass it on to the lieutenant. You say Vance could be the guy. You say maybe, then you say probably. So what is it? Fifty percent? Eighty? Thirty? What?"

"Will you please watch where you're driving? God, I thought cops were good drivers. Don't you have to go to school or something to learn to drive?"

"I've never," Canelli pronounced gravely, "*ever* had a traffic accident."

"You've probably caused a hundred."

"Dolores. I'm getting you home by eight-thirty. So will you please answer my question?"

"How about sixty percent?"

"Is that what you're saying? Sixty percent? Is that your answer?"

"*Shit,* Canelli, I already *told* you. Sixty percent."

"You don't think it's the mustache, do you?"

"The mustache?"

"Vance is the only one of the four guys that's got a mustache. Do you think that's what you were looking at?"

Exasperated, she sighed. "All I can tell you is what I already said. Of the four guys, he looks like the closest. The next closest is the one with the beard. The doctor. He—" She interrupted herself. "There." She pointed. "Turn on Guerrero. Get in the right lane." She looked over her shoulder to see if traffic was clear.

Elaborately resigned, he made the turn without comment.

"It's two blocks now."

"I know."

As he drew up in front of the house, Canelli checked the time.

"Twenty-five minutes after eight. As advertised."

"Good." Frowning slightly, she sat squarely, looking straight ahead. Her nose, Canelli noticed, was small and slightly up-tilted, an appealing nose. Grace's nose was bulbous, and had once been broken in a field hockey game.

"Listen, Canelli . . ." The frown deepened, the generously curved lips compressed, as if she were framing a complicated thought, searching for the words. "I don't know whether I thanked you for getting Oscar out of that place."

"You thanked me."

"Yeah." Stiffly formal, she nodded. "Yeah, I thought I did."

Another moment of silence descended. Deeply aware of each other, they both stared straight ahead. Finally, speaking softly, she said, "You want to come in for a couple of minutes, say good night to Oscar? I think he, uh, likes you."

Pleased, Canelli smiled. "Sure. Just for a minute, though. Great. Thanks."

8:25 PM

At this time, in this place, the entirety of his life had come down to this: two elemental problems, both of them related to a nickel-plated .45-caliber Colt semiautomatic pistol.

The first problem: where to hide the gun so the police would never find it.

The second problem: explain to himself why he hadn't dropped the gun through a sewer gate. Or dropped it in a trash container, or a box of debris. Why hadn't he taken a shovel with him on Wednesday night? Why hadn't he driven from the Bell house to Golden Gate Park on Wednesday night, and buried the gun?

Why was the gun here, concealed in bedding stored on the top shelf of his wardrobe closet—the first place Hastings and the others would most certainly look?

There was only one reason—one logical answer.

The answer was murder.

One more murder.

Was it a statement, a fact? Or was it a question?

Aware that his legs and arms were heavy and his neck unaccountably weak, as if the muscles were hardly able to support the weight of his head, he rose from the chair and went to the window and looked out into the gathering dusk.

Questions and answers . . .

Lights shining from household windows, streetlights glowing in the darkness . . .

When he'd been a child, he'd had to go home when the streetlights came on. Whatever he'd been doing, he'd had to go home. Stay out too late—wander so far from home that he couldn't return soon enough, and he risked a spanking.

A spanking when he was very small, a beating when he was older—old enough to take the beating, but still so young that he must be home before dark.

In the broom closet in the hallway just off the kitchen, his father had kept a braided leather whip. When the offense was serious enough, his father used the whip instead of his hand. Once, in the summertime, when he'd been wearing shorts, the whip had drawn blood across the calves of his legs.

And once, when he was in high school, when he'd come home on a Saturday night, he'd heard his mother screaming. He'd found her on her knees in the bedroom, her nightgown shredded across the back by the braided leather whip. Eyes wild, legs braced wide—drunk—his father had stood over her like some demented slave master, lashing a slave.

Called by the neighbors, the police had come that night—come and gone.

And now the police could come again—come for him, not for his father.

8:50 PM

"Sixty percent, eh?" Dubiously, Hastings rubbed his jaw as he stared out through the cruiser's windshield at Vance's apartment building. With darkness, more than half of the buildings' windows were illuminated, with shadows inside, moving.

"She said she thought it was between Vance and Pfiefer."

"What I'm wondering," Hastings said, "is whether she's telling you what you want to hear. You get her kid out of juvie, she wants to appear cooperative."

"Yeah." Heavily, Canelli nodded. "Yeah, I thought of that, too. Except that she picked out Vance when he was just walking along the sidewalk, before I even saw him. And in fact it wouldn't've made any difference whether I saw him or not, being that I didn't even know what he looked like. So when you think about that, then you have to think about—" Suddenly Canelli broke off, pointing to a nondescript green van just pulling into a parking place across the street and extinguishing its headlights. "Hey, isn't that the electronic surveillance van?"

Hastings nodded. "You haven't heard about Operation Fingerprint, I guess."

Canelli frowned. "Operation Fingerprint?" Turning, he anxiously scanned his superior officer's face. Had he missed something, some essential interdepartment bulletin?

In return, Hastings smiled. "Don't worry, Canelli." Quickly he outlined Friedman's plan to lift fingerprints for a match-up of prints found on the cartridges in the Llama's clip. As he spoke, he saw Friedman leave the van and cross to their cruiser. Grunting laboriously, Friedman got in the rear seat as both Hastings and Canelli turned to face him.

"So?" Friedman asked. "Anything?"

"According to Dolores," Hastings said, "Vance might've bought the gun. Sixty percent, she says."

"Sixty percent, eh?" It was a skeptical question, dubiously asked. Then, gesturing to the apartment building, Friedman asked, "Is Vance in there?"

"I don't know," Hastings answered. "He came in at about a quarter to eight. That's when Dolores Chavez eyeballed him. I got here about eight-fifteen. I tried to call him on my car phone, but all I got was a machine."

"Maybe he's screening his calls. Could you get into the lobby, try his buzzer?"

"I didn't want to stir him up."

"So we could be shooting a blank here. If he's at home, it's no go. And it sounds like he's at home."

Hastings shrugged. "There's no guarantees in this line of work. Or have you forgotten?"

"Is the back covered?"

"No. Are you all set to go?"

"Yes. We've already done Pfiefer," Friedman said. "No sweat. Except that I got a couple of drug dealers' radios from the property room. And they're not all that great. I got a good lock person, though."

"Lock person?"

"A lady locksmith," Friedman answered. "Very nicely packaged. She said she worked with you a few weeks ago. Another, uh, touchy job, up on Nob Hill. Illegal entry, in other words."

"Ah." Remembering, Hastings smiled, nodded. "Nicely packaged, no question."

"Okay." With the air of an executive getting down to business, Friedman leaned forward, spoke crisply, concisely. "I've got Alan Bernhardt and the lock lady and a fingerprint guy in the van. Bernhardt and I have civilian walkie-talkies, like I said. At Pfiefer's, I got a couple of precinct guys to cover the front and back. We rang Pfiefer's bell, and got no answer. Pfiefer lives in an apartment building about like this one"—he gestured to Vance's building—"only fancier. Sylvia, the lock person, and Bernhardt—they were posing as a locksmith team, if anyone got curious—they let themselves into the lobby, no sweat. They also got into Pfiefer's luxury apartment, no sweat. Bernhardt picked up a couple of drinking glasses, took them down to the van, got the prints lifted. He replaced the glasses and got out, everything as slick as a whistle. So—" Friedman gestured. "So that's what we're going to do here, same plan. Let's use surveillance channel three. Canelli, you take the back, and tell us when you're in position."

"Yessir."

"Okay." Friedman swung open the car's door. "Let's do it."

8:52 PM

He opened the big steel-clad door marked REAR STAIRWAY, glanced back down the deserted corridor, then stepped through the heavy door, letting it close slowly on its pneumatic cylinder. He stood motionless on the textured steel landing for a moment, listening. Silence. He touched the unfamiliar cold steel bulk of the pistol thrust into his belt, zipped up his leather jacket over the pistol's bulge, and began slowly descending the staircase. On the metal stairs, the sound of his running shoes was muted.

The three flights of the service stairs were functionally lit: large incandescent bulbs protected by wire cages. At the first-floor landing, one door led outside, one led to the garage. Slowly, cautiously, he drew the huge bolt that secured the outside door. He rotated the knob, pulled the steel-clad door open. Once outside, he eased the door closed on a book of matches. If no one used the utility door during the time he was gone, then he would return this way. Otherwise he would walk to the front of the building and enter through the lobby.

He was standing in a paved accessway that led to the street. He wore a "Save the Whales" baseball cap, and was careful not to look up at the windows above as he walked quickly to the street, where he'd parked the Buick. As he walked, he took the set of rental-car keys from his pocket: two keys attached to a large plastic tag. Did he have his regular keys? Yes, he must have them; otherwise he couldn't have locked the apartment when he left.

Had he locked the door when he left? Specifically, precisely, he couldn't remember. But habit was like that: the conscious act became subconscious rote. And, yes, in his left pocket, where he always kept them, he felt the reassuring bulk of his regular keys. The keys were strung on a key ring she'd given him last Christmas. A stocking stuffer, she'd called it. Fourteen-karat gold.

The keys in this pocket, the big nickel-plated pistol in his belt: both of them symbols. One symbolizing security. One symbolizing a way out.

He was standing beside the Buick, which was parked on the street, half a block from the accessway. Strangely, he couldn't remember walking from the utility door. It was as if he'd somehow levitated from the door of the building to the Buick. Yet he could remember the smells of the accessway, the bits of garbage and refuse left by the garbage trucks.

What was the word for the sense of smell? Olfactory? Yes, olfactory. On a quiz show, that random bit of knowledge might win a prize.

The first key worked in the Buick's door on the driver's side. He swung the door open and looked up and down the quiet street before he slid into the car. He was careful to keep the keys in his hand, ready to insert into the ignition. Once, years ago, he'd lost the keys to a rental car. He'd had to wait for two hours, until a man on a three-wheel motorcycle brought him a new set of keys.

Now, in the warm September night with the stars just emerging in the darkness overhead, two hours would be a lifetime, the end of everything.

A lifetime?

Or two lifetimes?

He put the key in the ignition, trod twice on the accelerator, twisted the key. Instantly the engine came to life. General Motors. His salvation. He switched on the headlights, maneuvered out of the parking space, carefully checked the traffic, and drove into the stream of light traffic. He would be a little late arriving at the yacht harbor. Five minutes late, maybe more, depending on traffic. Why? For this most important meeting of his life, why was he running late?

It was the gun—whether or not to keep the gun. The gun could endanger him; the gun could save him. Pick a number, take a chance. If they found the gun on him, he would be finished. But if he left it behind, and they found it and tested it for ballistics, they would surely arrest him for murder. So he must throw the gun down a sewer, or into the ocean from the seawall beside the yacht harbor.

But without the gun, the big, lethal .45 automatic, he couldn't protect himself, defend himself, save himself. And so, standing with his hand on the doorknob of his hallway door, immobilized, knowing he'd be late, he'd tried to decide. But indecision followed indecision, compounding. In minutes—only seconds, perhaps—he'd felt utterly exhausted, as if all his energy had been short-circuited, drained away by the agony of indecision. Leaving him here in this strange car, driving through the warm September night with the pistol thrust in his waistband.

9:15 PM

Crouched awkwardly below the window line of the surveillance van, Friedman keyed the walkie-talkie.

"Alan. How do you hear?" He released the Transmit button, listened to the crackle of static, tried again.

"Maybe you should get out of the van," Hastings offered. "All this metal doesn't help."

Impatiently, Friedman shook his head. "Wrong. I've got the goddamn thing hooked into the van's outside antenna. The problem is these concrete buildings, all that reinforcing steel."

"Too bad we can't use our radios."

Friedman shrugged, tried Bernhardt again. "Maybe they're in the elevator. I think elevators are the worst of all." He tried once more. This time, faintly, a scratchy voice answered.

"Yeah. Pete. Gotcha. Out."

"Maybe he's in the corridor," Hastings offered, "and doesn't want to talk too loud."

Without comment, Friedman nodded. Beside him, with his equipment arrayed on a small fold-down table, John Ames, the lab's senior fingerprint technician, yawned as he glanced at his watch. In the driver's seat, Hastings switched on the van's radio to the surveillance channel, keyed the microphone, which he held in the palm of his hand. "Canelli. How do you hear?"

"Loud and clear, Lieutenant."

"They're inside the building."

"But they aren't on this channel. Right?"

"Right. They've got civilian equipment. So you communicate through me."

"Roger."

"What's your position?"

"I'm parked across from a dead-end alleyway that leads to the utility area. It's the only entrance to the building back here. Is the subject inside his apartment?"

"We don't know yet. Bernhardt'll ring the bell, then he'll go inside if the apartment's empty. That's what he should be doing right—" Hearing Friedman talk into the walkie-talkie, Hastings broke off, listened for a moment. Then: "Bernhardt's inside, Canelli. So Vance obviously left. Bernhardt's going to give the place a light toss for the gun. Then he'll find a couple of drinking glasses, things like that, bring them out to be printed. Then he'll put the stuff back. So it'll be fifteen minutes, something like that. Clear?"

"Yessir."

Hastings switched off the microphone and turned to Friedman, who was glowering as he unwrapped a cigar, dropped the wrappings on the floor of the van, and jammed the unlit cigar in the corner of his mouth. This mannerism, Hastings knew, was one of the few visible indications that Friedman was irritated.

"I *think* Bernhardt's inside. Mostly what I got was static, with a voice saying something."

"Well," Hastings offered, "if he isn't inside the apartment, then he'll be out in a couple of minutes, probably. So relax."

"Hmmm."

9:20 PM

She was looking past him, beyond him, out over the waters of the bay. Even though the dockside light was dim, he could clearly see her eyes. Stranger's eyes. Once lovers. Strangers now. Bound together now by fear, a bond stronger than love.

Love?

No, not love.

A compulsion, yes. An addiction, certainly. But not love. He knew that now. Too late, he knew that now.

From the nearby yacht club came the sound of laughter, counterpointing the sound of music: soft, civilized rock, carefully calculated to please the younger yacht-club members without jangling the nerves of the affluent oldsters.

The Sound of Music . . .

It was a movie made more than twenty years ago, in a distant age of innocence. His innocence. Lost.

Lost . . .

A squeeze of the trigger, blossoms of blood spreading on a shapeless cotton housedress, and everything had changed. Forever lost.

He saw her eyes shift, saw her expression change, sensed her body stiffen as she said, "You can't leave. If you leave, they'll know. Don't you see that, for God's sake? They'll *know.*"

"If I don't leave, they're going to arrest me. I can see it in Hastings's eyes. I can hear it in his voice. He's already questioned me twice. Both times, he asked about you—about us." As the words registered, he saw her stiffen. Had he planned this—planned to frighten her, therefore to test her? Or did he only want to rouse her, break through her reserve, anything to spark those calm, cold eyes. Even making love, even in climax, her jaw clenched, teeth exposed, head thrown back, eyes tightly closed, her reserve was never threatened, never breached—never shared.

Strangers, standing on a dark, deserted dock.

Slowly, deliberately, she turned to face him. She was frowning slightly, as if she were troubled by some small, trivial problem. She spoke slowly, precisely. "How much does Hastings know about us? How much did you tell him?"

"Nothing. I didn't tell him anything. But he—he knew. God knows how." His voice, he realized, was rising, thinning. In response, he saw contempt chill her eyes. *The eyes are the windows of the soul,* someone had written. How long ago had it been since he'd first lost himself in these eyes?

Lost then, out of passion . . .

Lost now, out of fear.

"Have you still got the gun?" she was asking.

He nodded, reflexively touched the bulge beneath his jacket. Following the gesture, her eyes widened. "You've got it now?"

Was she frightened? For the first time, frightened?

"If I'm going to run, it doesn't matter. I'll need a gun."

"It *does* matter." She spoke urgently, sibilantly. "They can compare the bullets. It's all they'd need."

"In Mexico, it won't matter."

"Mexico . . ." She pronounced the word as if it were an obscenity.

"I need money."

"*You* need money?" Contemptuously, she was mocking him. "*You?*"

"It's Friday night. I'd have to wait until Monday to get some money."

"Are you asking me for money? Is that why we're here?"

"I need ten thousand. At least."

"If you can't get it before Monday, neither can I."

"You could, if you wanted to do it. But you won't. Will you?"

"I don't want you to run. If you run, it'll lead them to me."

"Then come with me. We'll leave tomorrow morning."

"It's like signing a confession if you leave. Don't you see that, for God's sake?"

"They won't know until I'm already in Mexico. I've already thought of a name. Charles Wade. Beginning tomorrow, at the airport, I'm Charles Wade. But I've got to have cash. Credit cards can be traced. You've got to get me some cash."

"You're crazy." She spoke quietly, coldly matter-of-fact. Emphasizing: *"Crazy."*

"They won't arrest you. They'll come for me, not you. So you can still talk. But I've got to act. I've got to act before they act. They—Christ—they could be following me right now."

"*Following* you?" Involuntarily her head came up, her eyes swept the nearby rows of parked cars.

Aware of the wayward pleasure he was experiencing, aware that he wanted to see her eyes register fear, he continued, "They could have my phone tapped. Or my place could be bugged. They have tiny microphones, you know—battery-powered transmitters."

"You suspected all this, and you told me to meet you? Christ." Incredulously, she shook her head. "You *are* crazy. Do you realize what you're doing? Do you realize that—"

"It started with you. Everything. You know that, don't you? It was your idea."

"So if they're following you, then you thought it'd be nice if they followed me, too. Share and share alike. Is that it?"

"I didn't say they were following me. I said they *could* be following me. I'm—Christ—I'm a suspect, don't forget. Not you. Me."

"So you're carrying the gun. The one thing that can incriminate you, and you're carrying it." As she spoke, she gestured to the seawall, close beside them. "Christ, throw the thing away. *Now.* Give it time. *I'll* throw it away." She stepped closer, extended her hand.

Quickly he stepped back, saying, "If I were staying, I'd throw it away. But I'm going. So I need the gun. Fuck it. And fuck you, too."

As if she pitied him, she shook her head. "Do you know what you're doing? You're imagining things, that's what you're doing. The police question you, and you think it's all over."

"I pulled the trigger. Where were you when I pulled the trigger? Did you see her eyes turn to stone?"

"We agreed. Long before that, we agreed to—"

"Words. Talk. You talked. You made promises. But I pulled the trigger."

"Ah—" As if she understood, she nodded. Then, again, she stepped forward. Not to take the gun, but now to touch him on the forearm, a belated lover's touch.

Did she suspect that he'd brought the gun because he knew he might kill her to save himself?

Did she sense that he couldn't do it?

Not here. Not now. Not with the music from the yacht club coming so clearly in the warm September evening.

9:35 PM

As she saw him leaving her, walking away in the direction of the yacht club, the rhythm of his strides uneven, his shoulders drawn forward, head lowered, frightened and defeated, his words began to resonate, as fateful as footsteps on a fresh-dug grave:

It started with you.

It was your idea.

Yes, it had started with her. And so it must end with her.

Before he could run—before the police could question him—she must end it.

Now. Tonight.

9:55 PM

He switched off the headlights, switched off the engine, set the hand brake. Just ahead, on the opposite side of the street, he saw the entrance to the accessway. Surprisingly, only a few cars were parked nearby. Was it significant? When he'd left here, an hour ago, there'd hardly been a parking place. Did it mean that the police were watching? Or did it mean that, Friday night, there were parties to go to, movies to see, people to meet?

While others partied, he would pack a suitcase, draw the drapes, turn off the lights—and leave. He would drive to an automated teller machine, clean out his checking account, clean out his savings. In the rented Buick he would begin driving south. He would cross the border at San Diego, just another one-day tourist, shopping. Paying cash for gas and motel rooms, he would drive to Mexico City, where he would take the license plates from the car, and leave the car for car thieves. Charles Wade, tourist. Before he was missed, sometime Monday, he would be safe. Charles Wade, calling her from Cancún. Telling her how to send him the money: cash at first, then checks.

Charles Wade, running.

While others partied, made love, watched a movie, he would be running. Whatever mess he made, others would clean up.

Job to job, apartment to apartment, city to city—all his life, running. After his father had left—disappeared, one afternoon in May—his mother began moving. Job to job, apartment to apartment—always smaller apartments, always darker apartments, always cheaper apartments. Until, like his father, he had left her, too. He'd been sixteen. His mother had just been paid. She'd cashed her check, and had gone out to buy groceries—and a bottle. He'd gone to the scuffed bureau they shared and pulled open the second drawer from the top. There, among the tangles of her underwear, he'd seen the nest of money, all bills, no silver. He'd left her a twenty-dollar bill, and taken the rest. All afternoon, when she was at work, he'd thought about it, planned it. He'd filled two shopping bags with clothes and hidden them beneath his bed, ready. Like tonight, it had been a Friday. Like tonight, the weather had been soft and warm, Indian summer in New York City, on the Lower East Side, where everything and everyone was for sale. Especially teenage boys with firm, rounded buttocks.

Why was he reluctant to leave the shelter of the Buick? Was he sensing danger? Unconsciously sensing danger? He glanced at his watch. Ten o'clock. By midnight he would be on the road. By morning he could be in Tijuana. Another town where everything was for sale.

10:00 PM

Friedman slid the van's door open and waited for Bernhardt to give him the clear plastic evidence bag containing two drinking glasses. "Any trouble?" Friedman asked, handing the evidence bag to the fingerprint technician and then gesturing Bernhardt inside, so the van could be closed and the interior lights switched on.

"Smooth as silk." Bernhardt smiled, nodded through the windshield toward the woman who stood on the sidewalk nearby, keeping a discreet distance from the undercover van. She wore a bomber jacket and tight blue jeans. A small red metal toolbox rested beside her on the sidewalk.

"The lady has a way with locks," Bernhardt observed.

"Have you looked for the gun?"

"No. I'll do that when I take the glasses back." A tall man, Bernhardt knelt on the floor of the van, his eyes following the fingerprint technician as he began working.

"Don't let her inside the apartment." Friedman gestured toward the locksmith.

"Right. There's a stairway. She stayed there."

Approvingly, Friedman nodded. Now both men watched the technician as he carefully applied the black fingerprint powder to the glasses, then delicately brushed it away. In the front seat, monitoring the radio, Hastings sat facing forward, eyeing the lady locksmith and her tight blue jeans. In the rear of the van, the technician rotated the glasses, examining them closely. Then, satisfied, he began applying the strips of Scotch tape to the fingerprints.

"How do they look?" Friedman asked.

The technician shrugged. "Average, I'd say." Working quickly now, he stripped off the tape, checked the result, finally nodded, satisfied. He began cleaning the glasses with a cloth as Friedman turned to Bernhardt.

"Can you hear me on that goddamn radio?" Friedman asked.

Bernhardt shrugged. "I hear you a little. Enough, I guess." He took the walkie-talkie from his jacket pocket. "It's very sensitive on the squelch, I've found."

Friedman nodded. "I'll keep that in mind." As he spoke, the technician handed him the bag with the clean glasses inside. He handed the bag to Bernhardt, who turned toward the door. With permission from the fingerprint man, Friedman switched off the interior lights and slid the door open.

"Don't forget the forty-five," Friedman said. "Give it fifteen, twenty minutes, a very light toss, no fuss, no muss. Right?"

"No fuss, no muss. See you soon, guys." Bernhardt nodded to the two lieutenants, stooped, and stepped out of the van. A moment later the tall, loose-limbed private investigator and the petite locksmith were striding toward the building's lobby. As Friedman watched them trip the lock and enter the lobby, the primary radio, mounted beneath the van's dashboard, came to life.

"Surveillance Four? Are you on frequency?"

Hastings recognized the voice of Bill Sigler, one of three communications supervisors. Whenever Sigler came on frequency, something significant had happened.

Turning away from Friedman, who was talking to Canelli on another channel, Hastings keyed his microphone. "Surveillance Four. Hastings." As he spoke, he turned down the volume of the primary receiver, then leaned closer to the speaker while Friedman continued talking to Canelli.

"Yeah," Sigler was saying. "Lieutenant, I know you're on surveillance. But I've got a lady holding who really wants to talk to you, plain language. I told her I'd try to get you."

"What's her name?"

"Her name is Hanchett. Barbara Hanchett."

As if some subliminal switch had been closed, both lieutenants stiffened. Quickly, Friedman signed off on Canelli as Hastings turned up the primary radio's volume.

"Okay, Sigler. Put her on. You'll be getting it on tape. Right?"

"Right."

A moment passed. Then, clearly, a woman's voice: "Lieutenant Hastings?"

"Mrs. Hanchett. What can I do for you?"

"Can you come over here, Lieutenant? Now? Right now? I've, uh—I've got something to tell you." In her voice, Hastings could plainly hear the tightness, the tension. Was it fear? Simple anxiety? Something else? Clearly, Hastings could picture Barbara Hanchett: a cool, calm, utterly controlled woman. Controlled—and controlling, too. A drawing-room dragon lady. Questioningly, Hastings looked at Friedman, who was looking intently at the primary radio's speaker. Finally, Friedman raised his double chin a half-inch and slightly tilted his head, signifying that he favored proceeding cautiously, deliberately.

"I can probably be there in a half hour, Mrs. Hanchett." Hastings hesitated. "This is an open line—it's being broadcast on a discreet channel, but it's still being broadcast. It's also being taped, by police communications. Do you understand?"

"Y—yes, I understand."

"Okay. So now I want to ask you—are you in any danger? Any physical danger, now? Right now?"

Her reply was a short, harsh laugh. In the laugh, Hastings

could hear the edge of hysteria. "No, I'm not in danger. It's nothing like that."

"Then what's so urgent, Mrs. Hanchett? What is it that can't wait?"

"What's so urgent," she said, "is that I can tell you who killed Teresa Bell."

In Friedman's eyes, Hastings could see his own expression mirrored: equal measures of caution, excitement, and quick calculation. For once, Friedman was sitting erect, not slouched. His eyebrows were raised: all the excitement Friedman ever allowed himself to reveal.

"Okay." Hastings spoke distinctly, deliberately. "Tell me. Who is it?"

"It's Clay—Clayton Vance."

10:10 PM

Vance was walking down the alleyway as if he were suspended in time and place, cocooned from the night's noises and sights and smells. The pavement hardly made contact with his feet; the concrete walls rising on either side might have been stage scenery, make-believe, without substance, without reality. Yet, as he walked, he was aware that his senses were drawn unbearably taut, a thin, shrill song. Steadily, the steel door was drawing closer. In the darkness he could see the seam of light between the door and the frame—the seam into which he'd inserted the book of matches, more than an hour ago.

10:12 PM

As Hastings released the Transmit button of his microphone, one of Friedman's walkie-talkies came to life.

"Lieutenant," Canelli was saying, "he's here. He just got out of a Buick back here. He's walking down the back alley of his apartment building."

Urgently, Friedman handed the civilian walkie-talkie to Hastings and used the departmental walkie-talkie to tell Canelli what they had just learned from Barbara Hanchett. Turning away from Friedman, Hastings spoke into the civilian walkie-talkie: "Bernhardt. Alan. Come in." He released the walkie-talkie's Transmit switch, tried again—and again. On the surveillance radio, Canelli was saying that Vance had just pulled open a utility door and was entering the building. Friedman, the theorist, handed his microphone to Hastings, the field commander. In seconds, responsibility had shifted.

"Can you get in that door, Canelli?" Hastings asked.

"I doubt it, Lieutenant. I can't even see a knob. I bet it's an anti-burglary door. You gotta ring to get in, I bet."

Irritated, Hastings demanded, "Then how'd Vance get in?"

"He must've blocked it open."

"Okay. Jesus. Stay put. If he comes out, take him. Clear?"

"Yessir. That's clear." Canelli's voice was chastened; Hastings had hurt his feelings.

"I'll get reinforcements." Friedman reached awkwardly over Hastings for the microphone that would connect him to Communications. One last time, Hastings tried the walkie-talkie. Finally he heard a static-garbled man's voice. Was it Bernhardt?

"Alan. Is that you?"

An unreadable response, then nothing but static.

"If you can hear this," Hastings said, "I want you to get out. I want you to leave the building by the front door. The subject has returned. Repeat, the subject has returned. Get out. Leave by the front stairway. *Now.*" He switched off the walkie-talkie and handed it to Friedman. Across the street, two couples were just leaving the lobby of Vance's building. Quickly, Hastings threw open the van's door. "Keep trying Bernhardt. I'm going inside." Sprinting across the street, Hastings caught the two couples as they clustered around a parked car. He showed them the shield, demanding, "Which one of you lives there?" He gestured to the apartment building.

Hesitantly, as if he'd been called on to answer a difficult classroom question, one of the men raised his hand. He was short, fat, and bald. And probably half-drunk.

"I want you to open the door—the lobby door." As he spoke, Hastings grasped the man's thick forearm, turning him back toward the building. "Now. Right now."

"But—"

Lowering his voice as he propelled the man roughly forward along the sidewalk, Hastings grated, "This is police business, asshole. *Important* police business. Run, don't walk."

10:13 PM

At the third-floor landing, Vance turned the knob on the metal-clad fire door. Slowly, cautiously, he drew the door open, stepped into the deserted corridor. Above the elevator doors, a Lucite bar glowed green: going up. He stepped back inside the open service doorway. The green light blinked out; the elevator was going higher, to the fourth floor. Once more he stepped into the corridor, let the fire door close on its pneumatic cylinder. Beneath his jacket he could feel the pistol. He'd been carrying the pistol for more than an hour, as if the heavy metallic bulk were an essential part of himself. The gun was identical to the army-issue .45 automatic, the gun he'd earned a sharpshooter's medal with, in the National Guard. A round was in the chamber, and the safety was off. Cock the hammer, and the semiautomatic would fire until it was empty, eight shots, one shot for each squeeze of the trigger.

As he walked down the corridor to his own door, he took his keys from his pocket. Was the corridor always so quiet? Until now, he'd never wondered. Until now, he'd never—

At the far end of the corridor, from the doorway of the carpeted staircase that served the front of the building, he heard something move, caught a fragmentary glimpse of a hand and a sleeve, now quickly gone. In the open doorway of the front staircase, standing as he'd just stood on the landing of the rear stairway, someone was concealed.

A policeman on stakeout?

A burglar, waiting for someone to leave an apartment empty?

A killer, waiting?

He was standing at his own door, his key ring in his hand. Covertly eyeing the front doorway, he shifted the keys to his left hand; with his right hand he lowered his jacket's zipper. As the zipper bottomed and the jacket came open, he touched the butt of the .45 with his right hand. As long as he remained facing the apartment door, he could draw the gun unseen. When he turned to face his assailant, the gun would be in position. Draw back the hammer, aim, squeeze, fire. Eight shots.

With his head still turned to face the apartment, he angled his gaze to his left, so that any movement in the hallway door would register in his peripheral vision. With his right hand on the .45's butt, he used his left hand to insert the key in the lock. He began to rotate the key—and went hollow at his center, the emptiness of instantaneous panic. Because there was no resistance. The door was unlocked.

It was important, he knew, to remain calm, somehow to replenish the void within. Cold, complete discipline, all the difference, now. He could have forgotten to lock the door when he left. Imagining what Barbara would do during their meeting, distracted, he had forgotten to lock the door.

Either he'd forgotten—or someone was inside. There was no other possibility. Meaning that he must now return the key to his pocket, then begin turning the doorknob. In the next seconds he would—

The door refused to open. The lock was free, the doorknob was rotated to its stop, but the door remained closed.

Bolted, from the inside.

10:14 PM

Inside the lobby, Hastings looked at the elevator, looked at the stairway door beside the elevator, considered, then pulled the unlocked staircase door open and drew his revolver. Wishing he had a walkie-talkie, some connection with the reinforcements that were on the way, he began climbing the stairs two at a time, the carpeting muffling the sound of his steps. At the second-floor landing he stopped, listened. Was someone on the stairs above—the third-floor landing? Was it a sound, or was it his nerves? Someday, he knew, crouched in an alien hallway with his gun in his hand, he'd realize that he'd grown too old for field command. Aware that the butt of his revolver was slick with sweat, he began slowly climbing the stairs, looking up. At the landing between the floors, back flat against the staircase wall, revolver raised, he stole a quick, furtive look. Sylvia, the lady locksmith, stood beside her red tool kit on the next landing above. Hastings covered half of the distance separating them before she suddenly turned, eyes wide, startled. With her gaze fixed on the revolver, her mouth came open. Hastings urgently raised his forefinger to his lips, sharply shook his head. Three double steps took him to her side. "Where's Bernhardt?" he whispered.

"Inside the apartment. And there's someone at the door. Is it him?"

"Muscular? Good-looking? Dark blond hair? About forty?"

Eyes saucer-wide, she nodded. Carefully avoiding the tool chest, he gestured urgently down the stairs. "Get down there," he whispered. "All the way down. Get outside. *Now.*" As she nodded, then reflexively stopped to pick up her tools, he shook his head. "*No.* Leave them. *Go,* dammit."

She frowned, hesitated. He grasped her shoulder, hard. "*Go.*" She blinked once, shrugged, obeyed. Hastings stepped around the toolbox again, raised the revolver, swallowed hard—and began inching toward the open doorway.

10:15 PM

As Vance released the doorknob, he heard the mechanism click, the sound so loud it might fill the corridor. Inside—whoever was in there, lying in ambush—they had surely heard the sound. Blood hammering in his ears, he stepped back, raised the Colt, looked toward the front stairway door. One was in his apartment, waiting. One was in the nearby doorway, watching. The police—surely the police.

Or had Barbara hired killers? After he'd called her, she would have had time to call the killers, give them their orders. She'd been terrified when he'd said he was leaving. She would do anything to save herself, to keep him from going.

With his eyes fixed on the open doorway sheltering its unknown occupant, he began backing toward the rear service stairway, back the way he'd come.

Someone hidden in his apartment, with the door bolted, blocking that avenue of retreat, of sanctuary. Someone hidden in the hall doorway, blocking retreat down the front stairs.

Leaving only the rear stairs.

If there were two of them, only two, then he could escape.

But were there more of them? Had one of the killers let him enter the building from the rear, springing the trap? In the alley, was someone hidden, waiting?

Only a dozen strides separated him from the fire door. Less than a dozen, now. And now his fingers touched the metal of the door. But should he go through the door, committing himself to the steel-and-concrete confines of the service staircase? With one of them below him and two of them above, he would be helpless, caught in their crossfire. Should he open the door, conceal himself, play the doorway game, cat catch a rat?

Cat catch a rat—

It was a game he'd played as a child.

The sudden memory, a wayward flash from long ago, was touched with hysteria.

Were they winning, then?

Was he losing?

All his life, even playing the games of childhood, he'd lost. Casting him up here now, cowering in this alien doorway, cat catch a rat.

Once he'd been the cat. But now he—

In the front hallway door he saw a flicker of movement, just a flicker. Then he saw first parts of the whole: first a shoe, then a leg—followed by a jacket-clad arm and a hand—

The hand holding a gun.

A revolver.

A short-barreled revolver.

A policeman's weapon.

10:15:30 PM

With his foot and arm exposed—and the gun exposed—Hastings took a last look down the carpeted front stairway, drew a deep breath, stepped clear of the doorway. Vance's apartment, he knew, was four doors ahead, on the left. What was Bernhardt's situation, inside the apartment? Had Bernhardt bolted the door from the inside? If he hadn't, he could be a captive—a hostage.

Friedman was in the front lobby. Canelli was covering the rear, standard police procedure. And help was coming, already on the way. In minutes, Friedman would begin sending in the reinforcements. So it was only necessary to—

At the far end of the corridor, something had moved—a hint,

nothing more. Was someone leaving an apartment farther down the corridor, also on the left? Or was someone—

The doorway to the rear stairs. It must be the fire door where someone was hiding, showing only the point of a shoulder, part of a face.

A man's face. Vance's face? Someone else, a stranger?

With his left hand, Hastings drew his shield case from his pocket, draped it over the breast pocket of his jacket. Then, gripping the revolver firmly in his right hand, slowly and deliberately, the sheriff advancing down the dusty Western street, he moved across the corridor to the left wall, then began advancing toward number 305, Vance's apartment. At any moment, Friedman would send the reinforcements in. He would send a man to reinforce Canelli. He would send two or three men up the front staircase. Tactically, therefore, Hastings should wait. If Vance had a gun—the .45, a killer handgun—then the odds were too long.

But where was Bernhardt? Was Bernhardt in danger? A captive?

He had reached number 305. Cautiously he gripped the doorknob, turned, heard the latch click, felt it release. The door was unlocked. He stepped back, drew a long, deep breath, blinked to clear his vision, swallowed once—and pushed at the knob. Nothing. Whoever was inside, Bernhardt or Vance, he'd bolted the door. Gently, Hastings drew the door fully closed, slowly rotated the knob until there was no more pressure. Then he glanced back at the front stairway. Had he heard sounds from the front stairway? Holding his breath, he listened. Except for background street sounds, he heard nothing.

Who was inside 305? Bernhardt? Vance? Both?

Who was concealed in the open service doorway? Could it be Canelli?

Always, it came down to this: crouching in a strange corridor, fighting to subdue the panic that rose like bitter bile. Hide-

and-seek, a deadly game of guesses, loser leaves on a gurney, dead or dying. And if the cop was the winner, the reward was another hallway, another game of guesses. Another winner, another loser. And always there was the shameful secret: the paralysis of fear that could freeze the limbs in their sockets.

Meaning that it was necessary to move forward. Not back, to safety. But forward, toward whatever waited in the shadows. Because others would come. Others would see—and would know.

10:16 PM

If he moved forward, took two steps into the corridor, raised the .45, aimed, fired, he could kill the detective who was flattened against the hallway wall, hand on the doorknob, eyes fixed on the door of 305. A split second, no more, kill or be killed, and Hastings would go down.

But instead of stepping forward he was stepping back—one step, two steps—surrendering his view of the corridor, surrendering his advantage. Meaning that he must turn, go silently down the stairs. Before more police arrived—before Hastings appeared above him on the stairs—he must be in the alley. Two choices: go for the alley, or fire on Hastings.

Kill or be killed.

10:17 PM

Canelli raised the walkie-talkie, keyed the mike, spoke softly: "Lieutenant . . ."

"Go ahead." Friedman's voice, too, was soft. "Anything?"

"Nothing."

"Nothing here. Are you sure there's no other way out?"

"Not back here, there isn't."

"Okay."

"I'm still in my unit," Canelli said. "But I thought I'd get a little closer to that door, if he comes out. There's a dumpster back here. And I could—"

In the alleyway darkness, the light changed on the steel door.

"Canelli? What is it?"

"I think someone's coming out," Canelli said. "I'd better go." He released the Transmit switch, turned down the volume, holstered the walkie-talkie at his hip. Slowly he pushed the cruiser's door open. Thank God, the dome light was disconnected, score one for the motor-pool mechanics. Or had the bulb simply burned out, the luck of the draw?

Eyes fixed on the steel door, Canelli drew his revolver as he slowly, soundlessly advanced, angling toward the dumpster with its thick steel sides and its deep, safe shadows.

10:17:20 PM

From the metal stairs rising two flights above, Vance heard the sound of footsteps descending: Hastings, closing in, blocking escape. Looking up, Vance saw a hand clutching the railing, giving up one grip for another grip, a foot farther down.

Years—months—minutes. All of them gone. Leaving only this: seconds, kill or be killed.

Or surrender. Throw down the .45, beg them for mercy, offer his wrists for the handcuffs.

Or escape. One last chance, through the alley.

He turned his back on the stairs, grasped the knob of the steel door—

Pulled it slowly open.

10:19 PM

Still midway between the open expanse of the alley's entrance and the safety of the dumpster, exposed, Canelli saw the sheen of the flat steel door disappear, replaced by a rectangle of darkness.

And a leg, emerging from the darkened rectangle.

And an arm.

And a hand, holding the gun: the big, deadly automatic. Vance turned to face him.

Dropping into a crouch, revolver raised, the approved stance, Canelli shouted, "Drop it, Vance. *Now.*"

10:20 PM

Standing motionless on the second-floor landing, risking a momentary look down over the railing, Hastings heard Canelli shouting to Vance.

A shot. A muffled cry. Another shot. And another. Hastings's shoes rang on the steel stairs, echoing in the ringing silence after the shots. At ground level, the outside door was standing half-open.

Headlong, Hastings kicked the door open wide, flattened himself momentarily against the rough concrete wall beside the door. Above him, a single light in a wire cage illuminated his position. He was exposed: bad tactics. Vance firing from the cover of darkness: good tactics.

"*Lieutenant. Watch it.*" Canelli's voice, barely audible, choked with pain. Canelli, down.

Instinctively, a diversion, Hastings fired into the alley, aiming high, to draw fire. Five shots in the revolver, the hammer resting on an empty chamber, good police practice. Four shots remaining. Now he must—

Answering fire: two deafening, close-range shots, from the big .45. Sparks flew on the fire door, just above his head. Throwing himself forward into the alley, diving, rolling to his left, Hastings saw movement in the darkness: Vance, running. On his elbows, aiming, Hastings fired once, twice. A short-barreled revolver fired double-action, a waste of ammunition, only two shots remaining. He heaved himself to his feet. Was Canelli badly wounded? Bleeding to death in the darkness? Could Canelli—?

A blaze of lights: two criss-crossed pairs of headlights. Shouts, a wild rattle of shots, one of them a shotgun, massive, booming. Instant warfare. And a man screaming. Vance, terrified, giving up, his silhouette sagging as he fell to his knees, screaming, "No. Stop. *Stop.* I'm shot. *Shot.*"

And Canelli, lying full-length on the concrete. Face down. Motionless. Revolver still clutched in his right hand.

"Ambulance," Hastings shouted. "Ambulance, goddammit. Officer down. It's Canelli, goddammit. It's *Canelli.*"

1:45 AM

Wearily, the doctor stripped off a bloody pair of surgical gloves, dropped them in a refuse bin, lowered his gauze mask around his neck, drew off his green surgical beret, and shook out his medium-long, dark brown hair. Unmasked, his face was a young man's, hardly more than thirty years old. Alert, perceptive eyes and a mobile mouth in a face as lean and handsome as a daytime TV doctor's. His green surgical gown was blood-streaked. Burdened by fatigue, his shoulders hunched, the doctor's arms hung slack at his sides.

"You from the police?"

In unison, Hastings and Friedman nodded.

"Well, your guy . . ." The young doctor frowned.

"Canelli," Friedman said.

"Yeah. Canelli. Well, I'll tell you . . ." Infinitely weary, the surgeon shook his head. "I'll tell you, about five minutes more, and he'd've bled to death. One bullet punctured a lung. No problem. But one bullet ruptured the femoral artery. That's the big one that supplies the leg. The rupture was right up near the groin, so pressure didn't work. If those ambulance guys hadn't done it just right with the plasma extenders, you'd be looking for another cop."

"Inspector," Friedman corrected. "Canelli's a homicide inspector."

"My mistake." The doctor raised a hand, then let it drop, as if the effort to finish the gesture was too much. "I've been on duty for twenty-seven hours. As Friday nights go in ER, this one was the shits."

"But Canelli'll be okay," Hastings pressed.

The doctor nodded. "Barring complications—clots, like that—he'll be fine. He won't be walking for a while, though. Or doing any deep breathing, either."

"What about the other one? Vance?"

"He's got multiple gunshot wounds, most of them superficial. What was it? A shotgun?"

"Buckshot. From about fifty feet."

"Ah." As if he were filing the information for future reference, the doctor nodded. "Buckshot. Yes."

"When can we talk to them?"

"Is Vance a criminal? I gather he is, by the two guards."

"He's a suspect."

"Ah." As if he were committing another fact to memory, the doctor nodded again. "Yes. I see."

They were standing in the corridor that led from the emergency room to surgery. A gurney and its crew came rushing down the corridor. The patient on the gurney was a young black woman whose hair was elaborately done in bejeweled cornrows. Her half-closed eyelids were fluttering, her gray lips quivering. Sections of her torso were becoming blood-soaked. The two detectives looked at the young woman, then looked quickly away. The doctor hardly looked.

"So when can we talk to Vance?" Friedman asked.

The doctor shrugged. "There's nothing very serious wrong

with him, aside from the aftereffects of shock and minor blood loss. If he were my patient—a private patient, I mean, that I felt obligated to protect, mostly for his psychic good health—I'd say you shouldn't talk to him before, say, twelve hours, just to be safe. But if you're willing to take the slight chance of causing him distress—bruising him, we might say, psychologically—then I'd say you could talk to him anytime."

"Like now?"

The doctor shrugged. "Sure."

"Good."

2:02 AM

"Jesus," Friedman muttered as they walked down the hospital hallway toward the uniformed guard standing at the end of the corridor. "I'm bushed. I just can't take these late nights anymore."

"You want to go home?" Hastings asked. "I'll get the guard for a witness."

Doggedly, Friedman shook his head. "No. If we can get something before Vance gets a lawyer, it's money in the bank." As he spoke, he nodded to the young, alert-looking patrolman standing beside the door marked POLICE WARD. The patrolman nodded cheerfully in return, using a key attached to an enormous plywood fob to open the door for them. Of the three beds in the ward, only one was occupied. Eyes closed, snoring slightly, Vance lay on his back. His breathing was shallow, his face white.

Just inside the door, Hastings hesitated. "He doesn't look so good. Maybe we should come back."

"Don't worry." Friedman gestured, a signal that they should proceed. "By the way, was Vance given his rights, do you know?"

"I didn't do it. And Canelli didn't, that's for sure."

"It sounds like Canelli almost bought the farm," Friedman

observed. "Jesus, what'd we do without Canelli to kick around?" He went to Vance, touched the suspect on the shoulder, then gently shook him. Instantly, Vance's eyes came open. He blinked once, blinked again, then turned to look at the detectives, who stood side by side, staring down at him impassively, implacable symbols of the law's unyielding phalanx. Just as impassively, Friedman recited Vance's constitutional right to refuse interrogation. When the recitation was concluded, Hastings spoke:

"How're you feeling, Vance?" He said it coldly, clinically.

Beneath his brave guardsman's mustache, Vance's lips were pale as he muttered, "I hurt."

"You almost killed Inspector Canelli. Do you know that?"

No response.

"I have to tell you, Vance, that when someone shoots a cop—almost kills a cop, like you did—he's a marked man. Do you understand that?"

Still no response.

"This gentleman"—he moved his head toward Friedman—"he's a lieutenant, just like I am. We're the co-commanders of Homicide. And we're here—both of us—to tell you that we're going to throw the fucking book at you. Us—the DA, everyone—we're all out to get you. Because when someone shoots a cop and doesn't suffer for it, then the next bastard with a gun in his hand is going to pull the trigger that much quicker. So we're going to make an example of you, Vance. You think you're suffering now? This is heaven, compared to what's coming."

"The only way you can help yourself," Friedman said, smoothly picking up the beat, "is to cooperate. Beginning now. Right now, right this minute. That's why we're here, to give you a chance to make it easy on yourself. Otherwise, it's your ass. We walk out of that door, and it begins, for you. If you start to bleed, or you need a drink of water, or you have to take a crap, and you ring for a nurse, nothing will happen, not for an hour or two. But that's only the beginning. When you get out of here and go to the county jail, where you'll be held for your pretrial hearing, you'll be put in a cell with the biggest, most brutal, most drugged-out sex offender we can find for you. And I guarantee you, Vance, that in about a week—a month, maybe, at the outside—you'll have AIDS. So it doesn't matter what happens to you in court. Because you'll already be a dead man. If you keep yourself in shape in the prison gym, do a lot of exercises in your cell, it might be ten years before you die of AIDS. But you will die. And the way you'll die, you'll wish you'd killed Canelli and got the death sentence and gone to the gas chamber, quick and clean."

"Of course," Hastings said, "we'll deny we said this. We'll deny this whole conversation."

Vance's voice was hoarse, no more than a whisper. "I want a lawyer. I've got a right to a lawyer."

"That you do, Vance," Hastings said. "But what Lieutenant Friedman is telling you—what we're trying to make you understand—is that if you cooperate with us, then we'll do our best to protect you while you're locked up. But hiring a lawyer—refusing to talk until you get a lawyer—that's not cooperating." Heavily, Hastings shook his head. "That's making it harder for us, not easier."

"Which means," Friedman said, "that we have to make it harder for you. That's just the way it goes." Now Friedman, too, lugubriously shook his head.

Except to blink, Vance made no response.

Posing now as the suspect's protector, Friedman continued in the same dire tone, "I hope you remember this, Vance. I hope you remember that we tried to help you. Because you're different from most of the guys who wake up in this ward. You've never been to jail. You might not even believe me, what I've been telling you. But when you're in that jail cell, getting screwed—getting AIDS—you're going to remember this little talk we're having here. But by then it'll be too late. You'll already have the virus. You'll already—"

"I believe you." In the early-morning hospital hush, the words were almost inaudible.

Hastings and Friedman exchanged a quick, covert glance. Was this the turning point, these three whispered words?

"Well, then?" It was a delicately asked question, delicately timed.

For a long, fateful moment the man in the bed remained mute, staring at the darkened ceiling. Then, clearing his throat nervously, he said, "It was Barbara. Right from the start, it was Barbara."

In the moment of charged silence that followed, Friedman inclined his head slightly toward Hastings. The message: Hastings should make the next move, attack from a different quarter, while Friedman watched, waited, calculated.

Hastings spoke quietly. "There's no proof that Barbara's involved. You, we've got cold. The Llama you bought killed Hanchett. You didn't pull the trigger, but we've got your fingerprints on the expended cartridges, because you loaded the gun. And the forty-five you bought killed Teresa Bell—and almost killed Canelli. So you're in deep shit, Vance. But Barbara?" Projecting regret for the hapless suspect, Hastings shook his head. "There's no proof. Nothing."

"She planned how it would happen. She planned everything. She knew about Teresa Bell—about the Bells' child. She—she set everything up. Those guns—she gave me the money. And afterward, when she got the insurance money and all the rest of it—all the stocks, all the real estate—we were going to live in Europe. Spain or Italy. We were going to—"

"That's bullshit," Friedman interrupted harshly. "*Bullshit.* You might not be the world's greatest intellect, but you're obviously not stupid, either. Are you telling me that you risked the gas chamber for promises? Blue sky, for Christ's sake?"

"I did it for *us.*" Vance was speaking more distinctly now. Color was returning to his face.

"Ah." Friedman's irony was a masterpiece of scorn. "Ah, I see. Love. You did it for love."

Vance looked away. His hands had been resting limply on the counterpane. Now the fingers began to twitch fretfully. His eyes began to blink, his mouth moved irresolutely, as if he wanted to say more—but feared the impulse. All promising signs.

"Christ," Friedman said, "that trick's older than the shell game. 'Help me get rid of him,' the wife says, 'and we'll take the money and live happily every after.' Usually on the Riviera." Marveling, Friedman shook his head. "And you fell for it. So here you are, with buckshot in your ass. And there she is, sleeping between silk sheets, probably, in Pacific Heights."

No response. But Vance's eyes were darkening angrily. His hands were clenched, no longer fretful. As if overwhelmed with pity for the suspect, Friedman turned to Hastings. "Should we tell him?"

Also projecting a negligent, contemptuous pity, Hastings snorted. "We may as well. He'll find out in court." He looked down at Vance, let a beat pass. Then: "She called us this evening. Barbara Hanchett. She called me at about ten o'clock. She told me you killed Teresa Bell."

"No." Vance began doggedly shaking his head. "*No.*"

"It came through our communications center. I've got it on tape. Every syllable. We'll play a certified copy of that tape for you, with police calls before and after. She set you up, Vance. On police radio. At about ten o'clock tonight."

"*No.*"

"Yes."

Saturday, September 15

9:15 AM

"This," Friedman said, gesturing to the Hanchett town house, "is very nice. Very nice indeed. A million and a half, two million, I'd say, in today's market. Wouldn't you say so?"

"At least." Hastings swung the cruiser into the Hanchett driveway and switched off the engine.

"What always intrigues me," Friedman said, "is why they do it, these rich people. Imelda Marcos. Donald Trump. Leona Helmsley. What're they after, anyhow? Why do they do it?"

"They do it because they want more. It's the American way. It's greed. Otherwise known as free enterprise."

"Hmmm." Speculatively, Friedman eyed his colleague, conceding, "That's pretty good. Is that an original line?"

"No."

"Ah." As if he were relieved, Friedman nodded. Then: "Did you call the hospital?"

"I stopped by this morning, on my way to the Hall. He's fine. They've tested him for brain function already."

Friedman frowned. "Brain function?"

"Because he lost all that blood. If the brain is starved for blood for any period of time, there could be brain damage. But he's fine. He'll be discharged in three or four days."

"I'm glad he's fine. Let's face it, Canelli needs all his available brain cells."

"Hmmm."

"I put a notice on the bulletin board, and talked to the deputy chief. I figure we'd get him a little TV. You know, a portable, with a battery pack. After we finish here, we can go by Electric City. A friend of mine runs it."

"Wait a minute. He's already got a TV in his room. He was watching the news."

"Well," Friedman countered, "he'll have to convalesce, you know, at home. He can use an extra TV then."

"What about flowers?"

"He'll get flowers from his family, whatever."

"Hmmm."

"What about Vance?" Friedman asked. "How's he?"

"No problem."

"Has he got a lawyer?"

Hastings shrugged. "I wouldn't know. I just talked to the doctor."

"After we leave here," Friedman said, "we've got to go by the hospital, see if we can get Vance on tape. If he doesn't have any money, maybe he doesn't have a lawyer yet. We could luck out."

"Have you got a recorder?"

"In my briefcase."

"Too bad we didn't have a recorder last night," Hastings said.

"That would depend on when we switched it on. I don't think a judge would be very enthusiastic about our interrogation technique."

"True." Hastings looked at the Hanchett house. "Should we try to tape her?"

Friedman considered. "Maybe not. Let's see which way she'll jump."

"You haven't talked to her, have you?"

"No. Why?"

"She's pretty tough. Pretty smart, too. And rich. That's a bad combination."

Friedman waved a casual hand. "That's negative thinking. The way I see it, we're on a roll. One down, one to go. Leave everything to me." He swung open the door, swung his legs out of the cruiser.

10:15 AM

"I'm afraid," Barbara Hanchett said, "that I don't understand this. I've already told you what happened. I've told you that Clay called me yesterday and said he wanted to see me. The yacht harbor, he said. He sounded terrible. I thought I should meet him, though. He's been acting so—so strangely, this last week, I was afraid *not* to meet him. So we met at a little after nine o'clock last night. He said he had to go away—that *we* had to go away. He had to have money so he could get out of town, he said. He was raving. That's the only word for it—raving. He said he'd gotten a woman named Teresa Bell to kill Brice so that we could be together, Clay and I. But then he had to kill Teresa Bell, he said, because she would incriminate him. And you—the police—he said you were after him. 'Closing in for the kill,' he said." Pantomiming incredulous puzzlement, she shook her head. "Those were his exact words, 'closing in for the kill.' Naturally, I humored him, put him off. I told him I couldn't get any money till Monday—not enough money to go to Mexico, or wherever he wanted to go. And then, as soon as I got home, I called you. So now"—she lifted a supercilious eyebrow—"now you're accusing me, as I understand it. I mean . . ." Exasperated, she lifted a manicured hand with a gesture calculated to project a well-bred inability to understand the limitations of the lower classes. "I mean, what're you *after,* anyhow?" Her voice was low and cold, her eyes haughty, uncompromising.

"What we're after, Mrs. Hanchett," Friedman said, "is the truth. We've got a man in custody who'll undoubtedly be indicted for murder. And he says it was all your idea. A conspiracy, in other words, to commit murder." Affably, Friedman spread his hands. "Now, that's a serious charge. And it's our responsibility, our solemn duty, to apprise you of what's happened, tell you that you're in jeopardy, and why. In fact, it's the law."

"I can hardly believe," she said, "that I'm hearing this." Syllable by scornful syllable, she measured the words like drops of poison. Her eyes were baleful as she looked at the two men in turn. "I saw Clay once a week. My husband went out to play, I went to Clay's place to play. It's what's known as an arrangement. Once in a while he came here. Sometimes we went to the movies. Occasionally, when Brice was out of town, Clay and I took short trips together. But that was the extent of it. That was all. Period. The end."

"That's not what Vance says."

She shrugged, eyed them again, then rose to her feet. "I'm afraid you gentlemen will have to excuse me. I'm going to call my lawyer." She frowned as she looked at Hastings. Finally: "You gave me your card, Lieutenant. But I think I threw it away. Would you mind giving me another? I'm sure my lawyer will want to talk to you."

10:30 AM

"Boy," Friedman said, marveling as he shook his head. "That's one cool lady."

Falling into step as they walked down the Hanchett driveway to their car, Hastings said, "I warned you. You remember that

I warned you." He opened the passenger door for Friedman, circled the car, slid in behind the steering wheel. "So what d'you think?"

"I think," Friedman said, "that everything Vance says is absolutely true. Actually, I never doubted it. But I'd like to predict—remember, please, that you heard it here first—I'd like to predict that Barbara Hanchett will never, *never* be indicted. The DA may question her—politely, over very dry wine. But that'll be the end of it. Jesus." Ruefully, he shook his head as Hastings backed the cruiser out of the driveway and began driving down the sedate, tree-lined street. "Jesus, a car salesman. You'd think he'd've been smarter. Logically, he couldn't win. She picks up the phone, and he's on his way to the gas chamber."

"That's logic, though. There's more to it than logic. You said so yourself, last night."

"Oh, yeah?" Friedman settled back in his seat and yawned. "What'd I say last night?"

"Love, you said. He did it for love."

"Oh, yeah." Friedman nodded. "Love. I forgot."